I0595873

Also by S.L.Mason

KILLING GODS

ALETHEA

CALYPSO

HERA

FATES

UNDERWORLD

ELYSIUM

POSEIDON

THESE HALLOWED HILLS

TRICK OF FAE

TEST OF FAE

THORNS OF FAE

TWIST OF FAE

TRAITS OF FAE

HERA

KILLING GODS III

Quick Quill Publishing, LLC

© 2017

This Book is a work of fiction.

All of the characters, organizations, and events portrayed in the novel are either products of the authors imagination or are used fictitiously. Its not about you.

Copyright 2017 Quick Quill Publishing, LLC

The distribution of this book without permission is a theft of the author's intellectual property. If you would like permission to use material from the book (other than for review purposes), please contact us at www.Quickquillpublishing.com Thank you for your support of the author's rights.

DEDICATION

~ 5 ~

To Elia my editor, without whom this book may never have
seen the light of day. And for telling me when it sucked!

TABLE OF CONTENTS

PROLOGUE

This isn't about my children or my children's children or their children. This is about an entire race. I know how that sounds. I birthed a new race.

Pythia

CHAPTER 1

SYDNEY

I felt like I was in a dream that I couldn't get out of. I never wanted anything more than I wanted to be able to look into those eyes at least one more time. I dreamed about them often enough and wished they were real, but actually seeing them, it felt like life was playing a trick on me and I hated the feeling that I was being played.

"Who are you?" I snarled.

"You know who I am," the man returned in all seriousness.

I wanted to head-butt him just for saying that, but I wasn't tall enough.

"You can't be him. He's dead! He's been dead for years. If he was still alive, he would have come for me. He wouldn't have left me alone," I yelled and my voice cracked on the last part. I was shaking. I tried to squirm away but he held me firm.

"I didn't leave you alone. You've never been alone. I've always been with you," he replied.

"If that's true, then why did I marry Gabriel? If you were there? You're not him! You can't be him," I screamed.

My eyes darted around the room and the furniture rattled with my emotions.

"Just because I wasn't there physically, it doesn't mean I wasn't there," Adrian responded.

"That's like when people say. 'I'm thinking about you' but never call you. That's bullshit!" I retort.

I've gone off the deep end, this isn't real. My mind has lost it and I'm just trying to protect myself. Travis is raping me. That's it. Self-protection, it's a delusion. Yep, that's got to be it.

The voice in my mind boomed.

< I've always spoken to you. >

< Go away, Voice! This has nothing to do with you.> I yelled.

< I AM THE VOICE! >

It rang out loud through the room and in my mind. He released me and I backed away from him, "It's not possible, this isn't possible," I muttered reaching for the door handle at my back. I depressed it, but it didn't go down, I moved it again in desperation, but nothing happened.

"Sydney, our whole lives shouldn't be possible and yet here we are," Adrian replied smiling.

"You can't be him," I whispered shaking along with everything in the room.

He's dead, I know he is.

Tears filled my eyes, "You're too tall and he'd be an old man. Old like me. You're young. You're not even 25," I sputter, over the tears slipping down my face.

That's it. He's a relative or a Doppelganger, or it's my mind fucking with me because I'm crazy.

With a low chuckle, he replied, "I'm not a Doppelganger. Let me show you! I'll explain. Just trust me and come with me." He then stepped back and offered me his hand.

It was like an echo listening to it in my mind and hearing the words come out of his mouth. My mind resisted as my body followed him. My chest burned with fear and hope, a feeling I'd learned to live without.

The door on the far side of the room opened the moment he touched it. It wouldn't open for me but it opened for him.

"How did you get that door open? I was desperate to open it five minutes ago and couldn't," I demanded.

He held up his arm. There was a bracelet on it, similar to the one Travis had given the kids.

"All doors on Alethea open, but you have to have a key, a bracelet." He supplied.

Travis hadn't given me a bracelet. He only gave them to the kids. He made sure that there was no way I could get out of this room unless he gave me one. That bastard just wanted the kids out of the room.

"What will happen to Travis?" I asked then chanced a glance down at the slumped form on the floor. Before kicking him for good measure. I snatched my shorts from the floor and wiggled back into them, the top button was gone, but the zipper locked in place. I tied the ripped front of my T-shirt together to hide my bikini top thankful the strings held.

"I don't know. Every now and again someone commits a heinous crime here, then they disappear. All their things disappear too. Usually, their whole family disappears." Adrian replied.

"What do you mean they just disappear?" I whipped my head back to look at Adrian. He was still gazing down at Travis.

"Gone like they never existed here, except in our memories."

Adrian's remark shook me.

So, they kill them?

Not that I cared all that much. Travis was obviously evil. I only wished that every sick son of a bitch could go with him. But his wife, she didn't deserve to die. So, they must do something else with them. But what?

I grabbed my pack and we stepped through the second door. It exited the white crystalline building and onto a stone pathway. All around there was a dense jungle foliage hanging over the walkway. The buzzing in the back of my mind returned with a vengeance.

The Adrian look alike, reached for my hand, clasping it in his own. It felt normal and natural for my hand to fit in his, so I let him. Following his lead, we walked deeper into the jungle. The path became overgrown and the stones had grass growing up between them, causing them to become raised and uneven. I unconsciously smoothed the walkway. My power over earth made it happen. The dark gloom of the jungle settled over the walkway as it turned to slick moss.

The darkness and the cool sticky air of the jungle surrounding us was engulfing. Holding my hand in his, Adrian stopped, took my other hand and looked deep into my eyes.

"Do you trust me?" his tenor inquired.

Part of me said that I should not trust anyone, but my heart beat a long-forgotten rhythm telling my brain that he was indeed the real Adrian. He was the reason I was there. Life is all about choices. Make one or one will be made for you.

"If you truly are the Adrian I remember, then yes, I trust you." I replied.

The air pressure around us changed and it became frigid. A blackness covered me. I heard a popping sound in my ears and then we were surrounded by a warm blue glow along with the scent of ozone.

I gazed up to find the source of the blue light, but instead, I saw the rounded dome of the ceiling in the pool cavern. I immediately glanced down at the perfectly round pool of water.

Adrian's smile washed over me. He released my hands and I felt the loss of his touch keenly.

"Did you bring a cell phone with you?" He asked.

"Yes, there's one here in my pack, but I think it's dead." I rummaged around my sack for a few minutes until I pulled out the cell. He pushed the front button on it and it glowed to life.

"I'm going to take your picture. Then I want you to go into the water and come back out. Then I'll take it again. Afterwards, all your questions about me will be answered." He stared at me through the hair that hung from his forehead and waited for my response, but since I was silent, he continued, "But I'm sure you're going to have a lot more and all of them will have nothing to do with me." He chuckled.

I nodded in agreement and awkwardly stepped back to the edge of the pool. I hadn't dressed for the meeting. I felt silly. Most of my clothes were ripped or hanging off of me. I stood there, probably blushing while Adrian took a picture. I was staring at him. I knew for sure there was a stupid smile on my face.

God, I'm too old for this.

In one swift motion, I pulled what was left of my shirt off and loosen my shorts. I had never had so little clothing in front of Adrian before. The only person who had ever seen me naked was Gabriel.

But it's swimsuit, Sydney. You're not naked.

No matter what I was telling myself, molten fire raced down my body. Why couldn't he have seen me when we were young before I had my kids.

Get it done for God's sake!

I stepped down into the pool. The water level reached my waist. I said a quick 'fuck it' in my mind and went under.

I slam my hand down on the bottom. Pushing off, I burst the surface.

Adrian was already holding a towel which he hadn't been holding before. He wrapped me in it, then he grabbed the phone and took a picture of my face again.

"You don't have to say anything. Just look at the pictures and tell me what you see." He tilted his head down and let the hair hang in his face.

The first picture was of me, but it wasn't me. The water wasn't cold but every fiber of my being shook due to what I was looking at. I touched my face, running my fingers down over the edges of my eyes. The skin surrounding them was tight and firm. I moved my hand down and realized that my lips were smooth and full. I looked at my body and my legs had muscle definition.

I didn't need to see the other picture. I knew what this place was.

The face staring back at me from the phone was the younger version of me, yet it was time-stamped just a few moments ago. The second picture was even more shocking I looked 20. How was that even possible? I was many things but

20 years old was not one of them. How does a 50-year-old woman go from looking 50 one day and 20 the next?

"Ponce de Leon did discover the Fountain of Youth, didn't he?" I remarked.

Adrian let out a deep throaty laugh. "Yes, he did, but then he lost it again."

"So, did he have the map made while he was here or afterwards?" I had a thousand questions.

He didn't answer my last question. He looked at me through the blond hair hanging in his eyes and I felt his urge to hug me, but he didn't. Instead he quietly asked, "So, you believe it's me?"

"Yes, I believe you." Wonder was the only way to color the picture that I was facing. After saying those words and realizing their meaning, my soul filled with outrage and my mouth started talking at a very rapid pace.

"But why didn't you come for me? Why did you stay here the whole time? Why did you let me marry Gabriel? Why did you do everything that you did if you've been in my mind and you've been alive this whole time why?" I demanded.

"No one is allowed to leave this island. Once you're here there's no way to get off. They make sure of it." He took my hand and squeezed it gently.

"You're saying my children and I are stuck here." The thought of being trapped lodged in my throat like a bone.

"No, I think I might have figured a way to get off the island, but I needed you and the kids here to do it."

With all the emotions running through my body, I hadn't noticed first that he said 'you and the kids'. My mind was hyper-focused on his words.

"What would my kids have to do with this?" I changed mental gears into defense of my children.

I dug deep into my psyche for the sound of their voices. Something frantic and deep pulled me.

"Do you hear that?" I asked.

"Hear what?" Adrian replied and clasped my hand.

"Like frantic crying. I can't identify where it's coming from. It's hard to hear everything in here." I searched the space for the reason.

The smile died on him and he said, "We need to go back."

"The kids will be going out of their minds. Is that the noise I'm hearing?" I asked as my heart raged with worry. I began to scrounge around the floor picking up my clothes the trying to put them back on in a semblance of normalcy.

"The structures around here impair your abilities. That way you can't really hear 'them'. It's like wearing earplugs," he shrugged and pulled me to him.

"What do you mean? The buildings around here work as dampeners?" I asked with a raised eyebrow.

"Yes," he glanced around as if he was embarrassed.

"How did we get here?" I glanced around for the fifth time.

"The same way Tristan gets anywhere. Teleportation," Adrian let that sink in.

"What is this place?" This was the question that burned in my mind.

"Alethea. It means 'truth'. However, you may know it by a different name — Atlantis." He never faltered with his reply, so it wasn't in jest.

I coughed and stepped back, raising my eyebrows and plastering a disbelieving smile over my face. "You're kidding, right?" the shock took the form of a laugh.

He didn't say a word. He just smiled. Looking in his blue eyes, I realized that this was just the tip of a very large iceberg.

"I should get back to the kids. They've got to be freaking out. I heard them banging on the door." My hands shake from the adrenaline racing through my veins.

Before I could think of anything else, Adrian grabbed my hand. The pressure changed and in a second, we were next to the door to Travis's office. He opened the door and instructed me to wait.

"Get out of my way!" Tristian shouted.

Both children burst through the door, wrapping their arms around me. Their minds were desperate to find out what happened.

"Mom, what the fuck?" Tristan's mind churned with every possible scenario while Issy's tears laid wet on my tattered shirt as she clung to me.

"Issy, it's okay. We're going to be okay," I assured her, petting her hair back.

After a moment of closeness, they froze and turned in unison to Adrian. Tristan stepped in front of Issy and me.

"Who is this guy, Mom?" He straightened his stance and puffed his shoulders out, creating a wall between us and Adrian.

"It's him, Tristan. You know the guy," Issy whispered and tipped her head at him. "The voice in Mom's head." She whispered.

Heat from my body rolled from my toes to my ears.

"What guy?" Tristan's voice faltered.

Before either of us could stop her, Isolde reached around and touched Adrian. A smile spread across her face that could have lit ten thousand suns before being replaced by a water fall of tears. She released his hand and stepped back.

"Why didn't you come to her sooner?" Issy asked and cocked her head to the side.

Adrian stared dumbfounded at her over what had just passed between them. "You know why," he sputtered.

"I want my mother to hear you say it out loud," Issy urged.

"I met someone here." He never looked away but rubbed each of his hands in turn with the other.

My heart hammered in my chest. "You met someone?" I whispered and mentally backed away.

Why did it matter if he met someone? I had married Gabe and had children. Guilt struck me in the belly. Everything I had lived, so had he. I covered my mouth with my hand. He had to live it. It didn't stop the wave of jealousy that threatened to take over.

"Yes, but it's not what you think, Sydney." He moved closer, reaching out to caress my cheek. Tristan pushed his hand back out of the way, creating a space between us.

"Why would you bring me here if it's not what 'I think'?" I whispered. I was jumping to conclusions, but I couldn't stop myself.

Issy pulled on my sleeve. "Mom, listen to him for a minute." Her other hand ran up and down my back.

Deep breath, in and out.

I had to slow down using my breathing, because objects in the room began shaking. The doors rattled in their frames. A few moments before nothing moved for me and now the whole room sounded like a xylophone.

"It's not what you think at all. She's special and important, but it's not like what we have. We have to go see her now," Adrian stumbled over his words and our connection rolled with emotions. There was fear, love, insecurity, uncertainty, urgency, I pushed them to the side, but they crowded in.

Not helping.

He pulled at my arm to coax me out of the room, but I held firm.

"Who is she?" I demanded and the doors started slamming back and forth in their frames.

The room felt like it was going to burst. The furniture was lifting and lowering as I breathed in and out.

"I'll explain in a couple of minutes," he replied.

Biting my teeth down, I hissed with jealousy. "Everyone keeps saying 'they'll explain later.' I don't want explanations later. I want answers now!"

Adrian stopped and turned to face me. "Alright. Here's your explanation. I'm related to her. She explained everything that was going on here and now she's going to help us."

Okay, now I feel stupid. Great!

I hadn't seen this guy for over thirty years and I was acting like an asshole.

CHAPTER 2

SYDNEY

To say that death cannot stop true love was the most ridiculous line I have ever heard, yet Adrian had been dead and that didn't stop me from loving him or finding him alive.

The pull on my arm brought me back to the island and the world I'd discovered there. Adrian led us out of the labyrinth of a building onto the avenue. We were closer to the temple than when we'd gone in.

I couldn't stop myself from gazing up the straight road to the temple perched there. The glaring white edifice blinded me for a moment, so I raised my hand to shield my eyes.

It felt like the dream but from a different angle. Instead of being in the sky, I was on the ground level. The dizzying perspective change threw me off. Of course, still having sea legs didn't help either. I closed my eyes to push the vertigo away before opening them again.

But the pyramid dominated the scene with its shining peak. Even though the jungle covered it, I could still make out the flattened sides and the angular corners. The water was pouring from the base of the temple and was giving off the floating quality akin to fantasy.

The face of Poseidon and his battle smile sent shivers down my spine. I couldn't imagine what it would be like to stand against him. You'd have to have a set of balls made of titanium and the size of Gibraltar to face him down.

"Sydney, we can't linger," Adrian urged me on.

That was the first moment I noticed his clothes. He was wearing linen shorts and a short tunic style shirt belted at the waist with sandals that tied on. The most interesting portion of his ensemble was the sword, he wore a belted short sword. It was strange and out of place, but this whole place was strange, so I let it be.

I didn't feel the urgency that Adrian did. He gave off a fear vibe in his every move. Adrian had always been a 'take charge' kind of guy but this was different.

"Where are we going?" Tristan demanded in his tone of distrust keeping his bulk between Adrian and his sister and I.

"To Emily and the boat," Adrian replied while pulling me along.

The fountain loomed in front of us, dry and cracked. It was out of place against the pristine care everything else carried. If you took the time to notice, the infinity symbol was everywhere on it.

"Why isn't there water in this fountain?" I asked as we passed.

Adrian shrugged, "It's been dry for as long as I've been here. The islanders say it never runs and Athena refuses to fix it." His lack of interest worried me.

"That's strange," Issy remarked.

"Who cares? We found Mom's island. Now let's get out of here while we still can," Tristan spat.

It wasn't like him to be on edge. Tristan usually took everything in stride. The sharpness of his tongue worried me. But he too now moved with a purpose in the direction of the boat. Both men moved in sync, Adrian pulling me and Tristan with Isolde in tow.

"What about your relative? Don't you want to get her too?" I asked while trying not to trip.

"She'll meet us at the boat. Don't worry. Aunt Emily isn't staying here," Adrian said.

It was my first clue as to the 'relative's identity'. Aunt Emily. I didn't remember Adrian's Aunt Emily disappearing. I thought she was still in our hometown. She was at Grace's funeral.

< She's my great aunt and not my dad's sister. >

< *Why don't you just move us like before?* >

People milled around the various pathways leading away from the main avenue. Some stared openly with curious smiles, others with pressed lips. All wearing clothes similar to Adrian with an ancient-world quality.

< *Never mind. Stupid question.* >

We passed over a bridge spanning on one of the watery channels. The edge of the water was met by a golden ban. It couldn't be gold, the saltwater would have corroded it away, but nothing clung to the pristine metal.

Adrian's steps slowed as we came in sight of the dock. Standing by our boat was a golden-haired man, in a toga with a quiver across his back and a gold bow with a silver bow string hanging from his shoulder. He turned to take us in but there was no joy in his eyes.

CHAPTER 3

SYDNEY

Seven men, all clothed in togas, approached us. Tristan cocked an eyebrow at Adrian and asked, "What's with the crazy get-ups?", but Adrian just shook his head and put his hand up.

< Tristan, cut it out! > I mentally ordered him.

"Are you the newcomers?" The gorgeous man in the toga asked.

Adrian rolled his eyes and moved slightly in front of me. "You know who they are, so why do you ask stupid questions, Apollo?"

"They are to come with me," Apollo ordered then laid his hand on the pommel of the short sword hanging at his waist.

Adrian repositioned himself between us and Apollo and didn't appear to have any intention of letting anyone near us.

"Why? Have we broken some law?" I demanded. I never used to have a problem keeping my mouth shut, but it appeared that was a thing of the past. My irritation rose, and I expected the island to rise with it but it didn't move.

"Athena wishes to speak with you," Apollo's reply wasn't a request. He held his hand out indicating the temple at the other end of the avenue.

I sought out Adrian's eyes, but he never gave me a side glance.

Athena?

"Athena, Apollo. Do you guys all think you're Gods?" I scoffed.

< Don't mock him. They are the Gods. > Adrian said.

< *Bullshit!! They don't exist.* > I retorted.

"Don't ask questions. Just come with me!" Apollo stood his ground firm and decisive. Racking my brain, I tried to recall what the Greek mythology said about Apollo. He looked the part, blond hair, bow and smoking hot. But I thought he was kind, so was he?

< Let me do all the talking. There's a lot more going on here than you know. > Adrian reached out again.

< *Like what? Are they going to toy with us?* > I internally giggled.

I thought that if these Gods were anything like the stories, we might very well be truly fucked.

< No. They stopped doing that ages ago. > Adrian's mind still reeked of fear.

< *Well, that's a comfort, I guess.* > I responded while squeezing his hand, to block out the dread that was now taking over me.

We followed Apollo up the central avenue to the base of Poseidon's Temple. All the Apollo want-to-be club of goons came with us. The edifice reared up in front of us and its massive size was intimidating. Every column was the size of a sequoia tree, only older. They were smooth and white with flecks of crystal shot through like veins, everyone the same, yet different.

I had never seen the inside of the temple and I had no idea what to expect after passing under these monolithic towers.

Every vision I'd had was floating from the outside high up in the sky. I reached for the dream to center myself, but it was gone. All these years I lived with it just out of reach but there. Now it was gone. Every scene that I had grasped onto as a getaway from the horrors of my life was gone. I yearned for the blue colors that were always there at the beginning of the dream along with the soft rocking of the waves. I realized that my escapes to the dream world were over.

The seven-man goon squad formed a circle around us, hedging and herding us towards the entrance. Tristan's mind pressed in and Isolde grabbed my free hand while Adrian held on to the other.

Walking beneath those massive columns, the entire island felt like a step back in time, a place removed from reality, almost like it was frozen. At any moment a Pegasus might fly across the sky. Actually, I wanted to see a creature from the Greek Mythos crossing my path because then I could pretend it wasn't real.

The walls were composed of more of that shimmering white star-like material. It permeated everything, even the ground. The far end of the temple merged into the reclining slope of the pyramid. All the walls reflected colors, so instead of having only white, there were reds, greens, and purples, just like a rainbow array. I wanted to take a closer look at the walls, but I couldn't take my eyes off the back of the two men in front of me.

The buzzing in my mind had turned into a roar and the pressure in my cranium increased. It consumed my focus. I saw Tristan rubbing his own temples several times and Isolde seemed to also have a problem with the internal noise.

< Adrian, do you hear that? >

< Yes, but I block it out. You need to, too. Go to that room inside your mind and close everyone else out. >

The deeper into the structure we ventured, the louder 'it' became. I felt Tristan's probing. I passed along Adrian's message as we reached a massive archway to a room. Whatever I had been drawn to, it was there. I only had to pass through the archway to achieve it.

The cornucopia of minds rebounded inside my skull, but I pushed the sounds to the side, closing myself off from the distractions.

Before passing through the arches, Apollo turned and stared at the four of us.

"Athena doesn't take kindly people who don't listen. She's in charge of this project and the council has the final say on your fate. If you don't wish to be wiped or worse, I suggest you show restraint and respect."

His earnest instructions sent shivers down my spine. *What does wiped mean?*

*****

It wasn't a room, but an amphitheater. It was massive. You could easily have put thousands of people in it.

We had entered the center of the 'lion's den'. Directly across from the archway, sat a raised dais with 12 seats. One seat was larger and higher than the others and upon it sat a woman. Every sound from the dais was amplified to the extreme. However, it didn't just amplify sounds, but minds too.

The woman was beautiful in a fierce way. She had long black glossy hair, dark blue eyes and full cruel lips that were set in a grim line of control. She sat on her throne as if she was marble herself. The whole thing was surreal. I glanced around and everyone here was wearing a toga except for us.

The whole scene reminded me of a scene from the "Clash of the Titans" movie when Zeus demanded the Gods help Perseus. However, no God was going to step forward to help us. There would be no demands made on our behalf.

I closed my eyes and filled my lungs with as much air as would fit, trying to clear my mind. Adrian held my hand. The reality of it still lingered in the background.

Here! He had been here, all this time.

I opened my eyes.

I'll be damned if they keep us here. Or my children.

Two of the 12 seats were empty. The rest were filled by an equal number of men and women. All of them gorgeous, perfect specimens. I've never seen so much perfection in one room without being in a movie.

"Apollo, you and your sister may take your seats. Are these the newcomers?" Athena's voice filled the room. It was a voice of command. She was comfortable leading and being followed. Her eyes never left our group.

That piqued my interest. His sister? I snuck a peek at her out of the corner of my eye. There was a female version of Apollo with a quiver and bow slung over her back. She moved with control. Every move like she was on the hunt, giving her a predatorial aspect. I was taken away from my thoughts by Apollo's voice.

"I brought them as you requested." The sound pounded into my person.

However, I wanted to focus completely upon the woman in front of me. She was clearly a force to be reckoned with. I couldn't help gazing around to see how many people were actually in this massive room. Probably thousands and they sat on the benches stiff as rods, each one with rapt attention.

Athena continued, "Do you know why you and your offspring have been brought to the Citadel?" The cool calm raised my heart rate.

Arrogant too. Nice.

"I don't know. You don't like outsiders or perhaps you're advocating rapist," I said and her eyebrows rose. It appeared that she didn't like sarcasm.

Too bad!

"I will not tolerate your insolence, human!"

But before she could continue, a woman with strawberry blond hair stepped forward cutting her way through the crowd to the front. She stepped in front of me, and I couldn't see her face, but I was sure she too was a beauty.

She stood proud and straight with her hands held at ease. Her entire demeanor emanated peace and control.

"Athena, you know she is not human. Do not accuse her of that, as if it's some kind of a slur." The woman turned to me. "You've been brought here *because* you are not human. You are more," she informed me.

My mouth dried at the sight of her. She was the woman from my dream. I recognized her calming voice, the one that kept urging me on for years. I shook my head to throw off the power of the dream.

"Adrian, what are they talking about?" I asked in a low voice and leaned closer to him.

Adrian was stilled facing forward without answering me.

< Block us all out, beautiful girl. They will learn too much if you don't. > he didn't flinch as he replied.

"Yes, Adrian. Why don't you tell us all about what you've learned in the 30 years that you've been here." Athena arched her eyebrows at him while her lips were set in a pinched half-smile.

"This is why I stayed, Sydney. I had to find these answers," he said.

What is he talking about? What answers?

"The blood tests are complete. What is the outcome, Hera?" Athena asked.

Hera? They must be kidding. Is everyone named after a God? And I thought no one was going to step up. Ha!

"You know the answer, Athena. They are all hybrids." She stated in a flat voice.

Wow, hold the phone!

"All of them?" Athena demanded, leaning forward with the wide shocked eyes.

"Yes, even Adrian," Hera stated.

A burst of air exhaled from Adrian. I didn't even notice he'd been holding.

Athena barked thrusting an accusing finger at Hera, "You did this, Hera! I know you did. How long have you known Adrian was a hybrid?"

The smile bloomed on Hera's face. She waved her arm in a sweeping motion. "Since the moment of his conception and before. I know every single hybrid on the planet," she responded while triumph oozed from her stance.

The scowl on Athena's face told me everything I needed to know.

She's my enemy.

Athena's head whipped in my direction to stare me down with hard as a diamond blue eyes.

"How dare you call me your enemy? I have done nothing to you or your kind. Hera is your enemy. She's the one who created you. I do not know what the High Council will say of this. Apollo, you and your men are to take the hybrids and place them in an area that is heavily guarded. Make sure the rooms are shielded. I don't want any of them using their abilities to get out." She ordered.

Athena's men moved into position around us. My heart sped up in anticipation of a fight.

There is nothing like being herded by the Greek goon squad. They were all living, breathing sculpted statues of heroes. The clanking of swords surrounded me. My eyes darted around to every man, each armed.

I'm a fucking fool! I thought realizing that I had left my gun on the boat and no one had searched me. I could have at least brought the flare gun.

< Don't beat yourself up, Syd. They would have taken it. They are like us. They would have known. > Adrian tried to console me.

< *Us? What are we?* >

< Think, Syd! We are hybrids. Demigods. >

I didn't respond to that affirmation. I threw a hard look over my shoulder at Athena. She lifted her head slightly and looked around at the rest of the council.

"Hera, you will come with me! We will dreamwalk the High Council together and you will explain yourself."

I chanced a glance over at Adrian. "What just happened?"

"We've been found out," he supplied with pinched lips.

Great!

"What does that even mean? We've been found out. Why are they calling as hybrids and who are these people?" I didn't get my answer because a blond woman that looked vaguely familiar, stepped out from the crowd.

"Athena, I request an audience."

Our group halted at the arch and I turned at the sound of her voice.

"You have no standing here, Emily. You're just one of the many humans trapped on this island," Athena waved her away.

Emily jumped in with both feet, along with her interesting accent.

"No, I'm not. I'm a hybrid and Adrian is my nephew. If you're going to lock them all up, you might as well take me too. I won't be separated from my kin. Then, you can do all the dreamwalkin' you want," she finished with a half-smile. She looked like the cat that ate the canary.

Note to self, Emily is trouble.

Hera spoke before I could take another step. "Athena, before you lock these hybrids up and dreamwalk the High Council, I would say one thing. Why don't you ask yourself why Adrian is here and how did he get here?" Hera moved closer to the dais. "Why don't you also ask how Sydney got here? Did you know they grew up together and were childhood sweethearts?"

Hera's calm front worried me and it appeared that I wasn't the only one that got that effect because all the color drained away from Athena's face. "What are you saying?"

"I'm saying exactly what you think," she replied slowly. "Before you go tattling to the High Council about what I've done, please keep in mind that something happened here that none of you expected. I am the only one who foresaw it. Adrian and Sydney are a true mating between two hybrids," she smiled in her triumph.

The room roared to life. Voices were yelling and calling out, anger and disbelief ricocheting off every surface. It pummeled my mind and Issy shook with the onslaught.

Athena's anger blazed through the room, filling the entire Citadel. It was like a fire pouring out of her.

"That is impossible! Hybrids cannot mate. Matings only happens amongst Themian's. You will not tell the council about this," she roared.

"I can and I will. I can hear their minds. They've been talking to each other continuously since the moment of their Awakening. They are a true mating. She has the twins - a boy and a girl. Only something more interesting happened, Athena. Adrian is the father of only one of those children," Hera smiled again in triumph.

All the blood in my body hit the floor at once and I turned to stare first at Adrian then at Tristan and Isolde. Their saucer shaped eyes and O shaped mouths made my heart beat through my chest.

How the hell do I explain that one?

Father Rizzo's words from the catacombs rang through my mind. *'Information is dangerous and people are willing to kill for it.'*

CHAPTER 4

HERA

"Did you give them Primordium?" Athena hissed, after regaining control of herself and the room.

"No, I did not give any of them Primordium." I crossed my hand in front of myself and clasped them to keep them from fidgeting.

This was the moment I'd been waiting for, for thousands of years. However, gambling was always Athena's preview. Her eyes were like thin sheets of paper that stared down, boring into me. I could feel the mental pressure she was putting on me. She didn't believe me.

"What is Primordium and why is everybody's panties in a wad over it?" Emily demanded and reached out to put her hand on Adrian, leaning over and whispering something in his ear.

The tension between Adrian and Sydney weighed the air down. He examined her face closely as her eyes widened and her pupils dilated.

"That is not the whole of it, Athena. Hera needs to tell you the whole of it." Emily goaded Hera on.

"Well, Hera I'm waiting." Her eyes flashed into tight lines of irritation.

"I did not give any of them Primordium. The fact that they knew where to find it is of no consequence to me. Perhaps you should've sealed the Primordial chamber, making it impossible for anyone who is not a shifter to enter, to begin with. What say you, Athena? It sounds as if you are not doing your job properly," I had to prod her to the point where nothing she did would ever work short of genocide because my people didn't have a stomach for another round of that.

"You dare question my capability? You, of all people? You, who are guilty of crimes that others died for and were imprisoned for? No, I didn't enclose the Primordium chamber.

I did, however, program the walls so no one without Themian blood could enter that chamber."

"My guess is that's your answer then. Isn't it, Athena?" I replied.

"They should have never been able to enter." Her lip curled at the side. Athena's emotions were off the board. I had never experienced her so on the edge.

Directing her ire at Sydney, Athena demanded. "How many times did you go into the pool?"

Sydney blinked, then straightened her shoulders and shifted her stance. "My children went in twice and so did I. What difference does it make? We went in the water for a swim." Sydney finished her words with a dry laugh. Her body was flooded with endorphins and adrenaline.

"How much time between exposures?" Athena asked then smacked her lips together searching for moisture that wasn't there.

"The kids, one right after the other, mine was" she turned her head to the side, "about 12 hours apart." Sydney remarked, "It's just water." Then shrugged.

"It is not just water," Athena remarked, "Hera, I don't know how, but you've done it again. You turned humans into immortals," she spat as if the very taste of a shared immortality was vile.

"You know they're not human. They're half Themian. That's how they were able to get past the ship's programs," I informed her.

Athena took to her feet. The emotions rolling off her were out of character. But Athena never liked to be outplayed and I had outplayed her. It ate her from the inside out. A part of me wanted to take satisfaction in my small win, but the war wasn't over and Athena still held the possibility for the winning hand.

"Take them away!" She ordered.

Apollo and Artemis herded Sydney out of the Citadel. I imagined that they would take her to the labs because they were the only rooms with enough shielding to contain her.

"Well, Hera, what are you waiting for? The High Council awaits," Athena held out her hand indicating an exit from the amphitheater.

Two Themian guards flanked behind me, at a distance, so I followed Athena through the ship, to her private quarters. The door opened at her bracelet and she moved aside for me to enter.

"Stay at the door and do not let Hera leave unescorted!" She instructed the guards and with that, the doors slid closed.

Athena took out the injector which carried the blue serum for an induced dreamwalk. Athena's chamber was laid out for the leader of the project to control most of the ship from this room if necessary. It was right down to the windows necessary for a shifter to move the ship from here.

The dream couches reclined in an alcove off to the side. I moved to my appropriate couch and laid back to wait for my injection. I could dreamwalk Athena anywhere, to anyone. I could dominate her mind into believing she had spoken to the High Council, but what then?

My children were on Homeworld 12 and I could not retrieve them without help. I was not a seer. I have to follow the logical path.

"I am sorry, old friend, but you only have yourself to blame," her eyes softened as she gazed down at me. She took my hand in her own and gave it a squeeze. "I only hope for your sake your children are spared."

Without another word, the cold metal of the injector met my skin and flooded my body with the drug. My heavy eyes closed on Alethea and opened in the council's chamber. It was vacant at the moment. I wanted to stroll out the lofty archway to see if there was a new ship sitting on the landing pad, but I shook the silly notion away. My nostalgia for Alethea's launch and my long-forgotten desire to make my parents proud was lost to the past.

I opened the many doors in my mind to the High Council and one for Athena then pulled them all into my mental construct.

The power of a dreamwalker is the power to put anyone to sleep at a whim and release them just as quickly.

I waited for everyone to take their places and Athena began. It was a long list of my sins culminating with the hybrid mating. She held nothing back. I was left to stand my ground with the quaking in my belly and locked knees.

"Do you deny these charges?" Otris, the leader of the High Council, asked.

"No, I'll confirm them. In the immortal words of Pythia, *I have birthed a new race.*" I replied with my head held high.

"Blasphemy! How dare you use Pythia to justify your crimes?" Leto burst and she turned to find agreement with other members. Many nodded.

Otris raised his hand for silence. "What are we to do with you? You were given clemency before and your response is a complete rejection of our forgiving nature. You could have rejoined Themian society by petitioning for it. We might have granted it."

I couldn't help but snort a mirthless laugh at him. "You would never have let me leave Alethea. It is a prison for me. Why did you not just send me to Tartarus with Poseidon and the others? They would have freed me through death. Why force me to stay and watch? Since when did Themia ever understands what 'clemency' is? In order to grant it, you must have empathy, something you are all lacking in," I stopped because I didn't want to cry and the lump in my throat warned me I was on the verge.

"We are not without understanding of justice, Hera," Momos offered his lackluster understanding of emotions.

It sickened me to experience the cold buffeting of suppressed feelings from the room. Each member of the High Council was unable to even fully express how they were feeling about the chair they sat upon. I was wasting my words here.

Let them make their proclamation!

"There is no place in Themia for your destructive influence. You and yours must go!" Therino's voice boomed around my simulated construct.

My mouth dried as my hands grew moist.

"I agree! Our society has no place in it for emotions. That does not make us evil, or wrong. The Great Division was not about emotions, but control. Hera has great control over her emotions. I believe her people do too. Her children have lived on Homeworld 12 for thousands of years and never once caused a problem," Athena stopped to let her argument sink in and continued, "This isn't about Hera's crimes. This is about her people and if they have a right to exist. If we are truly ready to study life and origin, then we must let them live, if only to study them."

My belly turned at her words. I would not allow my offspring to become lab rats. I opened my mouth to speak, but Ortis raised his hand cutting me off.

"We have made our decision."

CHAPTER 5

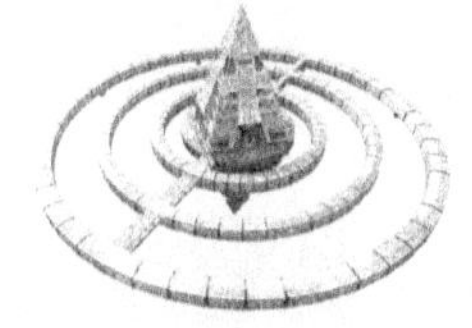

SYDNEY

Authority filled her every word. "We have spoken to the High Council and their reply was simple. Every hybrid must voluntarily leave the planet or be removed by any means necessary."

My belly tightened and my mouth went dry. I gazed over at Adrian.

What exactly does that mean?

My mind raced with the ramifications of her words.

"You will simply kill them off? Only because they do not wish to leave? You are barbaric!" The words were out of my mouth before I could think better. Outrage ripped through my chest burning a path to my eyes.

How dare she and some unseen aliens tell us what to do?

"I have no intention of killing anyone. You will take as many as wish and leave. All who remain will be given gene therapy to remove any and all remaining Themian genes, making them wholly human. There will not be a single hybrid left on this planet," Athena calmly explained.

Horror rolled through me. She would force Themian will on an unsuspecting population?

"What are you saying? How are we supposed to leave the planet?" I demanded gripping my tunic on the sides to hold my emotions and abilities in check.

The room rumbled with me. Many looked around at one another. The name Poseidon was whispered on many lips.

"With a spaceship," Athena supplied.

Oh, gee! Why didn't I think of that? My eyes rolled in my head to further emphasize my irritation.

"My son and I are not strong enough to shift everyone anywhere," Adrian's hand landed on my shoulder and he smiled quietly continuing his sentence only for me to hear.

< I will find a way. Don't worry. I won't let anything happen. >

< I know. What she demands is unreasonable. >

We weren't as subtle as we'd thought.

"We all hear you," Athena said and then moved her attention from us and continued while her eyes widened as her jaw clench down, "It's true, Hera. They are true mates!"

"I told you that they were a true mating of hybrids. If our race doesn't accept hybrids and the fact that we are not above them, we, ourselves, will be bred out of existence. We are equal in different ways. You do not understand that the hybrids have the best of us. They can reproduce at an alarming rate without having to be mated. They can overrun the Universe if they want to," Hera responded and the murmuring arose in the citadel. The Themian's shifted in their seats and whispered to one another.

"We're going to have to teach them the necessary restraint," a deep baritone informed the amphitheater.

We all turned at the deep timber of the new voice that joined the conversation. The man had glossy black hair that was pulled back, hanging in one long braid behind him. He stood taller than any man I had ever seen. His build was lean, with broad shoulders that tapered to narrow hips.

"Ixis, you have come to offer some insight?" Athena asked. She moved in her seat and repositioned her elbows on the armrests.

"By the order of the High Council, I'm here to collect all the hybrids. They will certainly leave the area and I will go with them." He announced.

A great rumble tore through the citadel. With many voices all speaking just one word 'no'. Most cried, or shouted, but all murmured at the same thing.

Hera shouted over the din, "Do you really think that your exclamations are going to change his view? Change his choice?" she demanded.

"Why should you go with them? You are our strongest shifter," Athena asked then took to her feet.

A radiant smile broke over his face and he turned to face our group. All that dark hair and reddish toned skin was nothing compared to the indigo blue eyes that lit up in his face. He extended his hands and Emily ran like a schoolgirl. Everywhere in the room the air filled with disbelief.

His strong-arm cradled Emily. "I have mated, so I will go with my mate and her people. We'll never be separated and you cannot force me to stay with Themia or to believe in our cause. I used to think we were moral, simple scientists that were looking to explore the Universe and discover new life," his smile melted away and he continued, "But we are not. What has happened here is a travesty. We came to this planet and lorded over them, trying to understand what had happened to ourselves." His mouth opened and closed several times.

Athena's nostrils flared. "You're mated to a hybrid? How long has she been living on the island here?"

Ixis ran his hand over Emily's hair and she leaned to him. "I've been mated to Emmaline for more than 70 years. I believed my work was always more important than our meeting. I knew that she was a hybrid. I didn't visit her in a dreamwalk because I feared that Themia would discover her, but I'm afraid no longer. Fear is something I learned from humanity, something all our people could benefit from. Fear helps remove arrogance. We have no fear of death. We have no fear of failure. We live so long and whatever we put our minds to, we never fail at. We just keep going until we succeed. It's the only reason Emmaline's alive today."

He turned to gaze silently down at her before he continued, "She was dying of cancer and I knew if I did not tell her to get the Primordium, she would have died, so my fear kept me from telling anyone and ending this travesty decades ago. I was still farming worlds, hoping to improve the Universe to make it more habitable for our life form. But I began to wonder how much hubris do I need? Our people have become self-absorbed children. We're willing to alter the Universe to our own desires," he released Emmaline and turned so his voice would carry into the far reaches of the cavernous space. "I have moved thousands of worlds in my lifetime, but I never really stopped to consider whether it might develop life on its own. Instead, I moved planets right where our people wanted them to be, so that in a couple of thousand years an environment would form for us to live on. We used them as we saw fit, like a virus altering environments. Instead of adapting to the Universe, we have manipulated it. It's wrong and we've done it on a grand scale. How many Galaxies, solar systems, and stars do we need to infest? I've moved thousands of planets and thousands more stars. I've visited a hundreds of thousands of Galaxies. The Universe is massive on a scale that our people can barely comprehend themselves. Yet, we alter it all just for us? No more!" He boomed his resolve.

Athena's shoulders sagged. She was beaten. Ixis was the oldest Themian on the island and his words rang true. On a deep level, I was awed by what he'd said - farming worlds, moving stars.

I looked over at Tristan. He'd moved a body, but I never dreamed that he might be capable of moving a world. Adrian moved me into the Primordium chamber, but that was a far cry from a planet or a star.

"So, you intend to go with them?" Athena replied.

"Yes. We created a new race of people. People with fabulous powers much like our own. As far as experience goes, they are young and untried. The High Council gave me permission to take one ship and all who will fit upon it. Human, hybrid, Themian, it doesn't matter."

Her head shot up with raised eyebrows and a retort on her lips, disdain dripping from her. "You lobbied on their behalf?"

"Yes, of course, I did. Any children I have will be hybrids also," Ixis said.

Her mouth was set in a grim line. "You have three days to gather all your people on the ship and leave the planet. It is important that the project continues. Once the planet is cleansed of the hybrids, and mind my words, there will never be another contact between us and the humans ever again, we are to observe at distance only, with no interaction. Anyone violating is to be exiled to Tartarus." Athena raised her chin and stepped forward proudly, then turned and left the room.

CHAPTER 6

SYDNEY

Taking a deep breath, I took in the scene. The room had a clear dividing line between the Themian's, hybrids, and sympathizers.

Hera smiled. "Well, Sydney, you're in charge. What would you like to do?"

I'm in charge?

I've never really thought of myself as a leader. How was I supposed to lead all those people? How many people were there?

< There are millions. > Adrian informed me.

I stepped back and looked at our group and addressed all the minds in our circle.

< Transport us all to a private space, please. >

The pressure around us changed along with a pop. A second later our entire group appeared in a large room.

"I hope you'll find this to be an acceptable private meeting place. After all, it's going to be part of our home till we find our own planet," Ixis said opening his arm at the pronouncement.

Emmaline gazed up at him with hungry adoring eyes. Seeing two people so engrossed in one another was somehow sickening, but I guess anyone who saw Adrian and I together would have thought the same thing, at one time.

However, that was not my prime concern. The matter at hand made me crazy.

"How do we identify all the hybrids and get them here in three days?" I bit my lip over the idea.

Hera instantly supplied her answer. "I will send a subliminal dream to every hybrid on the planet. They are all genetically linked to me. This is also how I found you," she smirked.

Isolde butted in. "Wait! Is that what you did to us? Never mind!" It was like she couldn't speak fast enough everything she was thinking. "But you can't just think to take people out of their homes. I'm assuming you want to ship them all here. That's great but we can't just take people away from everything forever," she concluded.

I had hardly glanced around the space Ixis had moved us to. It was a large trapezoid-shaped room with a domed ceiling. I paced for a moment before looking up to find the answers I was grasping at. However, what I encountered wasn't a ceiling at all, but a domed clear window into the cosmos. The pervasive black was speckled with stars, more than I could count in a lifetime. I glanced at my companions and the only ones not staring at the stars were Emmaline and Ixis.

Emmaline had her arms crossed and a smirk plastered over her face. She uncrossed her arms and reached for Ixis, then tapped her left temple. I knew what she meant. She already had seen it through Ixis. I gave her a small smile and shook my head.

Refocusing on the task at hand I continued. "You need to give people a choice. We need to find out what they want to bring with them. Not everyone is going to want to come."

I paced the room, soaking in the soft blue light. There was a lot of nodding around the group.

"One of the best ways to find out what people want is to tell them 'you have one hour to pack everything because you're never going to come back to your house.' We need to subliminally plant in their mind what they must to do, and get them to do it." Hera's idea was quick and to the point.

From the sound of her voice, I was sure that Hera had done this before. I wanted to know to whom and why. However, we didn't have the time for a walk down Hera's meddling lane.

"Doesn't this seem a little mean? Like we are manipulating them?" Isolde's hands twisted one over the other in front of her. She was always so sensitive to people's feelings.

"Issy, if we leave them here, the Themians will take what they are away from them. Wouldn't it be kinder to allow them to bring the most prized possessions so that the transfer isn't so painful?" Tristan asked, soothing her.

Issy raised her shoulders and sighed in acquiescence. "I guess so, but it's like they don't have a choice. I feel bad for them. They're all going to be so confused and angry." She grabbed her elbows and held herself.

"If you want, I can help block all this, Isolde. What we're talking about will be saving their lives. Just think for a second what'll be left behind after the gene therapy?" Hera placed a hand on Issy's shoulder and her ability to influence emotions worked its magic on her. Issy didn't flinch away. "These people don't understand the depth of the change. Hybrids enjoy better health. Tell me, have you ever been sick?" Hera asked.

"No, haven't broken a bone either," Issy said.

Tristan crossed his arms and joined the conversation, "I broke an arm."

Hera shook her head. "Your arm broke because you fell in such a way there was no chance to avoid the bone breaking."

Hera's intimate knowledge of our lives unnerved me. I didn't want to think about her tiptoeing through my mind ever.

"Most hybrids are never going to break a bone because the skeletal structure is too resilient. However, even if this happens, it's easy for a hybrid to quickly repair a fracture to the point that no one would ever even know that the bone was injured. Breaking a bone requires excessive force for us. As far as I know, all hybrids have inherited that ability. You all live longer, are healthier and most of you tend to be smarter. Would you really take that away from them?" Hera asked.

Tristan looked down and shook his head.

"Let's get this show on the road, Hera!" I stepped in. "You dreamwalk the hybrids and give them mental suggestions, but how soon can we start transporting people?" I wanted to know the logistics and I wanted this issue to be taken care of quickly.

Issy still looked strained. Every muscle pulled tight across her face.

"What about the wives and husbands that aren't hybrids? What happens to them? We tear their family apart? What if they all want to go but the other person doesn't, what then? What about the rest of their family? Mothers and fathers from the human side or adopted kids or fosters. Family is whatever you want it to be. We can't make humans come with us and we can't leave them behind if they want to come." Her point cut to the bone of the matter.

How do we conquer this one?

"Athena didn't say we couldn't take humans," I ventured. However, working the problem gave me a déjà vu.

"The High Council said we could take any who wish it," Ixis deep baritone cut through all doubts.

"Hera, add additional family to the list. I don't care about the logistics," I demanded.

"What about your father?" Adrian asked.

I turned to meet his eyes and the heat rose in my chest. "My father will never come with us," I spat out over the lump in my throat.

Hera came over to join us. Her eyes lingered on me, but I looked down and away. I didn't know what she was looking for and actually didn't care.

"Sydney, you have to forgive," she supplied.

Hera had a way of connecting to people I've never experienced before. Almost my entire life she had been trying to communicate with me and the sense that I know her lingered, clinging to my psyche like grease to a pan. However, on the issue of my father, I was completely irrational. My father and what happened to me all those years ago drove me to a place where I couldn't be anything but neurotic.

"I cannot forgive him, ever! What he did to me was monstrous." I rounded on Adrian and continued, "You lived through it. How can you even suggest we take him with us? He's a monster."

Hera worked her calming way as her hands cupped the sides of my face. "Sydney, your father, Edward, his mind, something is broken there. He can be fixed, or so I think. Doesn't everyone deserve a chance to heal?"

I jerked back. I knew she was using her ability on me and calming me using suggestive reasoning.

"I'm not sure I can ever bring myself to do that," I replied with a thick voice.

Emmaline joined our group. "Perhaps, I can help ya'll out? I don't think it's an issue of your father comin' or not." She had a strange twang in her voice. Everything came out clipped. She talked so fast that she cut the ends off words that slowed her down.

"Edward died a year ago," she stated. "From what Adrian told me, good riddance. I don't want to travel the cosmos with that kind of poison hangin' round," she added shaking her shoulders.

"You knew?" I asked Adrian cocking an eyebrow at him.

Emmaline continued before Adrian could, "Dewey went to his funeral. You remember Dewey, my brother? I told you about him," she said to Adrian and Ixis at the same time.

< I'm sorry, Sydney! I wasn't trying to hurt you but you are going to have to forgive and start anew. All business needs to be settled before we leave this planet. >

I turned away from everyone. Letting them see my pain was more than I could handle. So I did what I do best, I pushed it back out of the way. Swallowing back the flash of memories that came with the mention of my father-Edward, I changed tack and focused on the problem at hand.

< *I should let it go, but I can't. Healing is about forgiveness, and I can't forgive.* > I told Adrian.

He didn't reply, so I turned back to face the mountain of problems that fell into our laps.

CHAPTER 7

SYDNEY

The next time I searched for Adrian with my eyes, he was standing next to Ixis. They were talking, but it was just a buzzing in the back of my mind. I couldn't hear what they were saying. When Adrian ended eye contact with Ixis, he gazed over at me.

"Well, as long as Hera tells us who's ready and when, we can start moving people right away, in small or large groups, depending upon the family's size." Adrian rested his hand on Tristan's shoulder. Tristan stiffened but didn't shrug him off, so Adrian continued. "Ixis, Tristan and I are all shifters. The three of us must work together. Tristan and I are never gonna learn his level of control or become as strong if we don't work alongside Ixis. We need to do a lot of the heavy lifting ourselves to make this work."

I wasn't really sure how to react to that. Adrian's actions made it public, not only that Tristan was his son, but that he intended to take a leadership role in his life.

Tristan crossed his arms and scowled for a moment. "What makes you think I'm going to work with you?" he mumbled under his breath.

I stiffened at the public challenge and I realized that it could only mean a fight. Adrian shook his head with his little secretive smile, then shifted all four of us to a different room on the ship.

< *I don't like being moved without my consent.* > I huffed

< **Next time, beautiful girl.** > He replied only for me. Then he focused his attention on Tristan and started talking out loud.

"Tristan, I'm not your enemy. I know that I can never replace your dad, but I am your biological father and I can teach you things Gabriel never could have. You wouldn't be here without me. At first I didn't understand what Hera meant by a dreamwalk but I do now. I get it very clearly now and understand exactly how you came into existence," Adrian said and kept his ground.

The similarities between the two of them were striking. Adrian was taller by a few inches and broader through the chest, but Tristan was only 18 and he wasn't done growing.

Tristan uncrossed his arms and grounded his teeth down. "Is someone going to explain it to me?"

My chest heaved from the deep breath I had been holding. I looked away to the other side of the room. I didn't want to start this conversation.

"It's very simple, Tristan. Themian mates do not always live together. Sometimes they don't see each other for thousands of years," Adrian poured out his wealth of knowledge, only to be joined by a new voice.

"They work on different projects and have different interests, but their minds are joined and they live the same lives through each other. This is why we evolved to be able to reproduce over vast distances." Hera's intrusion wasn't unwelcome, but she seemed to be everywhere. "Our people discovered the dreamwalk. Mostly, it can only be done between mated couples and it's very rare for a dreamwalk to happen between two people who are not mated. I am a dreamwalker. It is a special gift. I can bring as many people into the dream as I wish, or have only one. Apparently, your parents dreamwalk too," Hera smiled when she finished her lesson in Themian dreamwalking.

"Great! What does that mean exactly?" Tristan huffed.

Issy laughed out loud. "Really, Tristan? You want them to spell it out for you? They somehow met each other in a dream and had sex, stupid."

"Issy, you make it sound so cardinal. It isn't like I posted on Tinder or something," I retorted over my embarrassment.

"But that's what you did, isn't it?" Tristan asked.

I sighed and ran my fingers through my hair absently. "Yes, but it was a dream, or at least I thought it was a dream. I didn't know it was real." Now I gripped my tunic with the desperation of a woman wishing only to hide under all the fabric.

"A dreamwalk means that you can be present in the other person's life, without physically being there. It's like a materialized astral projection - there but not there." Hera's interjections were fascinating and irritating at the same time. "Mated couples can have sex and thereby the female can potentially become pregnant and reproduce children. I know that your parents had no idea what a dreamwalk was. They didn't even know they were hybrids."

Tristan reached his hand up and scratched the back of his head, then pulled on the hair hanging in his eyes. On cue Adrian mirrored him.

"It's pretty simple. Sometimes I go to sleep thinking about your Mom and I wake up and she is there," Adrian offered, but judging from the muscle working over the jawbone on Tristan's face, it didn't help.

"How is that even possible that you can go to sleep and wake up where she is? By the time of my conception, my father had to be there. How come he didn't notice? I mean he was there, wasn't he?"

I took a deep breath and joined the conversation. "Adrian only dreamwalked me once, Tristan. I did all the rest. I went to sleep thinking about him and wake up wherever he was. If you want to blame someone for your existence, blame me and not Adrian."

There it was. I was the one to blame for all of this. It wasn't cheating, Gabe didn't know, I didn't know. But I did it, none the less.

"So, you were married to daddy but you were still thinking about this other guy? I don't even want to start with the fact that you were having sex with him in your dreams," Tristan spat.

"You know, Tristan, when you say it like that, it sounds so dirty and disgusting. That is not how it happened." I moved in front of him. Tristan had always been my sweet boy and suddenly that was washed away. "It was a dream! Let's take it this way. Imagine that you are sleeping and, in your dream, you see a pretty girl who is emotionally and physically available to you. Would you go for it in your dream thinking there were no ramifications for your actions?" I raised my hands with the question. "It's just a dream so you aren't hurting anyone and it's only going on in your mind, it's private, right?" I asked.

"Yes, I would do it if I didn't think anybody would find out. I'd be pretty embarrassed too if there was physical proof of my lust," he mumbled.

"Thank you for calling it lust, Tristan," I huffed. "You can be upset about it if you want to be, but the truth is that you wouldn't be here if I hadn't done what I did consciously or unconsciously. I woke up from one of those dreams and I was obviously with your father. So, of course, this is how your sister came to existence. We're hybrids and strange things are gonna happen to us. I guess it's just the nature of who and what we are. You can either accept that this is how you came into existence or you can punish me and Adrian, who by the way, really had no idea. You can do it for the rest of our lives or you can get over it now."

"What do you mean 'he had no idea'? Are you saying that you had an idea?" Tristian quipped.

Well crap! I really let the cat out of the bag now. Tread carefully, Syd!

"Yes!"

Fuck!

"So, all this time you suspected?" He was getting more impatient.

Fuck! This sounds so bad. There is no way to candy coat it.

"Yes, I've suspected for a while now. After you broke your arm, your blood type was wrong. You couldn't be Gabriel's. It's physiologically impossible because you can't be O- and have a father who's a B+. It's impossible. I knew Adrian was O- and you look so much alike. I suspected a long time ago, but I thought that was impossible." Issuing a dry laugh, I continued, "In the human world, what we're talking about is impossible. It could never happen. The Adrian in my world was dead. It was just someone I dreamed about. So, for me to become impregnated by two different men, was not something that I could even begin to comprehend." I sucked in a deep breath. "But in the Themian hybrid world..."

Issy cut in, "DemiGod world, mom."

I shot her a glare. "What we're talking about is not impossible. It's not crazy and it happened to me." I took another deep breath and hoped that this subject was almost over. "Whether I suspected it or not, it really doesn't matter because that's exactly what happened. I had no proof at the time. Why would I open my mouth and say anything to you or anyone else? Why wouldn't I just be quiet and keep my crazy suspicions to myself? After all, I thought I was the only one with my abilities. We live in a very different world today than the one we knew yesterday."

Presenting his back to me with his arms crossed, Tristan moved away from our group and Issy floated over to him. I looked at her petite frame next to his towering bulk and the stark contrast struck me. She wrapped her arms around him, but he remained stoic and withdrawn.

< He will get over it. You can't snap your fingers and change 18 years of a belief system overnight. > Adrian murmurs in my mind.

< *I know. My life is crazy. I love you!* > I responded.

< I love you too! Let's move some people. We only have 3 days and we are going to need every one of them. >

Tristan whirled around. "I can hear everything you two are saying."

"Then, you should know that we didn't plan this. Give Adrian a chance! Be mad at me if you need someone to hate," I offered, that feeling that my child might not get over it welled up inside me.

Tristan clenched his jaw, working the muscle over the bone. "I can't stay mad at you…" He came and hugged me gruffly. "I'll try to get over it, mom." He mumbled.

It was the best I was going to get on short notice. I kissed his bristled cheek and petted his hair. Adrian was going to have quite a time with him.

*****

Adrian moved us all back to the domed room to rejoin our crew. Crew, I guess that is what we are, now. I dragged my thoughts and eyes away from my children and saw a podium looking device perched in the center of the space. It was projecting a 3-dimensional star chart into the air above it. I smiled as I walked closer to the projection and was able to pick out Saturn and Jupiter. When I turned my head, I observed Emmaline playing with the display dials.

The projection changed from a flat holographic image to a tilted one, our nine planets all traveling around our sun on a flat plan.

I smiled at Emmaline. "Why does Adrian call you Emily?"

She absently snorted, then pressed a new button turning the image from just planets to a tracker for their solar rotations. I kept staring at her, waiting for an answer.

"First off, Emily isn't my name. I don't like it and never have. Grace called me that and I let her cause she was little and cute. Then she named her girl Emily, claimin' it was after me." She made an ugh sound. "Adrian's the only one who says it like he loves me, so I let him. You were always a sweet thing when you were little but even then, you called me Emmaline. Let's keep it that way. I earned every bit of them letters and I want to use them all to the fullest!" She gave me a knowing smirk and a hip thrust.

I regained my balance and laughed. I didn't remember Emmaline, but she looked like Grace, only younger and full of trouble.

"Well, take a look at that! What do you suppose that means? Is it broken?" Emmaline asked, then covered her mouth with her hand.

I glanced up at the holograph. Nine orbital lines on a fairly flat plan circled the sun, only to be intersected by an elliptical path that crossed the plane at an acute approximately 32° angle. The holograph didn't show what was on the other end of the orbit. It ended after Pluto.

"It could be a comet," I offered.

"I don't think so, but we don't have time to look into it. Ix says he wants a pow-wow." She winked and tapped her temple.

I glazed around the room and spied Hera sitting off to the side in a trance-like pose, in what I could only describe as a space lazy-boy. I wanted to snicker but I watched Ixis inject something blue into her neck and her eyes drifted closed.

"Ixis, you've been in deep space for long periods of time. What can we do to make it easier for everyone?" I asked not only to gauge his ideas but for my own peace of mind.

"Well, Darlin', Ix is an expert on deep space. I'm sure he's going to give us the low, low down. Just as soon as he's done bein' the movin' man."

Emmaline could make anyone laugh out loud. She had a nickname for everyone. Come to think of it, Adrian did too…

CHAPTER 8

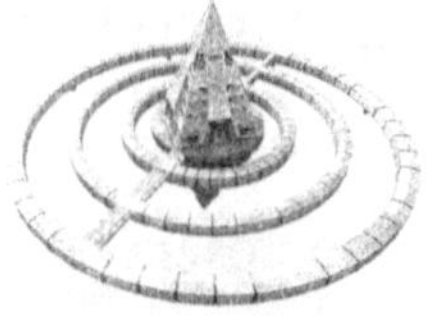

HERA

I drifted off into the dreamwalk, but the holograph of the terrain system nagged at me. It lasted barely a moment before Ixis gave me the shot. The dream drug flooded into my body, creating the feeling of floating.

This was the in-between and I usually stayed in it for a while. I loved the in-between because it was the only place where no one could reach me, where I was utterly free.

However, I didn't have time for that and if all went well, I would probably never need the in-between again. My heartbeat rose with the thought and my dream-self smiled at the thought of freedom.

The construct took form before me - the shining white citadel on Homeworld 10. It was the place where my fate had been sealed and it was always the building I chose. Even as a child when I could have chosen anything, I always chose that building. Not only did it represent power but the sheer size of it created a place with so many openings. With it, I could walk billions of minds.

The Themian people counted more than a hundred billion. The only way for me to dream walk all of them would be to change my construct to a planet. I had never needed one so large. I shivered at the thought of a day where I would need a construct of that size.

I floated and paced across the landing field of my fake Homeworld 10, passing under the arches and into the citadel. Focusing only on my bloodline, I watched as billions of opening in the walls disappeared leaving only my hybrids.

A tight smiled lined on my lips and I left it there. Several million windows remained, each one aligned under my children's names. The openings branched out like the roots of a plant reaching deep into the soil of an ecosystem or the fingers of a lightning bolt, splitting apart to reach the land while burning its way through the sky.

The thought of lightning still stung my heart. I would never be free from my thoughts of Zeus. Even on the eve of my success, he was present in my mind to torture me.

Two days with Sydney by my side had taught me one thing - pushing your problems to the background only gives you space to operate but it doesn't make them go away. I shook my head to clear the dark thoughts out of my way. I could exercise my demons afterward.

The windows waited for me and with one thought I opened them all. The voices of my blood poured into the silent world I'd created. Each of them muttered about something that seemed so important and was unaware of the change that was coming.

I whispered to them like I had my own children, of dreams and wishes, hopes and desires and how none of them could have come true in their world. I told them to pack and take all they had of value.

Some were greedy, others had nothing at all. A few only wanted one thing. One little boy asked for a pony. I smiled to myself and added his wish to the list of things to move as if I was the Santa Claus of hybrids.

Not all of them were asleep, but all answered the call of the dreamwalk. One man missed his bus stop from dozing, another lost her job, but all took the catnap and the message.

< Pack! We must leave. > I instructed all the hybrids.

Millions readied themselves.

Sydney had been small potatoes compared to this. I had never dreamwalked so many at once. The power filled me like a drug. I had the power to instruct them in any way I wanted, but none of them could give me what my heart desired, so I allowed them to follow my call and pack. Offering passage to all family members who wished to come also.

At the top of the pile remained my children. All eight doors were open wide and they could hear my call. I pushed all to the side but my children. They too began to ready themselves, packing what few belongings they cared for.

A thousand years should have carried so much more to show for their time. But they cared little for Themia and Homeworld 14. Their only interest was in leaving.

I wanted to go to them and share how close we really were, but without the completed task it was still just the wishful thinking of eons and nothing more. Fire burned in my eyes and belly.

To be so close…What if Sydney will not get them? What if Themia will not let us take them?

The old fears poured back in, stealing my joy. I pressed my eyes closed.

It's a construct, I don't need to fear here.

I breathed deeply and sent the first of my visions to Ixis to disseminate to Adrian and Tristan.

Breathing through the flashes of images, I moved from one family group to the next, allowing the strength of the dreamwalk to grow with every shift image.

Each family brings me closer to success.

CHAPTER 9

SYDNEY

"Is there a good spot to sleep until you start moving people?" I asked glancing around the shifting room.

Emmaline winked at me, and a second later we disappeared and reappeared in a small room with a couch in the center.

"I hate that!" I huffed then ran my hands up and down my arms to work heat back into them.

Emmaline laughed. "Awe, Darlin', that is the best part about being with a shifter. You can go wherever you want in a jiffy." She opened a door that let off from the room and pointed at the bed.

"Shifter?" I mused.

"Yeah! That's what Themian's call them, cause they're shifting from one spot to another. However, I like the term 'movin-man' better. They always have those big muscles and tight shirts." She hitched a half-smile at me with a twinkle in her eyes.

I couldn't help but smile back. I could bet that she loved to watch construction crews too.

"Look, when we're ready for ye, Tristan will shift ye back. Ix and Adrian will be in it hot and heavy." Emmaline petted my arm and disappeared leaving only a whiff of ozone and cold air.

I tried to sleep, but other than a light snooze it was a waste of time. I finally gave up and got up.

< *Tristan, do we have an ETA?* > I inquired.

< Two hours give or take. >

I left the room to wander the halls. I opened doors. There were hundreds and most of them led to more berths. I changed hallways from one ring to another. The connecting corridors were made out of more domed glass on the ceiling, giving me a view of the Earth and the Moon. I stopped to stare at the world that was my birth home.

I wondered how Adam and Eve felt when they were ejected from their garden home. My hand touched the glass. It wasn't cold, but cool.

What would these Aliens do if we didn't leave? What could we do to stop them? There were so many of them and so few of us.

My feelings of weakness angered and frustrated me.

Earth isn't theirs. The people living there aren't lab rats for them to watch over.

But if Hera hadn't interfered, I wouldn't be here. It was the chicken and the egg issue.

Fuck, I hate this!

I opened a few doors that lead to rooms filled with plants and a light similar to the Sun's. One was a red Sun and the plants were just as happy as if it had been a yellow one.

< We're ready! > Tristan announced.

< Okay!>

Tristan shifted me back to the domed room that I thought to be the bridge.

"The first batch is ready to be moved?" I asked.

The holograph was off and Tristan, Ixis and Adrian stood around the display controls facing each other.

"Yes. There's a family in North America and they appear to be ready," Ixis supplied. He looked as though he was as fresh as the rain and so did Trist and Adrian. Actually, Adrian could have been covered in shit and I'd still think he looked great.

< Nice! > Adrian left a smile out. Apparently, he read my thoughts about him.

I smirked at him. "How many are there?" I asked then moved over to stand by Hera's recliner.

"Fifteen," all three said as if their minds were locked together.

Well, that was creepy.

"That's an awfully large family especially for the modern times," I remarked.

"There are four generations," Adrian replied.

"Well, if it's the first one and it's ready to go, I guess we should do this," I remarked.

They all stared blankly and the pressure in the room changed.

"Just like I told you, picture them in your mind. Hera will send you a vision of all their faces. Keep the picture of their faces in your mind. I'll move the inanimate objects and you move the bodies," Ixis instructed.

Tristan froze. "Ixis, what am I gonna do?"

"Tristan, I want you to listen and observe how it's done. I'm going to bring you into my mind. You're not to move anything, go anywhere, do anything other than listen and observe."

I looked over at Hera. Her eyes opened for a moment and she smiled and shook her head in a reassuring manner.

"Sydney, you aren't really needed here. However, we do need to know where you want everyone transported to." Ixis asked without looking my way.

"Do they have a Citadel here? I'm assuming this ship is just like the other one."

"Yes, this should be similar in design to Alethea," Hera supplied.

"Also, our ship should have a name. Most people would find it reassuring if they knew exactly where they were," I said while looking at Ixis.

God, I hope this thing has a name.

Ixis smiled before answering. "The ship does not have a name because it was intended for the next set of projects. We can name it whatever we wish to. You have a name in mind?"

Issy's mind pressed in. She had something she wanted to share and was excited about.

"All right, Issy. What is it?" I sighed

"Odyssey. I think it should be called Odyssey. You know like Ulysses after the Trojan war. After all, if everything about Greek mythology is true but just a little bit different, we're on our own Odyssey, right? We are looking for another planet somewhere our new race of people can settle. We can't live in space forever," she shrugged.

"I guess we've kind of been on our own Odyssey for a long time, hey Issy? After all, wasn't Calypso one of the islands that Ulysses visited?" Tristan asked.

"Yeah! Mom, why exactly did you choose the name 'Calypso' for the boat?" Issy inquired, with a knowing smile.

"I didn't. Hera did," I announced then glanced at the woman in the space recliner.

Hera's smile widened. "Calypso was lovely but she had a taste for human men, always luring them to her. Her island was everything that anyone could ever want. It was like an oasis, a heaven in the middle of the storm. I wanted you to feel like your boat was a heaven in your storm. After Ulysses left Calypso's islands, he made it straight home. I wanted Calypso to bring you and your mother home." She had a secretive smile. When she finished talking, she laid back in the recliner.

"What happened to Calypso? Is she still on Earth?" Issy asked always looking for more.

Hera closed her eyes before responding. "No, she died. One of the human men she ensnared was able to break free from her manipulations. Being a siren, luring men to their deaths and enslaving them, has a price. When they wake up from the trance, they're angry. He was the only one who ever did wake up and she paid the price for it. Osiris suffered a similar fate. They brought it on themselves," she shook her head with those final words.

"One of these days, Hera, you're going to tell us the real story of the Gods," Emmaline muttered.

"When you tell someone the truth about something, it's like killing them. They were never Gods, to begin with," Hera heaved a sigh only to continue, "If I tell you the truth, I'll simply be killing them, all over again. Yes, I guess my people started this nonsense. They allowed humans to believed they were Gods. In Greek mythology, all of the Gods seem to be petty and small-minded. That is because we are. We got everything we deserve, especially Poseidon. Now, I only want us to focus on the future." Her honey blond hair fanned out on the head rest and she closed her eyes.

"Let's get on with moving our people," I remarked drawing them back to our situation and smoothing the white fabric covering my hips.

"Ixis, Adrian, move everyone into the Citadel! Issy, you're with me!" I ordered.

"I'm not sure I'll be able to handle all the emotions," Issy whispered and twisted her hands over each other.

Hera got out of her lazy-boy chair and stepped to the wall of the shifting room. She placed her hand on one of the panels. It slid open like something out of a scifi movie.

Creepy-cool.

Inside there were rows upon rows upon rows of bracelets, all similar in design to the one that Tristan and Isolde had been given on Alethea. She removed five then pressed a panel to close the drawer.

"You will need to wear this. I'll have the computer program it to help you block out whatever you want. This way, it will keep their emotions from overrunning you." She slid it over Isolde's hand and it automatically resized itself to fit her wrist.

"We should all have one of these bracelets." Hera announced, "It will give us full access to the entire ship, including the Infinium pool. The Infinium pool is the most important asset of the entire ship because it can save our race in every way. It can aid even someone who was severely injured unless, of course, their brain is damaged."

"What is the Infinium pool?" I asked.

"It's the pool that holds the Primordial waters," Hera responded briefly and continued talking about the bracelets, "The ship reprograms every bracelet so each one is genetically compatible to the user. This means that they cannot be passed to someone else. As I've said, the Primordial Waters are of great importance, so do not grant access to it to anyone. We have no idea what people are going to be bringing. We need to keep our ship safe in all possible ways."

My mind reeled with all the possibilities. We had no idea if the people that we were bringing, were good or bad. In every group, there is always a bad apple in the barrel.

"If you wish to find the Citadel, simply request the ship to help you. It will use your bracelet to identify your location and lead you where you wish to be," Hera shrugged when she saw that I didn't answer.

I grabbed Isolde's hand and led her into the nearest hallway.

"Take me to the Citadel!" I demanded and waited to see what happened.

The ship did not have a voice. It wasn't like all the Sci-Fi shows I'd watched, where it would say anything. Instead, my bracelet lit up with a blue glow.

"Issy, is yours glowing too?" I asked.

I waved it around for a few minutes, the child inside me enjoying the glow stick effect. I noticed that if I waved it towards one branch of the hallway it got brighter but if I waved it towards the other side it got darker. My cheek worked up into a half-smile.

"I guess we're playing hot-cool."

Issy snickered and waved her arm around.

It took us 15 minutes to reach the Citadel. We got there just before the first family arrived. However, their things were already piled to one side. The cavernous room was heavy with silence and carried the echo of an unused space. On the dais, there were 12 chairs. I glanced over at Issy but she was glued to the pile of things on the floor.

"Well, I'm not sure I like the chairs. They're weird. But the best way to rule is with a group of people and not a single person," I remarked dryly.

"Mom, you're our leader and not Hera or Ixis. Neither of which even seem interested in taking on the role. All the people that are coming, we're going to be the first people they see. They're scared to death. Our job is to calm them. So, the best way to calm them is to tell them the truth."

Issy's sober words chilled me.

"I'm not sure telling them the truth is going to be very comforting but it's worth a try," I said while rubbing my hands together and taking a deep breath. Then running my hands down my clothes. It never occurred to me I would be meeting a ton of people looking like a rag a muffin. But my rumpled clothes would have to do.

"Well, it doesn't matter. Comforting or not, mom, most people do better with the truth. Don't candy-coat it. Don't give them a line. Just be yourself, like when you talk to Tristan and me," she answered and gave me a smile.

The dais had three steps off to the side. I mounted them to reach the center seat. A family group appeared in front of us and they were indeed 15 souls.

They all carried the wide eyes of terror. I took in the small children that were clutched onto their parents. The only person in the group who didn't look the least bit frightened was a bright-eyed young girl with long black hair and dark ringed clear blue eyes. She smiled at me and I heard her loud and clear,

< Finally! > she sighed in satisfaction.

I was unprepared to hear anyone speak in my mind. I opened and closed my mouth and tried again.

"I know you're scared, wondering how and why you're here." I licked my lips ready to start again, but I was interrupted.

"I know why we are here. We are different and special. My name is Caroline and I've been waiting for this moment. I knew you would come. I dreamt about you." She smirked.

Isolde did a quick intake of breath before asking, "You dreamt about me?"

"Yes, I looked it up. It's called pre-cog, precognition. I also saw your mother's face and she told me that you would come. I'm so glad you came in the dream. Hera gave us a choice - stay on Earth or discover a new world. I chose you, we belong with our people."

She held the hand of an older man with the same dark hair and smile. She grinned up at him and he squeezed her hand.

For all the years that I thought I was alone, I didn't know how to accept myself. I looked at the young teenage girl in front of me who didn't seem to have had one problem accepting who and what she was.

How is that possible? It's so easy for her and for me it was a struggle every moment of every day.

"It's possible because I already saw in a dream exactly what I would do," she responded after hearing my thoughts. "Knowing one's future makes it easier to live life. When we woke up from the dream, I convinced my family to come with us." She stopped and reached her hand out to Issy. "I'll help you when everyone arrives. I know we're going to be good friends. I can't wait for the boys," Caroline finished the sentence with a giggle.

I guess that knowing your future makes it easier to figure out how to live your life every day.

There was a rumbling in the background every time a new group entered the room. Some could send and receive thoughts like myself and my children, but it was low like they sent signals on a different radio station. I opened my mind and listened. These were my people. If I was going to lead them anywhere, I had to know where they wanted to go.

I slowly opened all the conduits in my mind and the voices began to pour in, all filled with worry. First thing I had to do was to quiet them.

< I can hear all of you. You need to quiet your mind and relax. I'll be explaining everything in time. Let's wait until everyone's here. Till then, you're welcome to wander around in this room as much as you wish. You can move your things too if you desire. No one here will steal from you. You are perfectly safe. >

The room grew quiet and stilled, all except Caroline. They all turned to face me and the dais.

An old woman stepped forward from Caroline's group. "My mother told me that this would happen one day. That we would all be together, all of us that are the same. Which line are you from?" She asked.

"Lines, what do you mean?" I hated being out of step.

"Well, I was told that in the beginning there were five lines. And that all five lines sent their genes and special powers, like the one Caroline has. She's got sight. She can see what's gonna happen. Everyone belongs to one of the five, so which one are you?" She demanded, thrusting her chin out.

"I'm an O'Dear," I stuttered.

"Not your last name, girl. Your bloodline?" She demanded while shaking her head and making a tsking sound with her mouth.

She moved to my side with a speed a woman her age shouldn't have. Her blue eyes stared at me unseeing before a smile broke over her face. "Girls. You're from the girls, but you got someone else in ya, someone else's blood. That's what makes you so special," she finished with a pat on my hand.

"The girls?" I asked.

"Hera will explain. Don't worry! Caroline said she will," the old woman said.

"We're all that's left of our branch. People don't have as many children these days as they used to. After a couple of generations, we started to really die off. Everybody here can hear but only Caroline's got the sight," the older man I could only assume was Caroline's father said while looking at his daughter. After a moment, he took his eyes off of her and added, "We're going to take that corner over there."

It's an amphitheater. The room is round. I snickered to myself.

The old woman who spoke earlier turned around and raised an eyebrow at me.

"We know there are no corners in an amphitheater. It's just a turn of phrase. My name's Nell and you best treat me with some respects." She snipped.

She just nodded her head in a sharp motion and said something to the man who looked like he was probably her son. Then everyone in the family began picking things up, moving them off to the side of the room. They took over a grouping of benches, spread out several blankets on the stadium seating, laid the children down and took their seats.

"I would like to stay with you if it's alright. I feel I can be helpful when new people arrive. I may have seen them or I can comfort them," Caroline said while approaching the dais.

Issy immediately seized her hand, "Of course you can stay over here with us."

It was pretty obvious that they were going to be friends and in a short pass of time. I turned back to look at the new families that arrived. They were in various sizes and they appeared in different areas across the Citadel. They all had items that they were carrying in their hands or on their backs. There were also several piles of items that appeared in different locations on the stadium seating. The murmuring of the room grew with each new addition.

"Settle down! You are safe. Please, go find your things and stay by them." I nodded my head to Issy and Caroline, "Go talk to each group. I'll handle the one closest to me."

Both girls headed in separate directions, Issy towards the small family of three and Caroline to the large family of ten. I moved towards the six in front of me. I spoke briefly to each person in the family. Once they calmed down, they moved over to a pile of things and settled in for a long wait.

People began appearing quicker than we could handle. Nell stood up and probably using her loudest voice she said, "Now, there's a lot of us in here, each one having your own problems, but I don't think anybody should get their panties in wade. I am sure we all want to know why we're here, but you have to act like adults. Keep the children under control and mind your manners. Just stop and sit down! I'm sure we will all have a chance to figure out what the heck we're all doing here. Sydney's a busy lady, so don't talk to her too much. She's going to answer all our questions."

I needed help so I contacted Hera.

< Not sure we can handle all these people. >

< Call Emily. She's a calming force. She'll help. > Hera replied.

< *Thank you!* >

< Put your big girl panties on. It's going to be a long night. > Adrian snickered and a picture of me in just my panties flashed through my mind.

I smirked and shoved the door between us closed.

The room filled up quickly and the noise was deafening. I didn't want to send a message to everyone and scare them but I knew that at some point in time it was going to be the only way to keep this room under control because the cornucopia of voices rattled around in my mind, fighting for my attention, all seeking the same answers.

Finally, there were thousands upon thousands in the room, predominantly families both young and old. As I was looking over the room, I heard a voice.

"I'll be damned."

I turned my head looking in either direction several times to try and find the source of the voice. Then I saw an older woman moving in a determined fashion towards the dais. She had silvery long hair and piercing blue eyes. She looked vaguely familiar but I couldn't place her. She stood in front of me with both hands on her hip, legs spread wide with a big shit-eating grin on her face.

"Well, Ms. Sydney Rhiannon O'Dear, I should've known you'd be in charge of this mess."

I shook my head because I had no idea who this woman was.

"Do I know you?"

"'Do I know you?' Now that's the stupidest question I've ever heard. Of course, you know me. I'm your great aunt Melinda. You haven't seen me in like forty years and I'm old as the hills. Don't worry about it. We'll catch up mighty quick. However, let me tell you that you look awfully good for as old as your supposed to be. Must be all that clean living on a boat, right?" She finished her presentation with a wink and a shake of her head.

Melinda. I know my father had an aunt named Melinda. I haven't seen her since I was a small child.

As I was thinking and trying to put my finger on who the person in front of me was, the woman contacted me telepathically.

< Don't think I can't hear you. You are the loudest broadcaster I ever met. Too bad you can't receive too well or you would have heard your father years ago. He was an asshole. >

My eyes went wide. "You can hear me? How long have you been able to hear me?"

Her laugh burst from her mouth like a balloon letting out the air. "Your whole life. I asked Edward about you, but he never wanted to talk about it. He said Mary's daughter wasn't my business. Edward was the most spineless little shit I ever met. He didn't like anybody in the family talking to you and the kids. I'm certainly glad to see you here. Where are your brothers?" She tip-toed up and looked over my shoulders.

I didn't even know my brothers were there. In the back of my mind, I knew I was bringing all the hybrid to the ship, but I guess that the thought of my family being also hybrids never really struck me. To me, the death of Edward meant the death of all of them. I thought of Tobias. I hadn't seen Tobias since I left Florida on the boat the first time. My throat knotted.

I raised my chin to surveyed the room. I didn't even know what Matt and Edward look like. They were early teens when I left. Other than black hair they could be anyone here.

There had to be over a million people in the room. Even with my sight to zoom in on people, I would have needed days to find one of them. I didn't even know if Matt or Edward would even talk to me.

Off to my left and high up in the risers, there was a man with salt and pepper black hair sitting on the second to the top riser. His elbows were resting on his knees and one hand held the other. He was boring holes into me with his eyes. Two little girls jumped around him pointing in every direction. I took two steps off the dais in high gear and in a split second I stood next to him. He reared back in fear.

Every muscle in my face flexed into a smile. His face pulled up into a mirror of my own. I leaned into his wide-open arms. I fitted right into his embrace. For the first time in a very, very long time, I felt the safety of a big bear hug from a brother. I kissed his cheek and he kissed mine. I didn't realize how much I missed him. Tobias had always had the spicy scent of orange and drakkar. I pulled back only to be snared by his blue eyes.

"In the back of my mind I knew you'd be here, but I wasn't looking," I said.

"Don't worry, little sis'. I knew you'd figured it out eventually," his voice came out thick and raw.

"Where's your wife?" I asked my eyes darting around him and the two little girls for Arlene.

He stepped back and looked down and away shaking his head slightly. "When I woke up, mine and the girls' things were all packed. I tried to convince her it would be for the best, but she said we were all freaks. She never wanted to see me or the girls again. I thought she really loved me—"

My heart folded over in my chest. "I'm sorry, T."

"How will I tell the girls?" he glanced over at the twin figures hopping up and down from one row of seats to another.

Both girls stopped jumping, and each took one of his hands.

"Don't worry, daddy! We'll get a new mommy just for you." They smiled up at him with their O'Dear blue eyes and plump cheeks. I swallowed back the lump in my throat for them.

He crouched down to hug his girls. They couldn't have been more than 7.

"Girls, this is your Aunt Sydney, my sister. She's in charge here and I'm sure she'll help us."

His eyes stared at me with that same look I must have given him after our father beat me the first time. He needed answers. I had to give him some, just as I had to give all of them.

"Of course, I will. What are your names?" I asked and smiled over their heads at T.

The twins chorused, "Heather and Clover."

Their faces were smug with a smile. I stood up. It was time. Looking at Tobias, I knew everyone needed the same assurances.

How the hell do politicians do it?

I was ready for a nap when Adrian tickled at the back of my mind.

CHAPTER 10

SYDNEY

< Sydney, we have an issue. > Adrian's voice moved through me like a cool drink of water.

< *Okay. Shoot!* >

< Criminals. There are thousands in jail and thousands more in mental wards. We can't put them in with the main population. >

< *Fuck, I'll be right there!* >

Before I could finish my thought, I was standing in the shifting room and it was Tristan who shifted me there.

"Ixis, can you pull up a layout of the ship? Or do you have a recommendation?" I demanded and huffed.

God, I wish I'd been able to sleep earlier.

Ixis never turned away from Adrian. "The research section is the best place for them. Every room is secured and shielded. I must tell you that some of them are extremely violent while others are having delusions. They need treatment and observation," he supplied in a flat tone.

"Will it be enough to keep them from contacting anyone else or using their abilities? We don't want anyone getting out or mind fucking anyone." I couldn't even imagine what a deranged hybrid could do to an unsuspecting person. I shivered at the very thought of it.

My father had no powers, that I knew of, but he still managed to destroy me with every chance he got. I thought of Edward with my powers for a second, but I quaked at the thought. I needed to focus on the real issue and not memories from the past.

"Yes, the only way to leave the room is with a bracelet," Ixis replied.

"What if they steal one?" I asked.

"As I told you earlier, they are connected to each person's genes. They blend with the first person who puts it on. It won't work on someone else. They can't be changed with mental corruption," Hera informed me then rubbed her hand over her forehead.

"We can't just dump them down there," I said while biting my lip "Hera, find me someone to herd these cats."

Hera glance at me out of the corner of her eye. "Your aunt is the best choice. She's a scientist and has a degree in Psychology." She turned back to Ixis and Adrian. The mental focus of the three men along with Hera was enough to give you the hebe-jebes.

"Tristan, get her up here," I ordered and sent him an image of Melinda.

Aunt Melinda appeared with a pop. "Well, I never... Whose foolish idea was it to transport me without my permission?" She demanded, while her eyes were darting around the room.

I raised my hand and her eyes narrowed to razor-thin slits.

"How many are there?" Melinda asked.

Hera's face broke into a smile. "Thousands, but we can treat them all. I will work with you as soon as I am done here," then she turned back to the mental mind meld of the shifters.

Melinda heaved a sigh. "I'll do it. Can you send me to where you need me? Also, send my things to a set of rooms nearby. I'll need to keep a close eye on all the crazy people. Since you can pluck me off a planet and put me in a spaceship, you can move my things where I want them," she huffed and crossed her arms.

Melinda once again stood with her legs wide and both hands on her hips. She was a no nonsense lady. Ixis nodded his head taking up her challenge.

"I'll send you where you need to be."

Melinda rubbed her hands together. " Let's..." But she was gone.

"I don't have time for that chit chat," Ixis turned back to Adrian and mentally engrossed again.

I bit back a laugh. I was sure Melinda would have a word or two about that later.

"Mom, they are moving people again. If you want, I can shift you back to the Citadel," Tristan said staring at me but through me at the same time.

It was eerie to see my son so disembodied. I slapped my hand to my head.

"Crap! We've sent her without a bracelet. God damn it!"

I dashed to the wall, opened the panel and I pulled one bracelet out. I paused for a second and then grabbed a few more, thrusting them into my pocket. "Send me to Melinda. I'll let you know when I'm ready for the next hop."

With that, the pressure around me changed and then I heard a loud pop followed by a whiff of ozone.

The space I was shifted to, resembled a mall. Every unit had a single door and glass walls from the floor to the ceiling. Each of the doors came with a pass-through slot. They had bathrooms but the walls around them were frosted. The hallway went on forever following a curve, I stood on the outside of the curve.

Melinda leaned off to the side with her back against the wall of a lab. Both her arms were crossed with one leg crossed over the other. Her silver hair hung over one shoulder in a braid.

"Nice of you to show up and help. You want to tell me how to open a door or get out of this prison you moved me to?" The acid dripped from her lips.

I barked out a laugh. "Sorry about that. We have three days to gather every hybrid from the planet and leave. So, we're in a bit of a rush and therefore not everything has been well thought out," I stumbled over my words.

She pushed off the wall. "You think?"

"Melinda, I don't have time for this. We have 3 million people that need to be moved or the Themians are going to pull a gene cleansing on them. So, we're taking everyone. This bracelet will get you wherever you need to go. It will only work for you. I don't know when I will be able to see you again. If you need help, contact me and I'll see what I can do," I shrugged and offered her a tentative smile.

She slid it over her hand and on to her wrist, then waved it around by the lab door.

"How's it work?" she demanded.

"Just go about your day as if it wasn't there." As I spoke, I reached out, placed my hand on the handle and pull the door open.

"That's it? Must send out a signal to the ship." She tried a few doors to make sure it wasn't a fluke.

"I guess. I haven't thought about it. Is there anything else you need?" I asked with a smile.

"Some food in about an hour. Keep your eyes open for a lab assistant or anyone to help out. I'll take whoever I can get. And, Sydney, the conversation you just had with me, you better have with them too." She pointed up, thinking 'they' were on a floor above.

"I'll start polishing up my 'your life on Earth is over forever' speech," I remarked and rubbed my forehead.

"Tell Mr. Serious up there that I want criminals on the right and mental issues on the left. That way I won't have to guess. Also, if they could take all the files associated with each one, that would be nice. I'd like to know who I'm dealing with. My lab is on the right, for your information, of course." She winked at me and entered the lab with a backward wave.

I watched her amble across the room. It was full of equipment. Files, a small frig, tables and chairs, everything she could need was there. As I gazed over the room, and fixated my eyes on the floor by the desk. Next to it was an overflowing trash can. There were bookshelves filled with books that were shoved every which way. As a matter of fact, the entire room had piles of stuff everywhere. There was a lived-in look that the rest of the ship lacked.

I pulled the door open and leaned my head in. "Did you ask for the whole lab?"

"Yes, my work is my life." She replied raising an eyebrow to boot. "I didn't even have to pack. I must say, your guys sure do know how to move." She winked again. "Now get back to your work so I can do mine."

Shaking my head, I called Tristan.

< Take me to the citadel. >

His reply was instant. < Everything okay, Mom? >

< Yes! >

CHAPTER 11

SYDNEY

I felt an increased murmuring in my head. I looked in the crowd. Emmaline was sitting in one of the chairs there. Her face glowed with her new-found happiness. I could see Grace in her smile and that made me sad. Grace would have been here if she had lived long enough. Adrian's parents too.

Emmaline met my eyes and started walking towards me.

"I came to help you out. I know that Dewey's out there somewhere. He's millin' round lookin' for his kids. I came to talk about the blood. We need to tell everyone whose who and separating by family name won't do it."

"Can you send all of them this information?" I asked.

She quirked an eyebrow looking down at me. "What an asinine question. I probably can do it better than you."

I raised both hands in surrender. "I'll take all the help I can get, so go ahead and send them your thoughts."

Emmaline's approach felt different. It was like tuning in to a different channel.

< I want to tell you about the Blood that runs through your veins. My grandma used to say that this was what it was all about. There was a saying in our families "yea marry within the lines." They meant the bloodlines. >

She stopped and waited for the message to sink in.

< If you weren't in the family yea didn't know about it. Nobody in my family ever married outside the lines, till Dewey. >

Her eyes landed and stopped on an old man with blue eyes and a goofy grin. He crossed his arms and nodded his head at her, then mouthed 'I'd do it again'.

I snickered. Both of them reminded me of Grace. A heat pricked my eyes over it.

< At first there were only five families, five bloodlines. Hera had four sets of twins. Every set was formed by a boy and a girl. Sure, they all had kids too, but Hera kept them all a secret. She was scared that they'd be killed. Her children were called Demi-Gods. Zeus fathered every one of them. >

She looked around to see if everyone was listening and she scratched her head.

< I should go back a bit. You've all heard of the Greek Gods. Zeus, the king of the Gods was married to Hera. We are their offspring. Every one of us is a Demi-God. The Gods are real, but they aren't actually Gods, they're Aliens. Isn't that a hoot? What Sydney told you is true. Hera has spent the last 10,000 years hiding us from her Alien family, known as Themian's. A long time ago a guy you've definitely heard of, Poseidon, had children with a human too. They were called the Nephilim. The High Council, that's the people in charge of the Aliens, killed them all. >

I sat down on the dais and listened to Emmaline. She was a true storyteller. Of course, the fact that she could send out a calm over everyone also helped. The room settled down as if it was storytime at the library and Emmaline continued.

< The only reason we are still alive is because of my mate, Ixis. He's a full-blooded Themian. > Her cheeks turned red only at the thought of him. < We're the first true mating between a Themian and a hybrid. Sydney and Adrian are the first mating between two hybrids. >

There was such a pronounced silence in the room that it felt like nobody was even breathing.

< But let's return to the origin and leave the mating part for later. So, Hera and her children, they con-cocked a crazy plan. If they could keep their bloodlines alive long enough and with enough Themian genes in it, something was bound to happen. Now, I know that you're all sayin'. You think that I said she had 4 sets of twins. So, shouldn't there be 8 lines? Your mathematics are correct, but there are actually only 5 bloodlines. >

Emmaline gave me a short glance while she took in a deep amount of air.

< 'So how is it possible' you might ask. It is very simple. The boys took care of their own, while the girls all merged into one bloodline. They encouraged the lines to only marry into each other's families. >

People started murmuring and appeared to lose patience, so Emmaline grabbed their attention again.

< You probably think we're all crazy. But try to think of world history for a second. Marrying your first, second or third cousin wasn't considered all that strange a hundred years ago and two or three hundred years ago it was a must in order to keep money in the family and dynasties alive. >

And with that, the murmurs turned into yelling and the room erupted in chaos. Several men actually stood up with their fists raised.

I had to do something so I whispered under my breath, "Emmaline, tell them how old you are."

She closed her eyes and I watched as she released a flood of calm. Every line in her face eased away to be replaced with a serene smile.

< Please, everybody, look at me! I am 104 years old. >

A quiet covered the room like a blanket while all the people turned into themselves again.

An old woman hobbled to the dais. Her skin had a light coffee color. She lifted her blue eyes that were milked with cataracts. She carried the look of an Caribbean islander about her.

"My great-great mother be livin to be 1 and 27. She didn't be lookin' of even 60. She be leadin' the mens around for every day she could," she said giggling under her breath.

The sound of her voice told me everything I needed to know - Calypso. The old woman was a Cruzan from the Virgin Islands.

Her lips pressed into a toothless smile before she continued speaking. "Now, you be askin' how she look so young? I say she lookin' her age. You no, know your own stories." She chided.

She wagged a gnarled finger at the crowd. "You no be listenin' to your olden-timers. If they learned you up, you'd be known. In old times, the women be havin' the long livers. They be touched by the voices. They had whatcha all be calling the hearin'. Then ones day they bellies get full up. Later they havin' the babes. That how the long livers be comin'. My three times great mother she be one those. I no's you, Miss Emmaline, be a long liver. You be havin' the look bout cha," she said and nodded her head in satisfaction.

She raised and lowered her shoulders. The breath weighed heavy in her chest. A tall dark girl with long glossy golden brown hair and light eyes moved to her side. The old woman waved her off with one arm. "I be 96 and feelin' all me years. Now I be the three times mother. I just want to be see-in my great mother. She's here, I can feel her. When she come?"

< I'll be there when my work is done. > Determination colored Hera's reply and we all heard her.

Emmaline raised her hands.

< If you don't know your line, come to me. My family is the line of Perseus. We were the keepers of the records, known as the book. >

She chanced a glance at me and winked. That second it hit me.

Adrian's thing. He left me a giant old book written in twelve languages.

I winked back.

"Did you bring my book?" Emmaline asked with a smile.

"I didn't get rid of it, if that's what you mean," I responded and gave her a tight smile.

She patted my shoulder. "Let's hope not. I was starting to like you, but I can't stand anyone who'd throw out a book just because they couldn't read it."

I coughed to cover my shock. "I would never do that," I sputtered.

Emmaline answered the question of one of the hybrids pointing them to Ares group and then she turned back to me.

"I couldn't read it either, but I learned." She arched an eyebrow at me then strolled away her toga swaying with her hips, to be eaten up by the crowd.

Emmaline reminding me of Grace ended at looks. Personality-wise, Grace was a jellyfish and Emmaline is a titan.

CHAPTER 12

HERA

The dream construct materialized around me and it had a cooling fog. I used the fog to obscure our conversations in the dreamwalk. There were probably others as strong as me, but Helio was the only one I could think of and he would never betray me.

The forms of my children took shape around me and my heart fluttered with joy. Ares glared at me through his black hair, cutting me with his sharp blue eyes. Perseus and Eros waited alongside each other while Hercules stood with his arms crossed and legs wide. I could never get over the sheer size of him. He dominated any room he entered. In contrast, his twin, Hebe, was the picture of feminine grace. Eris moved to her twins' side in solidarity with a smirk on her face. She flung her arm over Ares' shoulder as if to rest on it. Hephaestus and Eileithyia lingered behind their siblings. They were always hiding in the background.

I hope one day they step into the light and find it worth staying in.

I took a breath and then began with what I had to say, "You must all assemble in one apartment. Pretend you're having a party or that you're getting together for a family dinner. I don't care what excuses you must make, but you all need to be together because Ixis is going to shift you," I informed them, but the reaction I had expected never came.

"Ixis? Why is Ixis going to shift us? You haven't spoken to us in weeks. Other than seeing you in a dreamwalk a few days ago, we don't know anything that's going on and suddenly now you're telling us to be prepared to leave?" Ares yelled. He shifted in the construct and huffed while Eris moved around him. They were like two binary stars.

Eros chided her brother, "Ares, be gentle! Mother has been fiercely fighting for us to be together. Now she tells you that our banishment is at an end and you're going to lecture her like a petulant child because she didn't talk to you for a few weeks? Let it go! I'm sure all our questions will be answered the moment we arrive, wherever we're going." She reached out to Ares but he moved out of reach of her calming touch.

"Eros is right, Ares. Listen to your sister!" I said noting we were all dressed in an earth fashion from before our banishment. I smiled, even in the dreamwalk we picture ourselves as more human than Themian.

Steam rose from Ares shoulders and head. He was too much like his father, filled with vim and vigor, but also quick to anger and rage. It would serve him well in battle, but it was not helpful in day-to-day life.

"Ixis mated to a hybrid named Emmaline." I could barely contain myself, bursting with all the fruits of our plans in my hands.

"Fantastic!" Eris mused, her delight in all the trouble that information brought was worry some.

"This is better than anything we could have ever hoped for," Hebe said clapping her hands in her childlike way and adding a little jump for good measure.

"Really? That hybrid is something. Not only did she mate with a Themian but she did it with their strongest shifter?" Peruses remarked at the same time with Hercules. They both turned and smiled at each other. Peruses pride shown through, his line had won that prize.

The taste of our success hung heavy and sweet in the air.

"Yes. And I have even better news. As I've always suspected, Adrian is a shifter himself and so is his son. So, we have three shifters that are all extremely powerful and will only grow more so over time. Therefore, make your arrangements and be prepared. Anything you intend to bring, must be brought with you at the shifting time. Find some way to get it here. You have three days." I glanced from one child to the next. "In three days' time. You all must be ready..."

Before I could say another word, Perseus cut me off re-crossing his arms in front of me. "Ixis agreed to shift us?" he demanded.

I chose my words with care. "Not in so many words. He agreed to shift all the hybrids to Odyssey."

Hercules raised his hands in irritation. "That is not what Perseus asked, mother! Did he agree to shift us, the children of Hera and Zeus?" He wasn't shouting, but the joy of the moment was lost with the fear of failure.

The construct changed with my mood. The air grew cold and ice tickled my nose. It wasn't real, but it felt that way.

"I have gotten us this far. Do you doubt me now?" I demanded forcing my dream self to stand still.

Ares chuckled, "No, mother. My brothers, just like me, doubt everyone else." The wheels of a plan were turning in his head. "If Ixis will not shift us, will Adrian or his son do it?"

I bit my lip.

Adrian and I have lived side by side for decades, so he might.

He understood the pain of separation and the willingness to scale any mountain to reach your heart's desire. Sydney was the real question. Would she risk it?

"Ixis will do whatever Sydney instructs him to do. She is the key. Adrian will not cross her and neither will her son. All our hopes rest with Sydney." I looked to each of the girls hoping they might attempt to sway Sydney if needed.

The naked truth wasn't always easy to say, but I'd said it.

"Now, all of you stand together closely and let me get a good look at you. We want to make sure that Ixis sees exactly who he is looking for. A clear picture in my mind will give him what we need." My heart swelled. Finally, we shall all be free. Seeing all of us together was my only wish.

They huddled close together and tears pricked my eyes. I took in every curve of a smile, the eight set of shoulders, the hair and eyes of my progeny, the coloring of Zeus in there smiles and attitudes.

I had never been so happy in my entire life. At that moment, every one of them stood strong and proud. The furtive glances that filled their eyes for so many years was gone. They were clear and ready. I fixed the image in my mind, ready to transfer it to Ixis when the time came.

Hephaestus pushed his sister forward.

"Mother?" she said.

"Yes, Eileithyia."

"I have been wondering about our children from all of these encounters. The last child I gave birth to… do you think she'll still be alive?" She gulped back her fear, working her fingers together and apart.

"Perhaps. How old is she?" My reply was guarded. I didn't want to get her false hope.

"She would be very old. I'm fairly certain she would still be alive, although she would be close to reaching her first-century mark." She worried over it, her voice cracking on the last remark. She knew most humans don't live that long.

"All the hybrids are on the ship. If she's still alive, she'll be there and if she's not, someone that remembers her will be. One of the hybrids said that 'the children of the dreamwalkers are long-livers," I offered this slim hope. It was all I could.

After Emmaline mated, we stopped reseeding the lines because our plan had succeeded.

"You must be talking about Hephaestus' line. 'Long-livers' sounds like something out of the Caribbean," Eris remarked dryly dusting her hands as if to get sand off them. She carried no love for islands and sand. Her taste leaned toward city dwellers and urbanites.

"They are called Calypso. Eileithyia" I said kissing her on her forehead.

Even though they were grown adults, many thousand years old, I still longed for those moments and breathed in the scent of each of my children.

Eileithyia was always more emotional than the rest of her siblings. For her to know that one of her children, her trueborn children, had survived was important. She said she didn't know the girl's name but it was a girl and it was a single birth. I didn't want to raise Eileithyia's hopes up on something that could or could not be true, so I decided that ignorance was for the best.

CHAPTER 13

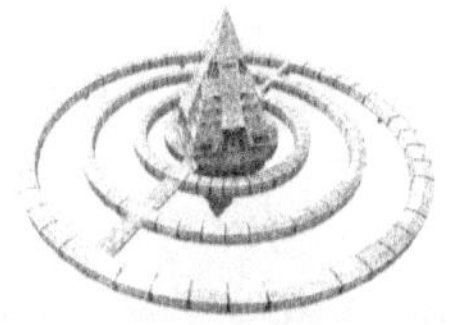

SYDNEY

< We are done moving people, so what's next on the list? > Adrian heaved a sigh and the weariness bled through our connection.

Before I could muster a reply, I was standing in the shifting room, as Ixis had informed me it was called.

"So, what exactly is on this ship, Ixis?" I asked because no matter how cool this place was, that feeling wouldn't last for me or anyone else.

"This is a standard project generation ship, engineered for long term interstellar travel. Every ship comes with a full company of living quarters. There are several geo-domes that recycle air and water," Ixis wanted to continue but I put my hand up.

"What's a geo-dome? And please talk to me like you would talk to an idiot. I know how to trade stocks for technology, but I don't know shit about most technology. Other than being very bad at tech issues, living on a boat in the middle of an ocean, for the last decade or so, left me further behind." I wasn't trying to be funny, but Emmaline giggled anyway.

Ixis gave her a very lovingly smile before he continued talking to me. "Eco-dome technology is like a mixture of an oxygen-creating piece of machinery and a bio-dome. You humans–"

Hera jumped in. "They're not human, Ixis. You know this," she spoke so low it could have been missed if anyone else was talking.

Ixis took the rebuke with grace. "Right, sorry! I know my mate is a hybrid. I just need to get used to calling you all hybrids… Perhaps we should come up with a better name?" He inquired.

I tilted my head to the side for a second, "I think we'll just stick with 'hybrid' for now until we find a better name. I think naming anything just has to happen organically."

But my reply was lost on Ixis and he charged on with the last thing he heard, "Exactly! An eco-dome or a bio-dome is simply an organic piece of machinery. It contains the soil, mountains, rocks, fish, insects, and every type of creature that you might encounter from the planet, or from Earth." He looked around the room gauging our reaction.

Adrian shook his head, "Are you're saying it's a giant piece of a planet? That there are several bio-domes and you're just not sure what planet we have a piece of and that it contains a lot of creatures that we may or may not have encountered before?" He finished his inquiry holding his hand on a part of his mouth. Then he turned to me and he said with an amused tone only for me to hear

< This is a nightmare! >

"Exactly!" Ixis remarked with a smile and Emmaline pulled at his arm.

"Okay, that sounds terribly frightening. Thank you, Adrian, for pointing that out. I'm scared shitless." I looked around at everybody from the room before speaking again.

"Anybody else frightened to death about the eco/bio-dome–geo dome or whatever it's called, that is filled with a planetary body that we may or may not have been encountered before?" I asked.

Everyone except for Ixis and Hera raised their hands. We needed more information and we needed someone to explain to us better how this worked and what should we expect to find.

"It looks like I am not the only one shitting my pants. But let's consider this situation a disease. When you are sick, you go to see a doctor, right? So, let's find the 'doctor' for our case," I stopped to see if anybody wanted to intervene, but since no one did I continued, "Tristan, go and find someone who knows about botany or ecology or geology or whatever the fuck we're going to need. When you find this person, go and explore these eco-spaces. Is there any way to keep everyone out of them until they've been cleared?" I asked looking up at an angle.

"Yes, of course. Simply inform the computer you don't wish anyone except for whoever you authorized to go in there," Hera replied but her 'matter of fact' tone didn't fill me with comfort.

Tristan disappeared from the room and I was grateful Issy was still dealing with our newfound civilization.

There were still things that I didn't understand about my situation so it was time to ask some questions. I glanced at Hera and then at Adrian.

"Why exactly was I chosen? I'm not saying that I have a problem taking control, it's just I don't understand why me. I'm not the oldest person here or the person who has the most knowledge. I don't know anything about this ship, or space or even interstellar travel, not to mention meeting and encountering new species. So why me?"

I felt a pressure behind my eyes that made me close them and in a second sleep pressed in.

Hera crossed her hands in front of her and clasped them together. "Sydney, you are the most powerful and that is what makes you the leader whether you like it or not. I am an empath and I have gained abilities over time, but what you have now is more than I ever had in my first years. Also, it may be more than I will ever have. I cannot move objects with my mind. I use the forces of the wind because they are my dominant power. However, you have called all the forces to aid you. You don't have to like it, that you're the leader. Being a leader, sometimes, you have to make decisions quickly and you made the best personal choices so far. As a hybrid, you've experienced more abilities than any of the rest. Even my children aren't as strong as you are." She stopped only to take a shuddering breath. "I don't like to repeat myself, but I will, so you can understand the situation. Whether you like it or not, you are our leader. I can't lead them because I'm an Alien. I can be the great mother of your people, but I can't be the leader. I can't make choices for all of you. I'm not part human and I'm only Themian."

She shook her head as if she wanted to be more. I didn't say a word so she continued, "Everything I do will be colored by who and what I am. My first determination is to protect. I may be unreasonable or irrational at times. I know this and have experienced it myself. I know you to be unreasonable and irrational when it comes to your children, but when it comes to everyone else you are not. I've seen you. You will fight for them with every breath of your being, in a way I never could. I wasn't trained to fight like you, with toughness. I have the ability to endure and I will, but you are something else. You didn't just survive, you became something more. I know your people need you, so keep that in mind and look forward," she finished and I noticed how her chest was heaving.

I couldn't tell if she was going to cry or hug me. Letting out a deep sigh she stepped back and waited.

"Adrian, I can't… think," was all I could muster and my eyes darted towards him.

"Awe, beautiful girl, I can't think of anybody else who'd do the job. I'm actually more frightened for anyone who crosses you. You have always fought your way out of everything. You do what most people don't, you play the long game. Whatever this is, it's a long game and we need someone who can plan for that. Not just react with a knee jerk reaction." He gave me one of his quirky half-smiles with a gleam of mischievous and I felt the urge to touch him but I was interrupted by Tristan.

< Mom, there's no way I can go through all seven of these bio-domes alone. >

< *Get help then, but just don't take anybody too young and too stupid with you. Okay? I don't want somebody to die just because they were young and dumb.* > I replied

< Don't worry! I'll try to choose the smarter ones. > He said and humor colored his send.

Issy walked into the shifting room rubbing her forehead.

< That wouldn't be you then. > Issy joshed him.

< Want to come along? > Tristan asked returning her tone of voice.

"Thanks, but I'm not interested. I think I'll stay here and see if I can help Mom and Hera. Anyway, I have a headache," she said out loud and to Tristan at the same time.

I glanced sharply at Izzy. She didn't have headaches without cause. She understood my concern from the look in my eyes so she turned to me and gave me a wan smile.

"Don't worry, mom! It's just a headache. I'm probably just tired."

I rubbed her shoulder and didn't say anything in return. I didn't want to be the paranoid mother. However, I needed to be sure so I focused on someone who could give me some answers.

"Ixis, is there anything else on this ship we should know about that is potentially dangerous and could kill anyone?" I asked.

"I don't believe so. However, perhaps we should review the layout of the ship. That might be helpful for all parties involved. In addition, it would make it easier for us to choose which bloodlines gets which sets of living quarters," his reply came immediately and while he was talking he already pulled up the holograph of the ship again.

The layout appeared in the air as a three-dimensional holograph and it floated in the middle of the room. I looked at it and the ship was massive.

"Please, color all living quarters in blue," I instructed and the layout immediately changed from a plain white schematic to white with blue blocks. There were seven different sections, not including the various labs and restricted areas such as the recycling technology, air purification and production, and the cafeteria or storage. Seven was more than we needed.

I considered that the blue zone closest to the shifting room to be the best place for our command group. That left six other areas for the five lines. Adrian and Ixis moved away from the main controls and I took over.

The terminal reminded me of an old 80's game console. I pressed a few buttons and it revealed the locations of different hybrids with bracelets around the ship, along with heat signatures of others. They were grouped in five different areas, all living quarters.

I smiled to myself. I guess I should trust that people are always going to pick out their place in the world, no matter what. I found it comforting to know that we could conform to our new world. But from what I'd seen and known about myself, hybrids are adventurous people.

The commotion in the background brought me back to the room and the next hurdle. Tristian had returned and was speaking in an animated fashion to the 'adults' in the room. He stopped and turned slowly to smile at me. My heart clenched as the man next to him gave me a similar smile.

Not having to deny what I had suspected for years, was a new internal war for me. Adrian side-stepped our son and extended his hand, which I happily took hold of.

In my mind, Odyssey was no different than my small boat. We just had a larger crew and all the crew was aboard. This being said, we needed provisions before we tossed the lines and shove off. My chest clenched at the idea that this was it, but pushing my fears to the side was what I did best, so I dove in. Our ship had to be in the best shape. I swallowed back all the knowledge.

We would never get another chance to do this.

Tristan started in and I gave him my full attention. "I've been through a few domes and they are on the far side of weird. However, two of them are Earth-like and one of them is empty."

I took the information in and as a leader I had to be, then started to give instructions.

"While we have several problems, most of which are pretty simple, supplying the geo-domes or bio domes or whatever it is Ixis is calling them, have primacy over everything else. They will provide air and water filtration and food, a lot of the food," I stopped to see if my Themian friends had anything to add, but they stood there stoic as ever.

"I don't know what is in some of them, but I'm assuming there are fruit and vegetables, unlike anything we've encountered before," I stopped again to see if Hera or Ixis had any input, but they remained unhelpful. The only one who made it clear that was listening to me was Tristan who nodded his head.

"I think that if we really want the hybrids — all of our people to survive, we need seeds, plants and sustainability," I grasped at the right words, not the catch phrases that had plastered the internet and news for the last few years. We really were going off grid in everyway a human/part human could.

Even though this talk felt like planning to run down to the local bodega to buy canned goods and toilet paper, it was definitely not the case. However, everyone blinked at me like they were actually waiting for me to go and buy all the things that were needed.

I wished there was a 'leaving the solar system' checklist I could go down, but unfortunately, there wasn't, so I just had to make my own.

I looked at each person in the room and added, "Well, do any of you have anybody that can help with this?"

Tristan pulled the hair on the front of his head, then smiled. "Yeah, there's a guy named Roger. When we were moving people, he insisted on bringing an entire double-doored fridge. He's an herb biologist— " Tristian's eyes stared off over my head for a moment, then he refocused on me. "Anyway, Roger says there's plenty of biodiversity in each of the domes and he'll spend the rest of his life inside of them. He literally packed a tent as one of the things he decided he needed to take with him. A tent!" Tristan laughed.

We all kind of snickered. His decision to bring his own place to live was not a bad plan considering he didn't know the lay of the land, or in our case the spaceship.

"Yeah, anyway, we will need lots and lots of viable seed, until we can start saving our own from fruits and vegetables. However, we can probably get by with prepackaged seeds," Tristan said stepping out of his comfort zone.

I realized that he was talking with this Rodger guy and I wished that I was better at receiving.

Tristan looked at Ixis and Adrian and continued, "Roger said we should just bring live trees, preferably ones that are, you know, a couple of years old. He gave me a very long list." Once again, Tristan pulled the hair on the front of his head. His eyes had dark rings around the sockets from the lack of sleep.

I rubbed my forehead to push back my own exhaustion. "We only have a day and a half to figure this out. I'm not sure how many people on this boat have slept in the last 48 hours, other than the children and I know we're all tired, but we can sleep when everything is done."

Adrian moved his hand across my back. It was comforting and almost relaxing. His hand stilled and he touched my mind.

< Sorry, I'll get a keg of coffee up here. >

< *Oh, God! Yes, please. One for me and one for the rest of you.* > I snickered.

I rolled my neck around my shoulders and continued the instructions. "Tristan, get Roger to organize a work crew for the empty biodome. We need a landing space, just somewhere we can drop off. After that, you and Adrian can start moving whatever comes first. I don't want to steal anything from anyone. You have access to all of our bank accounts, so pay whoever you can. If you take it from their warehouse, leave money behind in their accounts. I don't care what you do, you can even magically make money appear on the counters at the store, just pay for everything. We aren't thieves."

"You know that we could take a lot of these trees from the wild. Most of them will survive and we can deposit them wherever Roger instructs." Ixis's 'matter of fact' statement reminded me of how little he knew about humans.

"I don't want to take any genetically modified crap. I want to bring heirloom seeds and plants so they have a chance to survive."

The scent of coffee wrapped me in its tangy aroma and my eyes rolled into the back of my head as I pulled it in. I didn't realize that I'd stopped talking until the snickering reached me. My eyes snapped open and Adrian smirked at me and handed me a cup, placing a kiss on my neck making every fiber in me respond to his lips. I took a long draw on the hot cup and let it seep into my cells before continuing.

"We don't have a lot of time to go looking for trees and we need all of the trees now." I felt bad. If we had more time, I would have rearranged some of the trees on Earth to help the environment, but we didn't.

"Bring whatever trees you get argan oil from, avocados, mangoes and things like that. Also, strawberry bushes. Maybe the best thing to do is simply go to seed vault and make a withdrawal," I said and threw my hands up. It was a colossal undertaking and I was in over my head.

If you wanted advice on buying a stock or taking care of a boat I was your girl. But I was definitely not a farmer.

Tristan broke in to stop my overwhelming thoughts. "That's what I'm trying to tell you. Roger is really obsessed with this subject. We only need to get what's on his list. The list only contains stuff he doesn't already have. He's been saving for a long time. He actually calls himself a prepper."

"So what's on the exotic shit list?" I asked taking a sip of the magic brew in my cup.

"Stuff I never heard of, but when I asked him about one, he said that it's used for lotions and facial products. He said people wouldn't want to be without it. Sounded crazy but I didn't argue with him on the subject. He also gave me a long list of vitamins and minerals he said we should get."

Tristan was pacing the shifting room and was waving his hand as if he was having a conversation with someone other than us.

I moved in step with him. "Tristan, slow down! Okay, vitamins sound good but won't we get that from food? Take a breath and get this guy up here. I hate playing telephone." I stopped Tristan from pacing and he stood still.

A moment later, a strange little man with polyester pants held up by suspenders and a white button-down polo shirt stood before me.

"Tell her high and mightiness that…" he stopped speaking and blushed from his toes to his ear lobes when he saw where he was.

"Her high and mightiness would like you to start from the beginning of why we need vitamins," I retorted and waited for him to regrow his balls.

He cleared his throat and started talking again. "I'm sorry, I… I didn't mean to… I don't get out much." He wiped his hands on his pant legs and started again. "If the population remains static, we will be fine. However, humanity has never managed that. Population growth leads to soil depletion." He finished with a tight-lipped smile, then locked his thumbs behind the suspenders and stretched them out. A moment later he released them and they snapped back to his chest.

"Really? We have to worry about soil depletion on a spaceship?"

As if I didn't have enough to worry over. I'm not a fucking farmer!

Adrian heard my thoughts and intervened playing the role of my voice of reason.

"With population growth, it's not so much that we have soil depletion, but it works the same. We have a finite amount of minerals to spread around. If our population increases, we must share the same amount of vitamins and minerals between more people. That means that every person will end up with less." He did the suspender snap again, "This is why humanity hasn't been able to create a working bio dome or a colony on the Moon." He finished with a satisfied smiled.

I wasn't sure that was the only reason, but it was the most interesting observation I'd heard.

"Some of these minerals can be mined from asteroids or by visitin' planets. Don't forget Ixis actually helped create a lot of these worlds. Sounds like Mr Rogers has thought of everything," Emmaline remarked.

"Tristan, take Roger back down and see if you can find anyone who can work on the land," I said.

"Take the O'Neils. Their family seems to be the most familiar with farming," Adrian offered his opinion out loud so rarely, I tended to stop everything and listen. I looked at him and he continued, "I think making any one work anywhere for too long is a bad idea. We should rotate everyone. That way nobody feels like they're getting the shit end of the stick."

When he finished it hit me what he really meant. He didn't want anyone to go through with what I had - slaving away with no way out. I tilted my head to the side and he smiled at me. I smiled back.

"That works until people decide what they want to do. Rodger sounds like he's never leaving a bio-dome and Aunt Melinda will never leave a lab. I don't want anyone stuck, but we can't have slackers either. We should do rotations until people choose what they want to do." I rubbed my palms into both eyes and plunged in with the next list of shit that needed to be done.

"Do we know how many animals we're bringing?" I asked no one and everybody at the same time.

"Yes, we already have a list of all of those," Emmaline remarked, then she rubbed her fingers into her temples. "I should have gotten more sleep. Sydney, when Adrian said you were comin', I never guessed what a shit show you'd be stirrin' up. God, girl, you sure know how to rock a boat," she finished shaking her head.

"If everyone's off the planet and we have a plan to load up on supplies, then all we have left is information and entertainment," I shrugged.

Hera cleared her throat. "We can copy the internet along with all the entertainment if you wish, but most of the science in the Themian databases is better and correct compared to humanity's." She tapped a shape on the floor and a chair pushed out of the floor behind her. She sat down with a grin.

The floor was covered in geometric shapes and small circles and it looked like an abstract art from the '80s. The longer I stared, the easier it was to pick out a bird's eye view of furniture.

"Now, I'll be damned! I've been standing in this room for days and you never mentioned there were chairs," Emmaline scoffed, shooting daggers from Hera to Ixis.

Ixis calmly took her hand and something passed between them and Hera shrugged in a very human fashion, "You never asked!"

I covered my mouth to hide the smile that pulled on my lips. Emmaline narrowed her eyes at Hera and then me before turning around to a screen on the side of the room.

We each took a screen searching for the various trees, books, and movies we would need. Forever is a long time and I didn't want to leave without all the distractions possible. At some point, people would want more. More music, more books, fresh faces or landscapes. The longer I could kick that can down the road, the more time we had to figure out what the fuck we are going to do.

CHAPTER 14

SYDNEY

After gathering all the necessary supplies and all the hybrids who wanted to leave the planet it was time to go.

I called everyone to the Citadel. Looking around the dais, Ixis and Hera seemed uninterested in what I was about to say or maybe it was just they're Themian, and short on emotions. Adrian squeezed my hand and I opened my mind to everyone.

< Our three days are up and the big moment has come. We have what we have and we don't have time to take more. I don't think the Themian's will go to war with us, but I don't want to find out.>

Talking about war or fighting isn't the best way to calm people down, but at that time I needed it to make people understand the urgency of our leaving.

< The big question isn't what happens if we stay as we're not staying. The big question is where will we go from here. Where can we go, and what can we do when we get there. >

The room murmured and I continued.

< Ixis says that there are thousands of habitable worlds we could take over if we wanted to. We could explore the Universe and find our own habitable world. However, this option sounds a little crazy to me. We need to come to a consensus on the subject of where we are going and what are

we doing. Because of this, we're going to take a vote. Those of you who want to go and find our own Home world, please stand to the left of the dais and those of you who want to explore the Universe, please stand to the right of the dais. If you are undecided or if you have a different idea, please stand in the center. >

Mentally I was chewing on my fingernails. I didn't want to make any choices for people, because I didn't really know what I wanted to do. I've been wandering the Earth for the last decade with no purpose whatsoever, so how could I dictate to these people what to do with their lives? The idea of just keep on moving sounded good to me. I didn't just have an ocean to go and explore any more, but all of space and the cosmos.

"You don't seem to be making a choice yourself. Do you have a choice?" Melinda climbed the three steps in one move and elbowed me.

"No, Melinda, I won't be making any choices for anybody. But I'm sure you have an opinion." I placed the tip of my index finger in my mouth but didn't turn to look at her. Instead, I kept my eyes on the crowd. The families moved like schools of fish together, weaving their way between the other groups.

"Yes, I do know what I want to do," Melinda said smiling while moving in closer and cocking an eyebrow on one side.

I rolled my eyes. You'd think my great aunt was a nympho.

"You are welcome to have as many babies as you wish, just leave me and Issy out of it," I retorted taking a step back, in case whatever she had was catching.

"You're one of the few here that's really truly mated. It should be you the one having babies. Tell me, would it be so bad?"

Her smiled looked innocent, but I knew better.

"I've reached the point where I'm in charge of a civilization and also a mother for my teenagers..."

She cut me off. "Your teenagers are grown. They are actually adults capable of having their own babies. You have your life and you don't look a day over 22. Is being responsible for all of us so terrible?" She asked and pulled her thick braid over on shoulder to play with the end.

"Yes and no. Being responsible for you guys is a terrible feeling, but it'll get better once we decide where we're going and what we are going to do. And if you must know, for myself, I just want to be happy," I offered, knowing all along that was a lame choice.

My eyes trailed over Adrian and he smiled at the person he was chatting with, but I knew the smile was for me.

"Happiness is inside of you and you carry it around with you. You can't go somewhere and find it. If you are looking outside yourself to be happy, you never will be. Look inside your own house before you go to someone else's looking for something. You can't grow happiness." Melinda snapped.

Her words hurt. I had been running away looking for happiness for years. Finding the map was just me pursuing the happiness that always seemed to be just out of reach.

"Melinda, let's just get the votes, and then I'll tell you what I really want," I said with a tight-lipped smile wanting to close the discussion.

"Now, that sounds ominous." She winked and strolled to the other side of the dais then down into the crowd. She took a place in the center. I was sure she was not undecided and that she clearly had other ideas for our people.

The shifting of bodies came to a standstill when no one seemed to be moving from one side to the other. There were a lot of people standing in the center, more than I thought there would be. However, intergalactic travel versus a home world looked pretty even.

<Hera, count it out!> I had to concentrate to send the message to her.

"According to our tally, the same amount of people want to find a home world as intergalactic travel and exploration," Hera announced.

"I want to hear from the others and I mean those of you who have a completely different idea," I said breathing in and slowly releasing the air.

"I don't think we should leave at all. They didn't say we had to leave the solar system, so we could colonize the Moon if we wanted to. Or Mars," a man shouted.

Fear poured off of them and it was fear of the unknown. I could understand that kind of fear. Every time we put out to sea for the first year, I carried that fear with me. The fear we'd hit a storm, fear we would sink, fear that one of the twins would be swept overboard. But time and experience cured me of that fear.

However, I didn't want to learn to be very afraid of the fear of looking into the big black void and not knowing what's out there, so I repeated in my mind the statement that always worked for me in this kind of situations.

No guts, no glory!

I returned my attention to the man in front of me. "What's your name?"

"Charles," he muttered.

"Well, Charles, first of all, do you think humanity is ready to find out that Aliens have colonized their Moon or Mars?" I used logic because it was the only way.

He shook his head and hung it down taking a good look at the floor and shook it slightly. When he didn't answer, I continued.

"Going to the Moon, colonizing the Moon or Mars, would be easy." I glanced up at the room and saw all around heads nodding in agreement. "We wouldn't be that far from Earth. We could make visits to go around the planet and maybe even contact our friends. But we agreed to leave!" I let those words sink in. They created silence and they echoed around the amphitheater.

"They didn't say we had to leave the solar system. They didn't say that we couldn't colonize the Moon, that we couldn't colonize Mars. They are doing a science project here to discover the evolution of their species but also to study the human race and we're simply a step in the wrong direction. An oddity that shouldn't have existed, but here we are. I would like to know the answers to some of their questions too. Why I seem to, by all accounts, have been born a normal human being but then woke up one day and suddenly I have abilities. Those are the questions I would like answers to. How did that happen? Why my Themian genes waited to wake up and what woke them? Without the answers to those questions, we can't control our own evolution." I stopped because my throat hurt.

Voicing my own deep thoughts hurt, but they also rang true for the people I was looking at. It brought me comfort to know I wasn't alone in my need for answers.

I switched the discussion to the send because I didn't want my voice to break and also because the knot in my belly had reached my throat.

< So, we're going to leave this solar system and we will be the first even partial humans to get an up-close and personal view of Saturn or Jupiter. And you know what? If you guys want to go visit Mars, let's do it! We can fly by Uranus and take a look at its rings which nobody talks about. We can take a look at Pluto, it was considered a plant then a dwarf planet and then a moon. Apparently, people can't decide what it is, but we can go and look at it for ourselves. I hear the oceans on Titan are amazing. I also hear that IO is an amazing moon. From my point of view, we could either stay here and be stuck in the drudgery of the human mindset which is just barely capable of getting anywhere or we can go out there and find our destiny, whatever it is. >

I wanted to see all the things I'd just listed and even more, but it was not the best time for daydreaming, so I continued.

< Ixis says there are thousands upon thousands of habitable worlds, some of which he helped create himself. Let's go find one! We don't have to choose our home world immediately, we could just explore for a while. >

I moved the focus only on the people from the middle and I pointed at them. < You, who are standing here, you are saying let's do a bit of both and you are right. You want to go to a home world, but you have to explore to find one. Exploring increases the chances of finding a great one and this is the answer that makes everybody happy. >

I changed my position to face the left side of the room and addressed that group.

< You need to know that we are looking for a home. >

Turning to the right, I pointed to the final group from the room.

< Last but not least, you need to know that we can go and visit every part of the cosmos. Let's go do both! If we need more supplies, we can mine asteroids. If we need foodstuffs, as soon as we find a planet that is habitable, whether we want to stay or not, we could go there and harvest whatever we want, even if it's just minerals. We don't have to stay anywhere because we can do anything. >

I stopped talking and looking at just one group because what I was about to say was for everybody.

< We are all together in this and you all need to understand the level of freedom we have compared to the humans. Until the moment we find somewhere that we all really want to be, or at least what the majority will consider being a good place to consider as home, this ship is our home. This is

our world and we have everything we need right here. I know all this sounds crazy, but we're not human, so we have to stop thinking like humans. The humans that are living on Earth are not ready for what we're about to do. They are not capable of doing what we're about to do— at least not yet. >

I realized that the room was with me because all the faces were in rapt attention, people having their mouths hang open. A smile curled on my lips and I proceed forward with the speech.

< They are going to reach that level at some point and when they do, we can meet them on an even playing field or we can just avoid them for all time. The choice is ours to make. We are our own people. We have the bio-domes, but I would prefer that no one lives in them. However, you are welcome to go and visit them every day for hours, if you wish. We're going to need people who are willing to grow a garden, to go establish gardens. Also, if you want to put some plants in your room,

you should do so. We can do anything necessary to make this ship our home. If you want to paint the walls in your room, go right ahead and do it. Sparkly shimmering white is a bit much for me sometimes too. >

They all laughed and then to my amazement people moved to the center of the room.

< I will do everything in my power to make you feel comfortable here. All I ask in return is that if you have an issue, not to freak out and go all emotional. Rage will not help you. There are lots of people to talk to and anyone who wants to come and talk to me is welcome to do it. We will set up an hour a day where I will talk to as many people in a group or privately, depending on each person's needs. Hera is willing to talk to as many people as possible. She's eager to get to know all of us. We are all her children, so anybody who wants to talk to her all you have to do is to make an appointment. In the hallways, all over the ship, there are

computers and interactive terminals. You can't really see them because they're kind hidden, but they exist. >

People giggled.

< I think the best thing we could do right now is to pull out of orbit. Movement through this solar system can be slow because a lot of people want to see stuff. For example, I'd love to get a great view of the Milky Way. In the meantime, I need everyone to log into one of the computers. To do so you can just say your name. Once you are logged in, please let us know if you have an ability that you want to share or if you're trained for a job that you think we might need. We need all the help we can get because I can't run this big ass circus alone. >

Issy broke the silence and I let her.

"If you want to learn a skill that you don't know and you never thought you could learn, tell us that. We'll see what we can do about getting you trained for whatever it is that you wish to do. We are a society, so we need scientists, plumbers, electricians and painters, artists, writers, philosophers. We need people for every possible job, so if you ever wanted to do something but you didn't have the chance to study it, now is the time to say so," she said with a grin of satisfaction on her face.

< From what I understand, the ship is actually self-sufficient, so literally if you don't want to do anything all day long you could. However, I don't recommend that, that to me is a short trip down a very long rabbit hole of nothingness. From now on, we meet once a week, here in the Citadel, so everyone can air grievances or make announcements. >

CHAPTER 15

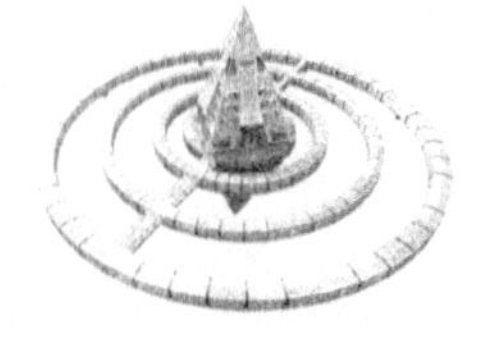

SYDNEY

"Now, that we're all gathered, let's fire up the engines and get out of here," I said staring up into the domed ceiling.

"The ship has no engines," Ixis remarked.

I gave Ixis a sharp look. "What do you mean it doesn't have any engines?"

"Themian ships don't need traditional engines. We have shifters and they can jump an entire spaceship, move an entire planet. Engines would be superfluous," Ixis replied in an even manner.

Emmaline smothered a smile behind her hand as she leaned over and kissed Ixis' cheek.

"Are you saying that this rust bucket doesn't have any way of maneuvering the ship without a physical presence of a shifter?" I demanded then pushed my hair off my forehead to hide my exhaustion.

The idea of being dead in the water without an engine terrified me. At least in water, I could use my power to move us, but out here in the void, I had nothing.

< You have me and I'm never leaving your side. > Adrian whispered in my mind.

"I cannot say that. Odyssey does not have engines in the traditional sense, we have maneuvering thrusters. They will reposition us in different ways, turning the ship around so that the shifting room can view different parts of the Cosmos. We can also use them to put the ship in orbit around a planetary body or to maneuver around various asteroids if it's required. However, if you're talking about engines for light travel, then no," Ixis finished with his facial expression unchanged.

I had hoped he would reveal that they kept engines for just in case something bad happened, but his lack of emotion said it all. The three men standing in the shifting room before me, were the only key to move us.

Tristan's excitement waited for no one. "You mean that we have faster than light engines or that we will be going with the speed of light?" His breath became quick and he bit his lower lip waiting for the answer.

"Yes, we're talking about engines that would do that. However, we do not have that physical machinery on Odyssey. Themian's have not needed that technology for a very long time. We travel using our minds and it allows us to move instantly. With my mind there is no time-loss."

His businesslike approach to our questions grated on me, but it was only because they were so absent of concern.

How could he not worry about losing control of the ship? But duh, he can control the ship, it is me who can't.

I gritted my teeth.

"Every project has its own shifter. What if the one guy dies?" I ground out.

"Every project has one main shifter, their strongest shifter, and there are always several underlings," Ixis explained clear and concise.

"So, we're your underlings?" Adrian finally broke his silence.

Ixis didn't turn away from me to address Adrian's concern but directed all his answers to me.

"I knew about Adrian before I approached the High Council. I did not bother to mention any of his abilities." Only when he finished the sentence did Ixis give a half-smile in Adrian's direction.

Adrian pursed his lips and crossed his arms and remarked dryly, "And I suppose that Aunt Emily is the one who was telling you all about it?"

Adrian didn't get his feathers up often, but this was rubbing him the wrong way. I wanted to reach out and take his hand, but he and I were too much alike. We liked to fight our own battles and looking weak didn't work, at least not for me.

"Don't be all like that about it, Adrian. It is not like I could help keepin' in touch even if I wanted to. Anyway, you kept in touch with Sydney, didn't you?" Emmaline barked defensively, crossing her arms and cocking a hip to one side then patting her Veronica Lake hair. It cracked me up how she continued to sport WWII hair styles with Greek clothes.

Before he answered he looked through his eyebrows at me, giving me a little sheepishly glance while hanging his head to the side. "You know I've been keeping in touch with her for years on purpose. It's not a fair question and Emily, I never told anyone about you ever." He didn't yell, that wasn't Adrian's way. Low and slow was how he got his point across. It was also how he always won. His calm had saved me every time.

I smiled to myself and took control of the situation. "All right, all these issues can be resolved later, somewhere in private, maybe." I arched an eyebrow at Adrian and Emmaline.

Issy, who looked generally annoyed with everyone there, crossed her arms and intervened. "We have every hybrid, human or Themian, right?"

"Yes. I found no others in my dream search," Hera replied, closed her eyes and then reopened them.

I wasn't sure if she was double-checking or praying. I shook my head because at that time it didn't actually matter anymore.

"Let's get this shit show on the road and let the exploration of the cosmos begin! Where should we go?"

"You said that the first stop is the Moon, but then what?" At that moment Tristan looked every bit the 18-year-old kid he was with his shining blue eyes and his glowing smile. Adrian touched his shoulder and Tristan didn't pull away.

"Well, we go see the rings of Saturn," I remarked and looked down at my clothes.

Hera cleared her throat before speaking, "You should inform your crew so they can find a good viewport before we leave. We won't be staying long and they'll want to see it."

"The shift is usually announced by the shifter," Ixis informed me. "But I do not have the ability to send the message to the entire ship, so Tristan will announce for me."

I was taken aback. Tristan smiled sheepishly and shrugged. "It's my thing."

< Odyssey is about to shift. If you wish, please find a viewport. > He sounded so grown up and professional.

I gazed through the domed crystalline glass of the room at the breath-taking view of Earth. The cradle of humanity sat quietly floating in the void. It looked so peaceful, but I knew better. The blue ball was filled with stress and strife, but I wanted to believe just for a moment that Zack, Maria, Nonna, and Trish were safe living their human lives. Completely unaware of the drama playing out in the skies over their world.

A lump formed in my throat. I didn't think leaving would matter all that much because Gabriel was dead, Adrian wasn't and I had the kids. But it did matter and it mattered very much. I had never made it to Machu Picchu or seen the cave drawings in Russia. I didn't dive in the underwater city off the coast of Japan. I would never find out how the pyramids were built.

I'll never see Zack again, and I didn't say I forgave him or I understood why he'd done what he did. I didn't spread Gabriel's ashes and now I never will.

Everyone I ever knew was there and would always be there. But I never would be again. I hadn't felt the tears until my neck itched. I realized that they were dripping from my jaw. Adrian pulled me into a hug and kissed my hair. Both kids came to my sides. I opened my arms to them and Emmaline joined us. Only Hera and Ixis didn't. They stood to the side, unaffected by the gravity of the moment.

"Are we ready?" Tristan whispered.

"Yes!" I replied gulping back my pain

< Shifting now! > Tristan announced.

Ixis closed his eyes and a stillness of concentration settled over him like a warm blanket. He reopened his eyes only to stare off into the distance. He reoriented his body to face a new direction in the shifting room. Not only was he facing away from the planet, but also away from the sun.

I gulped, as a cry climbed up my throat. The light from our golden sun bathed my face.

"Now!" Ixis said.

The heavy pressure of a shift filled the air around us pressing in on my body, my eardrums, sinuses, and lungs. As if I'd grown old all at once, my extremities chafed with icy tingles and a chill rolled over me. And just as quickly as it came it was gone, along with the glow of our sun. It was just gone.

There, before me, was the hexagon pole of Saturn and its icy rings floating around the gas giant. It was the most amazing sight I've ever seen.

But I couldn't stand to look at it. I sagged against Adrian and he shifted the four of us to our room. We sank to the floor and cried. I couldn't stop. I realized that I didn't want to leave.

What about Zack? Did I do the right thing?

*****

We slept for hours or days. I couldn't tell the exact period. However, when I got up, I couldn't miss the fact that I wasn't just in space orbiting around the planet I was born on. We were floating next to Saturn.

The hexagonal jet stream only held the storm at the pole that had been raging for millions of years. I looked at the pieces of ice that were twinkling in the dim sunlight that slowly filtered out here. It was a glowing ball in the void of darkness. No telescope could do the vision any true justice. I stared at the planet and remembered that I read somewhere that astronomers postulated that perhaps some of the rings were formed by the breakup of the Moon's coming too close to the gravitational well of Saturn.

If this is a mini asteroid field, it must be the most beautiful one ever.

I probably looked silly sitting there and musing over the ice and rocks floating in space. But as far as I knew we were the first hybrids ever to leave the planet, other than Hera's kids. But from what I understood, they were immediately shifted to a Homeworld and didn't get to see anything. So, to rephrase it, we are the first hybrids ever to see Saturn up close. Not to mention that there were also humans on board, making them the first humans to ever leave and go anywhere other than the Moon. However, history would never mention their name and people on Earth would never know of their existence.

I embraced this whole 'we're the first to do it' explorers. I never knew if that was what drove me to always go places and see new things, but it was energizing and terrifying all at the same time.

To be standing in front of such a fantastic view of the galaxy, in the cosmos, was greater than myself. I feel small and insignificant. I was never a fan of the saying 'small and insignificant', but I guess until you've experienced a moment like that you don't truly understand its meaning.

CHAPTER 16

HERA

From the shifting room, the rings of Saturn looked like floating diamonds. The pictures with the golden hues of the gas bands on Saturn didn't do the real experience any justice. The way they sparkled, filled me with hope.

I'd spent two hours in the Citadel meeting people. They were a slice of humanity in all its glory. Most of them were nice, scared, eager and brimming with hope. It was somehow refreshing to see new faces after all the years on Alethea.

I went to Sydney, but she hardly noticed me before I started to speak next to her.

"Well, now that I've achieved 50% of my plan, I'll tell you about the rest."

My announcement hit her like cold water from a mountain spring. Everything ran smoothly till that point, too smoothly something had to go wrong. In every situation, something no matter how small, always goes wrong. There was always a shoe that had to drop and I dropped that shoe.

Her head whipped around to stare at me. "50% of your plan? It was always part of your plan to get hybrids banned from the planet we were all born on?" Her eyes blazed with righteous anger while she demanded an explanation.

"No, it wasn't my plan to get everyone banned or removed or even found out. It was my plan to get a ship, get everyone who wanted to leave on board and take them with me off the planet," I replied simply.

It was a weak plan, a bit asinine one might say, but all I had was time and this was the only plan that I thought would work without dominating someone.

Sydney crossed her arms and retorted, "So, this is all about you?"

"Yes and no. It's about family. It's about the fact that when Athena found out that I had children, she stripped them away from me and then she isolated me on Alethea. She told me I would not see my children again until the project was complete. That could be several millennia if ever. I was given no guarantees my children would even live that long. When she told me, I knew that there had to be another way. I don't even know if she consulted the High Council," I tried to justify my actions, but I felt no guilt over them.

I looked deep into her eyes before I spoke next. "All I know is that she took a pod ship, shoved my children in it and had Micah shift it to Homeworld 14. I wasn't allowed to say goodbye. Hercules and Hebe had not yet reached their 18th year," my voice cracked with the last sentence. The pain of that day cut me to the quick even now. My chest aches for my children.

They were so young then.

"It's all about you, getting to your children?" She scoffed in disbelief and turned her back on me then paced the room for a few moments.

"Yes, it is," I retorted, with the heavy weight I carry in my chest.

I was ready for a fight. If she said 'no', what would I do then? I didn't want to find out, but I still had to push. I might be able to dominate her and still win.

"They're all adults, grown-ups. They don't need their mother anymore," she hissed.

"But they are hybrids on a planet filled with Themian's. They're isolated by themselves and treated like pariahs. They're not allowed to have a job. They will never meet someone and fall in love. None of them have mated. They are out casts for my mistakes and their birth!" I quivered with my fear.

She has to understand. I don't want to dominate her, but I am too close to let this chance pass.

"So you're in contact? This whole time you've been in contact with them and they know everything that you've been up to," she yelled.

Sydney wasn't just angry, she was enraged. The drawers in the walls vibrated with her emotions, some of them slid open and things flew across the room. I deflected two bracelets with the force of air.

"They helped manufacture most of what I've 'been up to'. What has happened would not be possible, as the Americans say, if we weren't in cahoots," I retorted then laid my hand on my forehead to rub the tension away.

She was standing over me, in a way typical of humans do when they are about to fight. Her hands were on her hips and she puffed her shoulders up to seem larger.

"So, you all concocted this, this plan? Are you serious? You and all your children suddenly decided it would be a great idea to hybridize swaths of Earth's population in an effort to be together again?"

The pedestal in the center of the room rattled and a hologram of Earth and its moon leaped to life. Then the hologram changed from one-star chart to another. It flashed through entire sets of star systems as if someone depressed the button and held it.

"So, tell me, what makes you any better than Poseidon?" her eyebrows pulled down, she didn't wait for my reply but carried on, "I will tell you." Wagging her finger in my face. "Nothing! Nothing makes you better than Poseidon. I mean, honestly, how arrogant are you? Suddenly, it's okay to go around impregnating as many humans as possible to spread your, your Themian hybrid gene?" She shouted and threw her hands up in the air in exasperation.

"It wasn't like that, Sydney," I stopped and swallowed back my rising fear and anger before continuing, "My children had already created their own hybrids before they were taken. Athena had no idea how old they were, so I told her they had not reproduced. I did that because I was afraid." Lowering my voice to hide the disgust I carried on, "You know what they did to Poseidon's children? They killed them, his children and their children and their children's children. Apollo and Artemis road across the sky and cut them all down, every man, woman, and child." I swallowed back the vitriol lurking at the back of my throat every time I think of the thousands of dead children.

"The level of butchery is beyond comprehension for you, but I witnessed most of it and rather than allow my children and their children and their children's children to be murdered, I lied — a lot." I too puffed my shoulder to appear larger than I am and faced off against her. "First, to hide the fact that I even had children, then I lied to make sure that Athena didn't know that they reproduced. I lied about everything. I've been lying for thousands of years," I shouted back.

"Then, you must be the most talented liar I've ever encountered. I really thought you just wanted to save us, but you don't care about us. All you care about is yourself and your children. We're just a means to an end," she spat it at me and it was like poison burning its way through my psyche.

I didn't know how but I'd hurt her. Tears filled her eyes and ran down the sides of her face.

I hung my head. She was right. My ruthless behavior misled them all and what little trust I'd build was shattered. The only way to fix it was to come clean and stop lying.

"Yes, it started out that way. You were a means to an end. My fear and anger over the whole situation drove me to do such a thing. I realized that my children would live well beyond a normal human lifespan. More so, I realized that we could do something about our situation but it would require more than one human lifetime, so I dream walked them all." The hollow sound of my voice enveloped the room with the weight of the plan I'd concocted.

She ran her fingers through her hair and walked from one side of the room to the other. That was when I noticed we had an audience.

She stopped pacing to glance at me through her eyebrows. "Exactly where were you planning on taking us once we were off the planet?"

"It didn't matter where. It was getting at that point. I knew Emmaline had mated with someone nonhuman, a Themian, but I didn't know who he was. I did know that the moment he realized she was threatened he would act to defend her. Themian mates can live without each other thousands of years apart. However, once mated they are irrevocably connected. I knew whoever he was, he was going to do anything possible to save her, including stealing a ship," I stopped to catch my breath and gauge Sydney's reaction.

Ixis and Emmaline stood off to the side wearing frowns. I gave them a brief glance before continuing, "The big question wasn't how I was going to get you off the planet. The real question has nothing to do with me and everything to do with you. You're more than half Themian. You're the child of a hybrid and a purebred. The real questions is, who is your father and where is he?" I deflected some of Sydney's questions.

"Don't try and shift the conversation by distracting us with inconsequential information. I don't care who my father is. So far none of them have been all that impressive. The only thing I learned from my so-called father was that life sucks, that it is filled with hardship and if you want to survive you have to just get over it, and fight." she retorted with her dry sarcasm.

"Did you ever wonder why Edward was the way he was? Why he was so broken inside?" I asked, reverting back to my Themian education, analyzing the data for answers.

"No, I mean yes, but that was a long time ago, when I cared. Those are questions with no answers so there's no reason to ask them. Asking that is an act of insanity and I've tried to do everything in my power to make sure my life sane." The room rattled again with her angered irritation over the mentioning of her father.

I backed off, because a war between us was not going to get me my children.

"Hera, you're saying that you were gambling with the fact I would come to Emmaline's aid? You gambled with our lives?" Ixis asked.

"Yes… I gambled with all our lives. Being a prisoner in any form, anywhere, is not living. Whether you all realize it or not, Ixis, you were imprisoned by the Themian way. Moving worlds and creating the Universe as the High Council saw fit— that was slavery. You just didn't realize until your eyes were opened."

I turned away from Emmaline's accusing eyes. "Sydney, you and all of the hybrids were enslaved to the human way of thinking and their way of being. Whatever abilities you inherited, you were all deathly afraid to use them. Hiding in fear is also slavery. Slaves fear for their lives constantly, they fear to stand up for anything. Being different is always strange and to be feared. That's the human way. However, it is not the Themian way." I was on a roll now. I could see the end and the years of hiding were almost over, so I couldn't stop.

"Adrian, you spend almost your entire life afraid. Not only that Sydney would find out that you're the voice in her head, but that she would hate you for it, even though it's impossible for her to do so. What's more, your irrational thinking trapped you on Alethea. You could've shifted yourself anywhere, at any time, but your fear locked you to that place."

I moved my speech to the next person in line. "Emmaline, you came to the island because Ixis told you to. You were dying. The funny part is that you weren't the one afraid to die, but he was afraid for you to die. You had no idea that it would kill him too. You went and drank the Primordial Waters. You were saved and then stayed on the island waiting for him for decades. Why didn't you tell Adrian who you really were from the get-go? Because you were afraid. Afraid to explain to him you hear voices too. Every one of the hybrids here has been locked in a cycle, enslaved by the very people surrounding them. I broke all your chains."

I looked from one face to another. I was desperate for them to understand. "I was forced to stay on Alethea for thousands of years. I was not allowed to see my children or my children's children as a matter of fact. Emmaline and Adrian are the only two of my offspring I've seen in thousands of years, except through the Internet or on television. Glimpses of people here and there." The last part came out as a moan, but I swallowed the cry back, pushing my emotions away.

"You were all very smart, my family." I opened my arms to encompass everyone in attendance. "You have managed to keep yourselves decently hidden, just enough not to raise too many eyebrows. Even you, Sydney, you made bad trades on purpose. You lost thousands of dollars to make it look like you weren't impervious and no one would get suspicious."

I stopped only for a second and then carried on. "My children and I were imprisoned by my Themian family whether you want to believe it or not. Alethea is a beautiful prison. By all standards, I should be thankful that I wasn't sent to Leavenworth. But a prison is a prison and it matters not whether that prison has walls or is a beautiful island. Anywhere that you are forced to stay and cannot leave without someone's permission is a prison and I've been imprisoned on Alethea for thousands of years. So, I made a plan with my children to break free, but in order for my plan to work, Sydney, you and Adrian had to exist." My gaze traveled from one to the other. "I knew it was the only thing that would scare the High Council. A hybrid-Themian mating wasn't enough. The High Council would let whoever mated live, while they cleansed everyone else." I said, then allowed my eyes to travel around the room and gauge everyone's reaction.

Adrian whispered something in Sydney's ear and she tipped her head. Tristan stood next to his twin with his arms crossed and his mind shielded from me. Issy was crying, with her face buried in her mother's arms.

"You can hate me all you want. You can think I'm selfish, that I used you, or I used everyone else. But I know that Athena would have carried out the High Council's orders had it not been for a mating and Ixis personally arguing our case. If all this didn't happen, we would never be off the planet. So, in conclusion, yes, I did all that and I'm not the least bit ashamed, I would do it again — every time." I finished.

Sydney cleared her throat before responding. "Well, at least you unabashedly admit your own crimes, but how exactly do I explain this to the rest of the people on the ship? Do you think all these people really want to hear that they're part of some Themian fracking experiment? That you Themians still use other species to experiment on, but on a grand scale because one human lifetime isn't enough for Themia?" She screamed, then stepped back as two wall panels ripped out of the wall and came at me.

I bashed them out of the way as if they were nothing more than a bubble on the wind.

"I have never gone around looking for a species to experiment on. Everything I have done was for love. I loved an imperfect man, a human, but I loved him nonetheless. I knew he was arrogant, and I still bore children for him. After what he did, there was no way I could stop the High Council from killing him." My throat tightened, "He was a human who became immortal and every quality in him that was good, died on the altar of immortality." I swallowed. "It supercharged everything and although he'd been keeping his arrogance at bay, it was clearly the most dominating characteristic. And that is what came forward. In the end, he deserved every bit of his fate, for all those humans he drowned and the animals he killed. It doesn't seem like that big of a deal now because humanity has so many billions of people all over the world. However, back then, there weren't that many humans and thousands of humans dying had the same impact as if millions of humans were to perish today." Time and scale didn't matter to Sydney and her emotions reflected themselves in the rattling of objects in the room.

"Zeus deserved to die, but that didn't mean his children did too. If they had just stayed away, Athena might never have known about them. However, the moment they all appeared, there was nothing I could do. I know Athena did not want to kill them. This is why she sent them to a Themian Homeworld and told me I'd never see them again."

Sydney stopped pacing and looked at Adrian. I wished I could hear what they were saying, but Sydney had improved her mental shields since we'd met. I was on the outside looking in.

She scratched her head, ran a hand across her forehead, then covered her mouth. "What's done is done, but that doesn't mean it's right." Her voice was low but easily carried around the room. "Whatever your reasons for doing it, you were still meddling. I don't have a problem with interspecies relations. I don't care that we're half-alien or half-human, Themian's or demigods. I don't care about any of that. We are a large swath of humanity that was altered long before we were ever born and none of that matters. What really matters is what we do now." She said it to herself, as if to convince everyone else it was true.

With that, she turned away from the crowd and tilted her head back to take in Saturn's view and sighed.

I could have held my tongue to see which way the wind would blow, but my heart wouldn't let me hold back, so I pressed again. "Well, you want to know where to go. Everyone wants to explore and everyone wants to find a Homeworld. I only want one thing and it is the only thing I will ever want. And that is to go to Homeworld 14 and get my children. Remember when the older lady was talking about meeting the great mother? She's pretty old and without any drugs, she's managed to live 127 years and didn't let anybody know. She was born before computers so that made it easier for her to hide her longevity. She's the last child created by one of my daughters and she wishes to see her mother. After you were born, we all decided it was not necessary to reseed the lines. After you and Adrian mated, we'd achieved all of our goals. Then it was just a matter of time..." I left my words to fade away.

She turned back to me. Her eyes were tired and filled with resolve.

"Ixis, make plans to move to Homeworld 14, wherever that is," Sydney commanded.

A holographic map appeared in the middle of the shifting room. The three-dimensional map contained several star systems but only one planet was lit up.

Tristan pointed at the glowing dot, "Is that Homeworld 14?"

"Yes, that's where we're going," Ixis replied with a smile.

"Wow! How far away is that?" He asked.

"97 million light-years, or in shifter terms, two jumps." Ixis kept his eyes on another screen, flipping through pictures until the screen settled on two different pictures. Both of them were planets, one with a red star and the other a brown one.

"You can make it that far in two jumps?" Tristan whispered.

Awe filled the room and the emotion rolled over me. It pushed the fear away leaving only and dumbfounded understanding of what 97 million light-years really meant.

"Yes. You will be able to do this too, one of these days. It's a relatively small jump, not like trying to go to the first Homeworld, if you even knew where it was," Ixis remarked.

Adrian gasped. "You don't even know where the first Homeworld is? How could you not know where you're originally from?"

CHAPTER 17

SYDNEY

Ixis needed rest and so did I. Actually, we all did. No matter how much I slept it would never take this weight from me. I looked at Adrian and he hovered. His eyebrows were pulled down with worry. I loved him. It was irritating because there was so much I wanted to say to him, to Tristan, and Isolde but I didn't have time. The whole situation was irking me.

I told Hera to dreamwalk her children and get the lay of the land before we charged in and steal them away. Hera had taken over a few rooms in the lab ring near Melinda and the loonies. No sooner had Hera laid down to dreamwalk her kids then Melinda arrived tight-lipped and pacing. It appeared that somehow she'd waited until Hera couldn't interfere.

"We have a real problem with genetic diversity. No matter what Hera says, there aren't enough of us to ensure the genetic diversity of our kind." Her eyes darted to the sleeping form of Hera on the dreamwalk recliner. "Themians don't have this problem and matings make it impossible. However, our human parts need genetic diversity – we're not as evolved," Melinda moaned in frustration.

"What's the point?" I asked rubbing my forehead. My brain just didn't feel big enough for this.

Two steps forward and three steps back. Every day had become a dance for forward momentum.

"I'm saying that if we don't keep track of the breeding lines and save as much genetic material as possible, we are going to have some serious problems with inbreeding." She stared me down with her hands on her hips.

I knew this game. She was leading me somewhere and I hated the slow lead-up. When people do this I just want to scream, to get to the point.

Stop with the story!

"Melinda, you brought me a problem. Did you bring me a solution to go with it?" I asked. I didn't feel this was an issue to focus on at the time.

Can't I have just a week or a few days of peace? Never mind, ten minutes will do.

Her small frame practically jumped with glee. "Yes! But first of all, I don't know how you and that man of yours did it. I'm not sure what Emmaline did. Some way or another, the three of you don't look a day over 23. There must be something you're hiding from me. Also, Hera says that she had lived for thousands of years. So, tell me, what is it I'm missing?" She demanded.

There was no reason to keep Primordium a secret. Eventually, everyone on the ship would find out. It can cure pretty much everything and provided the gift of immortality. But people didn't need to know about that. The only way to keep a secret was not to tell anyone. However, more than enough people already knew at this point.

It's not that I think the loose lips sink ships. But they do.

Once everyone realizes that Tristan and Isolde aren't aging, that I am not getting old, the whispering and wondering will start, then the resentment would set in. We were all hybrids, yet we didn't age like the rest of them. After that, it would be just a matter of time before I'd have a full-fledged mutiny on my hands.

"Melinda, you may want to take a seat for this one. It's a Themian story for children," I sighed.

She tapped one of the circles on the floor and a chair popped up. She plopped down and crossed one leg over the other waiting for me to speak.

"Millions of years ago, on the Themian Homeworld, they had something called Primordium. It's the Fountain of Youth, like the river of life, it turns humans into immortals." I bit my lip and waited for her response, but she never took her eyes from me. She only placed an elbow on the armrest and her hand on the side of her face in thought. Because she didn't reply, I had to continue.

"Themians are naturally born immortal. The only way to kill a Themian is to damage the brain beyond repair. This way, there's too much physical damage and they simply cannot heal themselves."

I glanced over at Hera's ageless form.

"Say someone is crushed by a building or falls from a great height. If we give the Primordium to them, it will bring them back to perfect health. It takes your genetic code back to whatever is supposed to be. It turns on everything that is good and turns off everything that's not. If you have a degenerative recessive gene, it will turn it off and if you have a desirable but recessive gene it'll turn it on."

Melinda leaned forward with both hands on her knees, but still, she didn't say anything.

"It automatically makes you, the perfect version of you, but with enough Primordium, you can make any hybrid or human immortal," I finished and pressed a circle on the floor for my own chair and sat down.

She blinked like a cat. Her mouth was closed and the only part of her body that was moving was just her eyes. I could see all the little wheels in her head turning as she stared off into vacant space. It was clear that she was working something over in her mind and that she wanted a plan. I let her be and after a few minutes, she spoke.

"Well, I wasn't ready for that. I'll have to think about this for a little bit and somehow use this information to solve our diversity issues. Yeah, talk to you later. I need to think," she said and then she stood up abruptly to stride away. She stopped for a moment and mumbled to herself then scratched her head and kept walking.

Not the most interesting knee-jerk reaction I had ever seen, but this was Melinda. Everything in her life had been well thought out. Scientists work on logic and not emotions or passion, but I expected a lot less logic and a lot more emotion.

The sucking sound of the lab doors filled the hallway as I left Hera's rooms. I could have asked Tristan to move me back to the shifting room, but I didn't. I hadn't taken a moment to check the "inmates".

I looked in every unit on either side - one side was all violence, the other side contained sad mental disorders patients. Some just sat there until they saw me, then jumped up yelling, pleading and begging. It was all a silent movie the glass blocked all sound. The people on the other side of the glass moved, opening and closing their mouths but in the hallway was nothing but silence. Every room was soundproof.

Hera said that she would help with all of the "broken" people. The only thing I knew so far was that not everybody down there deserved to be locked away.

Hearing voices isn't a good enough reason to be locked away. After all, if that was true I would be here with them.

Somewhere, down the hallway, was Mary— my mother. She was in one of those rooms and she was probably sitting and waiting patiently. She had spent her whole life locked in a room alone. My throat ached with the thought of it, but I was putting off, our meeting. I certainly wasn't ready for it.

< Sydney, I think I have the solution! > Melinda called.

< *I'm heading back your way.*> I answered and pivoted on one foot to retrace my foot steps.

The door swished, without the sucking sound that you always seem to hear every time you enter someone's laboratory. Melinda was making changes, but this was her domain.

"It's pretty simple. The solution to our problem is staring us right in the face," she said animated and I could feel the energy humming from her.

"And that is?" I hated it when people beat around the bush.

"My calculations for genetic diversity were based upon women and men of childbearing years. If we can turn women and men from whatever age they are into childbearing years, we should do it. If you take every old man and every old woman on the ship and give them Primordium, you turn them into someone who can have a child. And by doing that, you have more than quadrupled your genetic gene pool. So, I think we should offer the Primordium to everyone who's willing to become a parent." She nodded her head with the elegance of her solution.

I knew that she wanted a pat on the back, maybe even deserved one, but…

"Why hadn't I seen that coming? We can't tell them it's Primordium. We have to tell them it's some kind of gene therapy. No one needs to know exactly what it is or how it is we do what we do. It's too important!" I didn't know who I was I dealing with and I couldn't have a crazy person running off half-cocked over the Fountain of Youth.

I wanted to bite my lip, but Melinda would have seen it and I couldn't look indecisive.

She waved my answer off, "We can simply put them to sleep. When they wake up, they'll be changed. I can keep them asleep for a week if you want. Make them think that we used gene therapy on them in a hyperbaric chamber." She shrugged her shoulders and paced the room. She was lit up from the inside with her newfound answers.

I didn't answer immediately. At first, I just smirked.

Okay, we could make this work. Melinda and Hera already have tight control over the labs.

"A hyperbaric chamber," I repeated her words before saying my own, "That actually makes perfect sense. You put them in there for a little while and give them Primordium. They wake up in a week later ready to reproduce. However, Hera has the final say on who gets it and who doesn't. We don't want another Zeus. That is non-negotiable, got it?" I crossed my arms.

< Don't be so forceful! She won't cross you. This isn't a war. > Adrian chided me.

Melinda turned back to her work table and pushed half the papers to one side. "Yeah, I got it. It could work like that. I could devise an entire scenario so it will be plausible if anyone comes in and wants to see the process."

"We need to find a bunch of old people willing to have children," I murmured.

She clapped her hands together and her eyes danced in her head. We both burst out laughing.

"What? You don't think that every old crone in that big room wouldn't have a kid or two? Think about it. It will mean that they can relive their glory days and let me tell you that my name is the first one on that list. I'll have ten!" She barked and pulled her thick white braid over one shoulder.

Astonishment must have shown on my face as I sputtered out. "Ten?"

"Yes, I've always known I'd have my own football team. Even as old as I am, I still feel the desire. Now, I know I can. Question is who is the lucky young man?" she cackled and licked her lips.

A laugh boomed from my mouth. The lascivious old woman had a twinkle in her eye.

"Okay, Melinda. I get your point but we have to get everything under control up top before anything else. You cannot run off to have your way with some poor unsuspecting old man."

She shook her head, "He won't be old when I get done with him." She smiled a big shit-eating grin.

"Yeah, but he'll be really tired," I shot back.

She pushed my shoulder as I turned to leave.

"Hey, Syd! You're doing a good job so far. Now get out! I have shit to do," she said and then she turned away from me and back to her desk.

One worry solved.

*****

I returned to the shifting room and Adrian.

"All you have to do, beautiful girl, is tell the ship you want to make a ship-wide announcement," Adrian instructed me.

Working with Ixis had given him more knowledge about Odyssey than any hybrid on board, other than Tristan. I couldn't say the same about me, because I was still groping in the dark to find my way around.

"I know you keep saying that, but it doesn't come naturally to me. I'm not used to saying 'oh computer'." I rattled off in a Scottish accent.

Adrian threw his head back as a booming laugh burst from him. He shook his head and replied, "You don't have to say 'oh computer' with a Scottish accent? Sydney, it is very easy. Just say 'ship-wide announcement'. You have a bracelet that supersedes everyone, including Hera. You're in charge, beautiful girl, so if you want us all to meet, just say 'ship-wide announcement' and then tell everyone to be at the Citadel at such and such time," he kept repeating the same thing but I was still uncomfortable with it.

Shaking my head, I responded, "I don't know why you keep making fun of me." I pushed my lower lip out and pouted.

"You're so serious all the time and you make it easy for me, beautiful girl. You have been living on a boat with just you, but you are smart enough for all of this. I don't think Athena made it clear that you were in charge for no reason. I don't think she did it to make fun of anybody. Just accept it, Sydney. You're in charge and you need to make an announcement, so stop avoiding your responsibilities."

He stepped behind me and rubbed my shoulders, messaging the knots out and sending thrills down my body. I turned and glanced at him sheepishly through my eyebrows.

"Okay. I'm just getting tired of doing that all of the time. I want to take a few minutes and not to be responsible or in charge. I don't want to be constantly reacting to every fucking crisis," I said and I turned around.

His hands ran down my shoulders to rest on my hips, I stepped back from the close contact.

"If it makes you feel any better, beautiful girl, there are hundreds of people out there willing to do anything for the chance you're about to offer them. You will make them happy. People will fill the corridors of the ship with children. Hera says there are already more children on the ship then she had ever witnessed on any Themian spaceship. Ixis says he has never seen as many children. If we're going to have a race to populate a planet and have genetic diversity, this has to be done. As I said, there are thousands of people out there happy to do it, so, go make people happy. Don't think about this as a chore because it isn't. This is a celebration."

His voice was music to my ears and I didn't want to interrupt him, so I just let him talk and he continued.

"I honestly think that you shouldn't hold the Primordial Waters back from anyone who wants it. You could cure every person here of whatever ails them. More so, you could tell them exactly how it happened. I don't believe that anyone here is going to kill you for it. As a matter of fact, I think that some people might truly wish to stay the course. Aging teaches you a lot of things you're not going to learn from continuously being young and beautiful."

He didn't back away, but I knew he had never aged. Emmaline didn't mean to make him immortal. She just wanted to save his life, but little did she know that Hera had already dosed him. Adrian had never looked a day over 25 and never will.

"You mean to learn how to live with yourself?" I muttered.

I had learned that, but it took me the last three years to get there.

"Yeah, exactly. When all your beauty is stripped away, all that's left is really who you truly are, and you can either like yourself or you don't." He took my hand and kissed the tips of my fingers when he finished.

"What about you and me? Do you like me deep down?" I asked

"I don't like you," he whispered letting his lips trail the shell of my ear.

"What?" I squeaked and snatched my hand back.

"I love you! All of you, inside and out. Now, go make your damn announcements. Stop vacillating!" He stepped back, smacked me on the butt and left the room.

CHAPTER 18

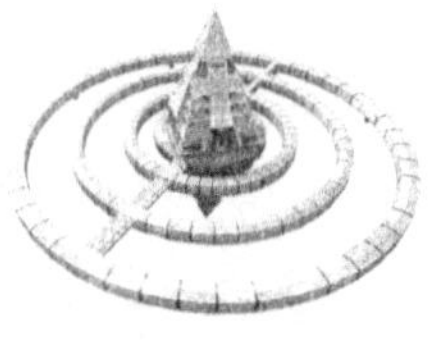

HERA

The layout of Odyssey was similar to Alethea but there were little differences. Alethea was a simple circle, and Odyssey looked more like the spokes on a wheel. They both contained the central pyramid, or rhombus, the shifting rooms in the same locations, but it was the little bits that really made Odyssey its own individual ship.

I'm not exactly sure why, but Themians revere the color blue and this is a fact that it has always been true. My mother described blue as the color of purity, as the thing that would wash away all mistakes. She also said blue would bring the truth. I guess, in Sydney's case, the color certainly did bring the truth for her. It brought her to Alethea.

It was time for that blue to bring my children to me.

Since my fight with Sydney, and her agreement to retrieve my children, I spent most of my time in my quarters. So far, my stay on Odyssey did not differ much from my stay on Alethea.

I was hiding because I couldn't let the shadow between Sydney and me extend to my children. I had to make things right and lounging around in my room, waiting patiently for Ixis to shift them, would not do.

I stared out at the black void. Even though I knew that every dot in that blackness is a star or a system, I still could only see the emptiness. I was aware that there are thousands of worlds out there, each with their own form of life but without my children it all meant nothing for me and I only felt alone.

I uncrossed my arms and looked at my reflection in the crystalline glass. My tunic reminded me of nothing but Themia and their antiquated styles. But that would have to do because I didn't want to waste time looking for the perfect piece of clothing.

I made my way to the shifting room, in search of Sydney and peace.

The center of the room was filled with the hologram of Homeworld 14's system and the white star that hung at the center of the system. Each of its five satellites moved in their counter planed orbits.

Sydney stood with one arm across and the other holding her chin. I reached out and placed my hand gently on her sleeve. She glanced down at it sharply and didn't seem the least bit pleased at the sight of me or the physical contact.

"I am sorry that you feel that I used you. You would do anything for your children and so did I. So, don't judge me so harshly! You were not obliged to walk for thousands of years in my skin. Yes, you are correct, this is a problem of my own making, but just remember that I really did do this for everyone and not just for myself."

She shrugged me off slightly, took two steps and turned around to glare at me.

"Hera, I understand why you did it. Doesn't mean I can't be angry for two minutes about it. I thought you were gonna be our Savior. I thought you were someone to look up to, someone who was actually trying to help. I had no idea you engineered all of this. And yes, it is true that I wouldn't exist without all this madness, but none of this would've happened to the human race. You decided it was okay to marry a human and it was okay to reproduce with him, then turn him immortal. That was all you and nobody else. I can't say the same thing about the rest of us. So, honestly, I just need a little longer to comprehend it. However, if you're willing to go to those lengthens for your version of love, I'm so relieved you're on my side. I'd hate to see what you do to your enemies."

My throat went dry. For the first time, I saw my actions from the eyes of another and I was ruthless. I had been looking at this problem as if it was the only way. I never even once petitioned the High Council.

But Sydney wasn't done, "After all that happened to Poseidon? You said you were imprisoned on Earth. Where did they put Poseidon and why is it that all of his children had to die? Why couldn't they just shift them on another planet? Why couldn't they sent them somewhere else to live out their lives?" She demanded.

"I don't know why the High Council chose death versus letting them live somewhere else. What I can tell you is that they were violent, every single one of them. They were all arrogant, dominating humanity and enslaving them. The difference between my children and Poseidon's is that my children worked for the good of mankind, even Ares. I know that the Mythologies paint him as some bloodthirsty warlord like his father. Ares is a bloodthirsty warlord, but he is not cruel as Zeus was. His thirst is to defend his family. He has no powerful aspiration beyond his talents. He would fight and defend the weakest for as long as it took, even if it meant his entire life," I concluded.

Everyone left the room, but I had hardly noticed their exit. This conversation was not over and not until I had all the details I needed.

"Zeus, on the other hand, would have sacrificed every weak individual he ever encountered to satisfy his lust for power. Poseidon's children were not different, they were the same. They rolled over entire continents. The impact was that many cities ended up having many monuments built to them. Look at Egypt and see everything I'm talking about. What they did there is on a grand scale that still exists to this day. You think that was done by people who were free or well treated?"

Ixis stood far off to the side, next to the exit. He had one hand placed in front of the other, waiting patiently for us to finish our disagreement. I caught his eye and he nodded perceptibly. There was nothing I could say to Sydney, Ixis had not already heard.

"My children, on the other hand, did not Lord it over anyone. Actually, we were defending humanity, constantly trying to protect them from Zeus and Poseidon. There is a reason why they were called heroes and Demi-Gods because that is what they were - Heroes." I raised my voice, I hadn't meant to.

The command crew came back. Adrian and Ixis took a position next to the center display module. Emmaline pulled a seat up from the floor and so did Issy.

"Mom, let it go! She is right. All her children are known as Demi-Gods and Heroes. Doesn't sound like bad people to me," Issy said as she leaned back in her chair and crossed her legs. She readjusted her skirt then placed her hands in her lap and pointed her toes.

"Don't play your cutesy games with me, Isolde," Sydney snapped and then she swiftly turned and looked at me with a raised eyebrow. "I'm not happy with you, but we are not fighting. So, how do you want this shift to work?"

She gave me a tight smile. She was trying.

"I really haven't given much thought about after their arrival. I am afraid my children have not been around other hybrids or even humans for so long I'm not exactly sure how they will react."

They were my children but I was almost positive that the only person they'd spoken to in thousands of years was me.

"Well, I'm sure that being swamped by a crowd of relatives wouldn't be my first choice." Sydney's eyes trailed around the room looking for confirmation. Emmaline nodded to her enthusiastically.

"All I do know is that when they do decide to finally meet, you must be gentle with them. They've spent a long time amongst only each other, they have lost the art of diplomacy in conversation. When you don't have to check yourself amongst family, you stop doing it. However, around strangers, they are extremely guarded and you will all be strangers. As they say in Las Vegas - it's a crapshoot."

Emmaline giggled, "Well, there's no reason I can think of why they should start checking themselves now. After all, we're all family, and it's not like I'm gonna hold back." She patted her spit curls, as if one was out of place, which of course they weren't.

I have no doubt in my mind that Emmaline would not hold anything back. I'd actually begun to wonder if she even had a filter.

"Have Ixis shift them directly into a set of family quarters close to my own. I want to make sure that they won't instantly be inundated," I requested.

I had arranged with Caroline to have food and beverages supplied to their quarters and I sent Ixis a mental picture of the rooms.

"They will be shifted within the hour. Prepare them!" Ixis said.

I exited the shifting room heading straight for their new quarters.

"Hera, wait!" Sydney called to me. "I don't want to be enemies and I want to tell you that I do see why you did all of this." She waved her arms around to explain herself better. "I would have done the same or worse for my children. I can't fault you and I won't hold it against you, but we are all your children now and I need to know that you aren't going to fuck the rest of us at the drop of a hat."

She closed her eyes, mentally pushing something away and stared back at me in the same piercing way Poseidon used to stare at me. I found it unsettling.

"I will always be on the side of my family," I answered.

"That's not good enough for me. I want you to be on the side of our people." Her comment took me off guard.

In my heart that was what I thought I had said, but she was right. My idea of family didn't extend as far as she implied.

"Our people, yes. I will always be on the side of our people. Do we have a name, yet?" I smiled.

She shook her head, with a half-smile. I pulled her to me and hugged her. She stiffened, then allowed me to hold her. When I pulled her back there was a glimpse of a young girl in her shy smile. I could almost see the girl she'd been before Edward had mistreated her. However, her wall of protection quickly closed like a curtain across her face.

"Go tell your children it's time. I want to get out of Themian space as soon as possible." She pivoted on her toes and disappeared before my eyes.

*****

Ten minutes later, I stood next to a viewport in my children's quarters. I opened my mind and made contact with Hephaestus.

< My dear boy, it is time. > I called.

His gruff voice answered back. < We are ready. >

Immediately, I switched to Ixis. < Now!>

The pressure in the room dropped and the scent of ozone grew. A second later the loud crack split the air and eight people occupied the center of the space.

My knees gave out from under me and I found I was kneeling on the floor. My chest was heaving with both pain and happiness. A cry ripped from my throat and my face grew wet.

The sweet faces all crowded around me, each holding me and the each other. It was a mass of bodies.

Eris and Ares didn't cry, but they held us as we held each other. I don't know how long we stayed there. I may have slept, but when we finally broke, the feeling of rebirth overwhelmed me.

"Children, my beautiful children!" I cupped their cheeks and smoothed their hair. Perseus hugged me as did each of the others in turn. I drank them all in. No dreamwalk could ever replace the scent of a child, the curve of their cheeks and the tilt of a head. The energy that came into the room with each and every one of them was as different as a blade of grass.

Hebe giggled and wiggled with joy, Hercules tried to still her but she couldn't stop from rushing to each of us kissing and hugging. It became a game.

"For God's sake, girl! If you hug me again, I may expel my lunch on you," Ares grumbled.

"You can't stop my love, brother. I will never be as happy as I am in this moment," she snickered.

Hephaestus and his twin lingered by the window staring out at the stars.

"This is space, the place where our people came from?" He asked.

I bit my lip and nodded 'yes' to his question.

"This is what we traveled through to reach the Homeworlds," I replied.

They all knew the stories, but seeing space for the first time is always memorable.

Eileithyia shadowed her brother. "It is nothing more than a dark sky with speckled light. I thought there would be more," she murmured.

"There is more, so much more. I want you to meet Sydney. She is our leader and will help us find a home world of our own," I pushed as much hope into my statement as I could.

"We will not have a home world for a long time," Eso stated in a flat voice.

CHAPTER 19

SYDNEY

I paced the ship most of the time, gauging the people and finding my way around. In many ways, it was more than a spaceship. It felt like a city.

Adrian sometimes came with me on my walks, but the ship needed a shifter on duty at all times, so it stretched our three thin. Ixis was used to being awake for twenty hours at a time, but Tristan and Adrian needed their sleep and I needed to walk.

The only way to get from one ring to another was via connecting hallways. They had domed crystalline ceilings, giving you a wide view of the cosmos. Now, that we were no longer in Themian space, the dull in between of the black void was all that filled half of the hallways.

I stared out at the vastness of space and my reflection stared back at me in an eerie blue. The woman I saw didn't look like me at all. My dress was a tunic and I could have walked out of a movie. I'd taken to wear my hair down, only because the wind couldn't blow it in my face. Wind, the boat... All my clothes were still on the boat. It was here somewhere, on this ship, but I haven't bothered to look for it.

We are alone out here. The Themians thrust us into the void with nothing more than a 'don't come back'. My nostrils flared as I pulled in a deep breath to push the irritation away.

We cannot be the only creatures out there.

The 'what if' game rolled around in my head.

What if we aren't alone? What if they are hostile? What if Themia changes their minds and wants to kill us? What if...

I placed my hand on the crystalline glass. I expected it to be cold, but it wasn't. We needed allies and information.

Themia could give us one, but not the other.

I turned back to the shifting room with millions of thoughts in my mind. Ixis was the only one on duty at the time. He never seemed to tire. He stood at his post and stared either into the cosmos or at a screen. He was not a man of many words, but Emmaline made up for that.

"I was sure you would find your way here," he said then turned from his terminal and toed a seat out of the floor. For the first time, I saw him sit.

"Am I that predictable?" I asked and toed my own chair.

"You and Emmaline are not so different. Also, your mental bled over is loud." He dipped his head with a toothless smile.

"Sorry about that. I'll work on it. Homeworld 1. Tell me about it," I said, leaned back and closed my mental doors locking everyone out then waited.

He crossed his legs, placing one ankle on the other knee and replied, "There isn't much to tell. We don't have the records. After leaving the first Homeworld, we were lost in the void of space. The oracle led us to a new home, Delphi, and taught us a new way to live. More than that, I do not know, but I do know where we can learn more," he stated and leaned forward. The smile that spread across his face revealed straight white teeth and laughing dark blue eyes. It struck me, Ixis is good looking. His reddish skin and long black hair framed a kind and intelligent face.

I didn't speak but leaned in myself.

"The Library of Alexandria," he smiled.

"That place burned to the ground in like," I scratched my head to think, "48 BC. Caesar burned it accidentally," I scoffed at him.

Really? Like we could go back in time and research. That is dumb.

"Not the human library. Alexandria – Homeworld 10's Library. That is the repository for all Themian knowledge. Vika, an acquaintance of mine, has been a member of the keepers for thousands of years there." His voice was calm and easy-going.

My mouth went dry and my hand moist, while my heart pounded in my chest. "There's a Themian library full of everything?" I whispered.

"Yes, if there are answers, that is where you will find them." He pulled his long black braid over his shoulder and played with the hair at the end, running the loose tail through his fingers, I'd seen Melinda do the same thing.

The wheels turned in my mind.

If they couldn't find one world, how many others have been lost to time? Where Themians always this way?

Hera seemed to think they evolved to this level but what if they haven't? Even though Father Rizzo's words echoed in my mind about the dangers of knowledge and how people would kill to protect it, I didn't care. If Themia didn't know where it was, maybe no one else did either.

"Prepare for a shift! I want to go to Homeworld 10 and the library," I ordered.

Ixis was up in a flash and was standing at the shifting podium. The room filled with a halo of a single star system, orbited by 27 moons and two planets, one of which had rings.

Ixis tapped the ringed world and said, "This is our destination, but I don't think we should orbit there. Perhaps near one of the outer moons?"

"Yes. Pick one." I swallowed to wet my mouth and squeezed my eyes shut.

"Shifting now!" Ixis' deep timber echoed around the room.

The feeling of cold and the pop at the end always made me queasy.

< **Where are we?** > Adrian demanded.

< *Homeworld 10.* > I responded biting my lip.

A moment later, Adrian stood in front of me in just a short belted tunic that was hanging around his waist. His exposed chest still carried the creases of sleep.

"Syd, we can't stay here," he breathed it out from between clenched teeth. Fear wreaked from his skin. A moment later, we were both in our room - the one place I'd been avoiding.

"You are our leader, but you can't endanger everyone for a bunch of books!" He yelled.

"That's not what I'm doing. They have everything here, all the information Themia has ever known. We need that," I shouted.

He grabbed my shoulders. I didn't pull away even though my first instinct was to do so.

"You don't know these people. They aren't all nice and even-handed. Hera and Ixis are different. The High Council can and will kill us all." He turned away from me and pounded his fist against the glass window.

I turned to leave. I didn't want to fight.

"Where are you going?" He demanded.

"Where ever I want. I'm not a child," I shouted at him.

"You are running away. Again. For Christ sake! You just can't stand to be alone in the same room with me. Can you?"

He shifted in front of the door blocking my exit. My eyes darted from the door to the bed in the next room and to the bathroom. This wasn't about Homeworld 10 or Themia. It was about me not talking to him. And that room.

"I'm not running away. I...I have work to do." I stepped around him heading for the door.

"No, you don't." He sidestepped in front of me and leaned back against the door.

"Can you please move?" I asked trying not to meet his eyes.

"When we are around people, you act like everything is perfect and that you love me. Don't get me wrong, I know that you love me, but the moment we are alone, you hide in the bathroom or run out the door. Why?" He crossed his arms locking his jaw down.

"If you're so smart, why don't you tiptoe through my mind and find out?" I spit the words out.

It was mean, but my default was to deflect and deny. I stepped back and turned to the bathroom. As I reached the door, Adrian appeared in front of me and I screeched.

"Nope, you aren't leaving this time. You don't get to shrug me off." He stated.

God, I hate shifters!

I thought I closed all my mind doors, but apparently, I didn't.

"You really do need to work on your mental blocking, beautiful girl," he said and stepped forward.

I took a step back, tilting my head to look in his eyes. I wanted to melt into them, to drown in those blue pools. I gripped my hand and the heavy wedding ring dug into my palm.

Gabriel.

I stepped back and Adrian followed. I couldn't breathe, I wanted to kiss him and hold him, but…

"He's dead, Sydney. He was human and he died. I am here," he whispered and his hands ran up and down my arms.

I shrugged him off.

"You were dead! Oh, but you weren't, were you?" I shouted. Anger and hurt welled up in me making my voice louder. "You left me and never came back," I screamed.

My chest ached with the remembered pain. I could still hear the announcement in the church that he had died. The vice on my chest ratchet down and I was gulping in air. The remembered taste of bile made my mouth water.

He cupped my face in his hands forcing me to look at him. "I didn't have a choice. I couldn't leave Alethea. Do you think I wanted to watch you with some other guy? Knowing he was touching you, kissing you…" his voice broke.

A second later, his lips crashed hungrily down on mine. His tongue invaded my mouth and I gave back in return. A second later, I turned my face away breaking the kiss.

"I wouldn't have been with Gabe if you had told me anything. All those times my father beat me, you… you were in my head. Why didn't you say anything?" I whispered while my body trembled.

"You didn't believe I was real. How fast would you have run away if I had told you? You would have better mental shields, for sure." He released a dry laugh and his hand moved down my arms, landing on my hips.

The fire from that simple touch raced over my skin creating a deep heat.

"But why didn't you tell me before you left? We were going to be married and you didn't trust me." I was gaslighting because I hadn't trusted him either.

"When the pot calls the kettle black..." he leaned his forehead against mine and his breath moved over my lips tickling my tongue, "I thought we had more time. I..."

I cut him off and stepped away.

"Then why the lawyer and the will? That was planning ahead as if you knew," I snapped and moved to the opposite side of the room next to the window calculating the steps to the door.

"My father took me to Langtree and had me make a will. He told me to always have a backup plan. He didn't know who you were, but he knew there was someone. It wasn't until after I was on Alethea I learned the truth."

"Yeah, what truth was that?" I demanded cocking a hip to one side.

"Emily didn't tell me who she was for years. She said something one day about me when I was little and mention my dad and only then did she come clean. Aunt Emmaline knew about you and me for years. She also told me that my father was a seer. I think he knew about us and what would happen, but he went down to Costa Rica anyway." Tears streamed down his face. "He knew and he went to his death," Adrian's voice cracked.

I was at his side, holding him and letting him know I understood his pain. He shifted us to the couch. We both cried. We cried for the parents he lost, for our lost time, for everything. After a few minutes we stopped and changed the subject.

"So, you weren't in love with Emily? I thought you were when you pushed me out." I smiled my eyes darting around the room.

He lifted his head and I could see from his wide eyes that he didn't expect that question. "Em? No! Even when I didn't know she was Aunt Emily that wasn't the case. I cared for her, but love... Sydney you are such a fool. I told you that I will never love anyone but you." He cupped my cheek again and my hand covered his.

The anger I'd been carrying since I realized he was alive went from a giant stone in my belly to a golf ball. It wasn't gone, but it was manageable.

"Tom told you to make that will?" I asked.

"Yes. Well, sort of. He said to make a will but not what to put in it," he quirked a smile.

"Why didn't you stop me with Gabe?" I asked and immediately looked away.

"By then, I knew everything and you were safer that way. That was what mattered the most."

I pulled out of his arms and got up off the couch. I noticed that the cushions were a weird, memory foam because the indentation from my body quickly disappeared.

"But you didn't have a problem sleeping with me while I was married to Gabe," I said and I ran my hand over my forehead.

We had gone over this with Tristan and my answers to him were perfect, but I knew deep down inside that I wasn't ok with my own explanation.

"Sydney, this is one fight I'm not going to have with you. I love you and have always loved you. I have never been with anyone but you. According to Themia's laws we are married and have been ever since the blue lights in the ski lodge." His voice was a deep growl.

My mouth fell open and Adrian moved to stand in front of me.

"If anything, he was sleeping with my wife." His teeth ground out his reply.

I tried to step back but I was against a wall. His fingers tipped my chin up and he pressed against me.

"I shared you only to keep you safe. I will do whatever is necessary to keep you and our children safe. You can't ask me to say sorry for making love to you ever. I won't! You are mine and I am yours." His eyes bored into me and my mouth was filled with cotton. "Is there anything else you want to argue over?"

I gulped back whatever retort I had. I wanted to say he didn't own me, but that wasn't true. He did own every bit of me and I wanted him to. However, his answer regarding my marriage with Gabe, made the situation sound so much worse. I closed my eyes to get a grip. Every nerve ending in me was on fire and he was the flame.

When I opened my eyes, I realized that my hands were on his chest. I met his sight and wiggled under his stare. The clasp holding my toga slipped down my shoulder and Adrian's eyes darted to the exposed flesh.

"I… don't want to argue," I whispered. "I'm tired…"

His hands slid behind me, one down and over the swell of my butt and the other up to my neck. I tiptoed up to meet his lips. I so wanted him, in the real world and not in a dream. The thin fabric of his tunics did nothing to hide what he wanted.

His mouth worked its way down my neck, nibbling and kissing everything in its path. I was like butter in his embrace and I only wanted more. My hands wound around his chest pulling him closer. Whatever belt held his tunic to his waist lost its battle against gravity and the fabric fell. Adrian shifted us to the bedroom, but my dress never made it.

CHAPTER 20

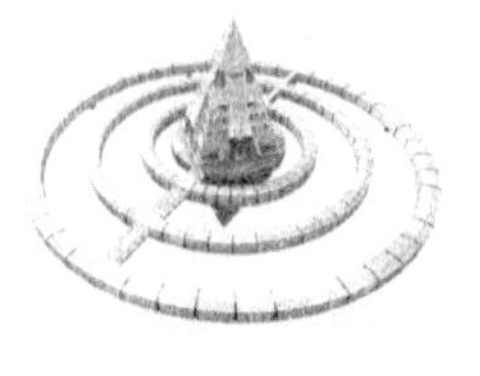

SYDNEY

The world had changed into a different place overnight. Being on Odyssey and wearing Greek clothes had somehow become normal. I smiled to myself and moved the necklace pendant right and left on its chain. It had a double pearl on it and Adrian gave it to me. He said that each pearl was for each of the children, that it was his gift to me. He found it off the beach on Alethea the day after I gave birth to the twins.

"Are you on the same spaceship as the rest of us?" Melinda asked while pacing the lab with her arms crossed.

I released the pearls, allowing it to drop back to my skin and nestle between my breasts. I took in her stance and wiped the smile off my face.

She stopped for a moment, then began again. "I've evaluated most of the mental patients and most of them are really not mental patients at all. A few clearly have issues, some of which I think might be resolved by giving them Primordium. Most of them were simply put into a mental ward because they heard voices or because they were overwhelmed by emotions. Others became violent because they could hear other people's thoughts." She stopped pacing again and her eyes were on fire. "They were raised in foster homes. They didn't know their families and they had no one to tell them what was going on. They were just alone and scared." Melinda stared at me waiting for a reply.

"Okay, so what do we do?" I asked and crossed and uncrossed my arms. The dreamy feeling from the night before still lingered.

"My opinion is that we should take every person that is relatively normal and just needs a little pat on the back and explain to them that they don't need crazy therapy. Then, we should release them into the general population and set them up with a friend. I'll start treating them but not as they were during their institutionalized period." She rubbed her head before she continued, "It's only scary if you think it's all in your head. Most of what's wrong with them, is that they need a little Primordium to clear the drugs that they've been on. Humanity pumped them full of crap and then wondered why they were so unhinged," Melinda huffed.

"I think that everyone on board of Odyssey should have a little bit of the Primordium. I think it would do everyone a world of good," Hera stated, then walked down the hall before returning.

"Really? You want to give Dewey a little pick me up?" Emmaline moaned with a smile.

Everyone laughed. Emmaline was always talking about Dewey as if he was the only thing in the world and the Universe, other than Ixis, of course.

"Why not? I think Dewey could do with a little Primordium. It would make him young again. Just like you," Melinda replied and then leaned back against one of the glass walls and crossed her arms.

"Thanks, but no one wants a young Dewey. Did you see what he did the last time he was young?" Emmaline scoffed and rolled her eyes.

"You really think he did that on his own, Em?" I asked.

"If I remember correctly, he said he was just carrying a gun," Issy laughed at Emmaline.

"Along with all of the other guys blowin' up Europe. When I think of Dewey being young, carrying a gun and also being part alien, I get worried. Don't you?" She pulled up a wicked smile, then adjusted her tunic. She was always fidgeting with her clothes.

"There are no hands-guns on Odyssey, Emmaline. Not that I think that there should or shouldn't be," I remarked.

"If we are going to an alien planet how useful would a gun really be?" Melinda retorted, pushing herself off the glass wall and on to her feet.

"If you think that no crazy half-alien hybrid brought a gun when coming here, you are out of your mind. Have you met some of those people out there? I mean there are a few hillbilly rednecks that look like they haven't slept without a gun in years and might be more in love their gun than they are with their wives," Emmaline giggled and slapped her knee and I followed.

"Are they crazy for sleeping with a gun? Or for sleeping with a gun on an alien ship?" I snickered.

She raised her eyebrows and looked at me as if I'd lost my mind. The other people in the room started laughing.

"It's crazy to me and I'm mated to an alien. Ixis is the most wonderful alien in the Universe, however, he is still an alien and I'm half-alien. It's all damn strange. I've been tryin' to swallow this pill since I was young and got my mind around it. What makes you think that the rest of these numbskulls are gonna do the same?" She asked while poking her thumb behind her, as though that was the direction of the delirious and demented.

"What? Should we confiscate all the weapons? I don't see that as an okay solution," I waved one hand at her and then changed my focus, "Hera, can a gun harm the ship?"

"No. Your type of guns cannot pierce the hull," she replied in her matter of fact tone.

I knew the answer before I asked but I wanted everybody else to hear it.

"I'm going with this. I believe everybody has a right to a gun. We're on a friendly alien spaceship but we don't know what we might encounter out there. I don't want anybody to register them. I don't give a crap if you've got one, but if you discharge it for no good reason on this ship I'm going to take it away pretty fast. Everybody is capable of protecting themselves in some form. So, as long as you act responsibly there's no reason for me to know about it or bother you about it. I also believe in the freedom to do whatever the hell you want, as long as you don't hurt anybody else."

Melinda opened her mouth to say something, but I put my hand up to stop her.

"Don't take people's things, don't steal, don't murder. These are pretty simple rules. I mean, if you're a murderer then we have some serious problems. I'm not saying I'll shove anybody out an airlock but if you are killing people yeah, I'll go there," I shrugged.

"We can do without taxes," Melinda murmured and we all snickered.

"You know that's one part of government we can absolutely do without. It's simple you know? We will have only one rule on this ship - don't be a dick!" I finished my rules and regulations outline.

Emmaline walked around the room with her hand over her mouth snickering, while Melinda grabbed her clipboard and checked something off an unseen list.

"Patients that aren't ill can be set free. That leaves the super bads and the criminals." She looked down at the sheet, tracing it with the eraser of the pencil.

"There are a couple I'm not sure about," Melinda said and pointed to the room down the hall.

A man stood next to the glass watching us. He gave me a smile that didn't reach his eyes and I shivered because it gave me the creeps.

Melinda's voice cut in, "Giving him the Primordium may not help his condition, but we still need to consider the gene pool problem. We still need to save as much genetic material for future generations as possible," she finished by clicking her tongue.

I looked again at the creepy man. He sat down in his chair and crossed his legs, but he never took his eyes off our group of women.

"I'm not sure that any of these will ever be released to the general population. I'm not sure we can cure their illness," Melinda added.

Hera took up the empty space in the conversation. "I've suggested several times, that Melinda should give them all Primordium and see what happens but she's resisting. Which is why we're coming to you. We need a decision and someone needs to break our tie."

I looked from one room to the other. Hera's tale of Zeus still rang in my mind. But she had given him three doses in 24 hours and we were only contemplating giving one. It would heal you or not, but she said immortality only came from the double dose.

"Ok, so my decision is the following. Give them all Primordium, the same amount you give everybody else. Everybody gets some. If there's even a possibility that we can cure whatever's wrong with them, then let's do it. Primordium realigns the genes and makes you the perfect you, right?" I asked and bit my lip.

"That's how it was always been described to me," Hera supplied. "I'm not a Primordium keeper. They study Primordium, the process by which it is made and how it is used on the Themian body for thousands of years. I would love to have a Primordium keeper right now. Their insight would be invaluable. I'm actually surprised they didn't send one with the ship"

I thought about Hera's remark but didn't answer.

"No one was willing to come with us," Emmaline replied and her words hit me. Ixis had asked for volunteers. Anyone willing to join our ragtag band, wandering through the space looking for a home was welcomed, but there were no takers.

"The only real problem is the following one. By giving everyone the Primordium, if they're half human and half Themian, which genes is it going to become perfect? Will it take a psychopath and make him a more perfect psycho?" Melinda's argument wasn't lost on me.

That is what happened with Zeus. So, what do we do if we get a new Zeus?

"That's what Melinda keeps saying and this is why she's resistant to give them any. She wants to try traditional therapies," Hera argued and I couldn't see why she wasn't against this too.

"There isn't a treatment for psychopaths. They've used shock therapy on them in the past but I don't think they found that very effective. I mean everybody here has seen or read 'One Flew Over the Cuckoo's Nest', right?" Melinda asked.

I could see how this fight had been going around and round.

"It's not really about whether it makes them a better psychopath. We need to find if they are redeemable and we have to find out one way or another, so everybody gets it!" I ordered.

"Everybody gets their chance at redemption. We will deal with the aftermath later," Melinda echo's sarcastically.

"Well, if someone's a psychopath and has the potential to run around here and become a serial killer, I don't see any reason whatsoever to keep them on the ship. I think death is a very good resolution. But if they aren't redeemable how are we supposed to justify feeding them?" I demanded.

"We're not murderers. I don't believe that behaving like one it isn't a great way to start a new society," Melinda shot back.

Isolde's voice rose over the group and the circular argument. "That sounds fine. If you wish, I can touch whoever the psychopath is. Then, I can see every crime they've ever committed. Would that make you feel better about jettisoning them out the nearest airlock? I'm absolutely going to tell you right now that I'm biased and I think that anybody who has the potential to become a serial killer or serial rapist or violent criminal like that, needs to go out the nearest airlock, genetic material and all."

The room became very somber. Isolde was not usually the one to sound so bloodthirsty, but her words rang true in my mind.

Do I really want to foster those genes? Do we want to run the potential of having another psychopath rollup in the amidst of relatively peaceful people?

"I will not help foster genocide in any shape. I have seen Primordium turn perfect human genes into a perfect psychopathic killing machine. That is exactly what happened to Zeus. It took everything that was bad about him and brought it to the forefront and the good was pushed to the side. Maybe those were the more dominant genes. I don't know. What I do know is that if that happened to anyone here, on the ship, I will not tolerate another Zeus. You weren't there. You didn't see what he intended to do. He wanted to commit genocide on a massive scale, leaving only a few humans so he could raise them up under the belief that he was a God and he could control them as slaves." Hera stared out the glass windows, but the only view was the white star in the Homeworld 10 system and the large moons floating nearby.

"Melinda, everyone gets some. Line them up and hand it out to them like candy. I don't care if it's just like a drink of water. Everybody gets it. If they are old they become young, if they are sick they become healthy, a psychopath might become normal person or they might turn into Jeffrey Dahmer. We will just have to wait and see the outcome," I stopped only to take in some air and then continued, "Also, no one's pushing anybody out of an airlock. I'll be the first person to cleanse the ship. I never believed I had such a bloodthirsty little girl or such a bloodthirsty empath," I murmured and looked at Issy.

*****

Adrian shifted me and I didn't protest. I was too tired from not sleeping all night.

We couldn't keep dead weight on the ship. There was no reason why we should waste resources on anyone.

Children are one thing. They're the future and should always be nurtured, but when it comes to psychopaths there's no reason in the world why we shouldn't toss them out the nearest airlock.

My father was completely fucking crazy and I would've happily tossed him out an airlock.

"You look like you swallowed something sour," Adrian remarked and pulled me into his arms.

"You guys put me in charge of a big ship. I know I have to make some decisions that I'm not always going to be 100% cool with, but..." I faltered.

He knew everything, but voicing it out loud changed it for me for some reason.

"Like what?" He quietly whispers in my ear.

"Jettisoning a few psychopaths. Like I'm not trying to justify it, but I feel terrible about it," I muttered.

"You should feel bad," he continued then kissed my neck.

I gasped and felt the anger rise up inside me. "Are you blaming me? Is there a better answer?" I demanded.

"Grace said we 'should' feel bad and the moment you stop feeling bad, that's when you really need to worry." He tilted his head down to make sure I was paying attention. "It means that you don't give a fuck and you've become the very thing you are throwing out the door. It's okay to be a realist and a survivor all at the same time, but don't lose touch with who and what you really are. You're not a killer, are you?" He asked.

His breath made the hair on my neck tickle a moment before he kissed my ear.

"No. It doesn't mean that I haven't killed or wouldn't do it again, but I'm not a cold-blooded killer," I murmured and pulled back the heat in my chest threatened to overwhelm me.

"Exactly! As long as you know why you're doing it and you're not getting any glee out of it, that's what is important - the good of the many outweighs, the good of the few. It's not logical to keep one person alive and sacrifice everyone else."

He turned my face back to him and glanced from my lips to my eyes and heat rolled over me. After the last night, I was surprised we could leave our room. However, the choice of the many over the few was a wet blanket for my lust.

Risking everyone for one person is wrong. If even one person died because I couldn't make the hard choices, I don't know if I could live with that.

Adrian wasn't talking about the criminals and mentally ill, he was talking about the ship and the risk I'd put us all in. "We have to move the ship," I said and hung my head.

"Yes, we do and I'm glad you agree. Don't worry! Hera can dreamwalk us to the library," he replied and kissed my hair.

I looked back up at him through scrunched eyebrows. "Why didn't I think of that?"

"Because you have me." He stole a deep kiss and left to dress for his turn in the shifting room.

CHAPTER 21

HERA

Sydney came up with thousands of questions and ideas. Keeping up with her was impossible. She wanted to find Homeworld 1 and to do that she wanted me to dreamwalk to one of the most protected places in all of Themia.

"I can, but I can't. You have to have someone to dreamwalk through. I can't just dreamwalk to a place. You need the mind of a person, even if that person doesn't realize that you're using them as a conduit. You will appear in their world and in order for that to happen, you have to have the person in place."

Sydney was not aware that one word from her mouth and every Themian for several hectares would know something was wrong.

"So, if I wanted to go back to Earth and find something, you would need a person there? You need someone on Earth you know so that your mind could attached to them and that person needs to be in the right place, like making a telephone call? You can't just call anybody up, you have to call the right person?" Sydney asked biting her lower lip.

Her tunic fell to her knees and she fidgeted with it. The tightness I'd seen around her lips was gone. I wish I could say the same. Even though my children were on the ship, I felt no peace and I was not sure I ever would again. At least not as long as we were still in Themian space.

"Exactly! It is like making a telephone call. You must have a person within the vicinity you want to go. Also, their mind would have to be receptive. I don't necessarily have to know them but I would have to have a way to contact them," I said and then toed a chair up from the floor and sat down. "Most Themians aren't mated and have never dreamwalked anyone. My ability is not as common as you think, so people may not even realize they are being walked."

I had not had a conversation like this in thousands of years. Explaining the dreamwalk to my children was the last time. I didn't want to think about mated dreamwalks and the need for clothes.

How embarrassing would it be to show up naked?

I rubbed my forehead. The hybrids in many ways were so young. I would need to add the dreamwalk talk to a long list of classes for hybrids. Perhaps I could get one of my daughters to give that one.

"Ixis knows someone on Homeworld 10!" Sydney said with her unrelenting push for forward momentum.

I turned away from her and covered my mouth with a hand. "I know many people on Homeworld 10. I was born there and I spent a great deal of my childhood there," I stated.

Hyprion is there. He would never leave, it is his home. My parents may be there, but they had made it very clear how they felt about me and my children.

I swallowed those memories away. This was my new life and I would have to embrace it.

"I don't believe they would be receptive, after all I am an outcast." My shoulders slumped.

Would anyone tell the High Council if they saw me?

"I don't care whether they like your choices or not. Can we do it?" Sydney demanded, then smiled, "Please!"

She was trying and it was hard for her. She wasn't like me. She didn't have the patience I had.

"I will send Hera my contacts information. She will have to be the judge over the usefulness of my choice," Ixis eyes glazed over and for a moment the blood vessel on the side of his head bulged. After that, he turned and headed back to the other side of the shifting room.

*****

A vision of a woman hunched over a screen, filled my mind. Her dark hair hung down trailing across a table with a pile of data chips off to one side. She pushed her hair back behind on ear before glancing up at me to smile. The vision ended with a name, Vika.

*****

I blinked to push back the malaise that came with things like this. Ixis must have mentally push hard to send that to me. Image transfers aren't easy, but he has been sharing

~ 276 ~

images with both Tristan and Adrian for months now. Perhaps the stress of all our changes had gained him this new ability.

"Maybe, you can tiptoe through her mind and figure out how to get into the library." Sydney clasped both hands before her as if begging but she wasn't. She was just acting as though as she was.

Sydney's pushing brought me back to the present time.

"You're going to take me with you, Hera?" She stared me in the eye and continued, "You know as well as I do, that two sets of eyes are better than one."

She smiled. I didn't understand her insistent need to make this trip. I began to shake my head but stopped. Issy mouthed to me 'books' and rolled her eyes. I smiled to myself. Sydney was a reader. So, of course she wanted to go.

I don't know why I haven't thought of it before.

I cleared my throat before answering. "Yes, but I want to take Issy with us. I somehow feel it's important that she come due to her creative way of finding information."

Issy beamed with my complement. "Thank you, thank you, thank you" Issy jumped with excitement, then regained control and replied. "I'd be happy to go."

Her hands gripped her earth clothing - shorts and a tank top. I frowned to myself.

"She'll stick out like a sore thumb, no offense, Isolde. Themians aren't stupid. They know we're makin' a play. You don't think they'll sit idly by while we go tiptoeing through their library, do you? I can alter my accent so I don't sound so Midwestern poe-dunk. Talkin' like a Themian is nasal and easy. As I said, Isolde would stick out like a sore thumb," Emmaline stepped into the discussion while crossing and uncrossed her arms.

"Well, then Emmaline, I think you just volunteered yourself to give Isolde the crash course in how to be Themian," Sydney replied with a smirk.

Emmaline crossed both arms over her chest, tilted her head to the side and gave Sydney the dirtiest look I think that woman had in her arsenal.

"I realize that you're in charge, Syd, but you're just a kid in my world and I don't appreciate you tellin' me what to do. Kids these days have no respect at all. In my days, I would've slapped that cheeky mouth of yours," Emmaline ground it out between her teeth.

"You can either take this as me telling you what to do or you can take it as a necessity for our group. Everybody has to do their part. Since you figured out how to mask yourself to blend in with the Themians, I need you to teach Isolde to do the same. Maybe while you're at it, teach her some Themian words so she won't stick out." Sydney moved toward Emmaline. "Three sets of eyes are better than two and Issy could be our best researcher. It will take twice as long for Hera to find anything on her own. This isn't the time to be fighting or arguing about whether someone can tell you what to do." Sydney wasn't pleading, but the please hung in the air.

"What you, Hera and Isolde are proposing to do is infiltrating a private library because we're trying to be preemptive—"

Sydney cut Emmaline off, "We have nowhere to go. Finding the original Themian Homeworld sounds to me like it would give us allies and maybe a place to stay for a while, assuming it's livable, but it also gives us a lot of insight into Themia. They are half of what we are. I don't know about you, but those are all answers that I would want to know any day of the week, so don't get your panties in a wad." Sydney said.

Emmaline narrowed her eyes. Sydney wasn't always the most diplomatic person.

But she rushed on before Emmaline had a chance to form a retort. "You're the best hope we have. I know you're a natural teacher. Adrian told me— you taught him everything he knows about Alethea. You saved him. I'd like to think you could teach one more person or maybe several people." Sydney reached out to Emmaline and took her hand in her own.

The two of them were like Nemean cats, fierce in a fight and hard to back down.

"Find a bunch of researchers in our ragtag group and take them all with you. Train them. We are going to need to start keeping our own records and libraries anyway," Sydney said as a matter of fact.

Emmaline didn't huff. She wasn't a huffer or complainer. She was a doer. She glanced sideways at Ixis and something passed between them.

"All right! I'll train this little ragtag group of library thieves. I'll even start the first hybrid library, but don't think that I'm gonna be okay with you tellin' me what to do. Y'all set me off. I still want a democracy. I understand someone has to make the final decision when it comes down the life-and-death. Nobody really wants that job and you're welcome to it.

Come on Isolde! Themian 101 starts now!" She grabbed Issy by the hand and drug her off.

I watched Issy trip behind and Emmaline cursing all the way. I turned back to Sydney, "You will need to train also."

She toed a seat out of the floor, flopped down on it and simply replied, "I know." as if she wanted to change the subject, she lifted the fabric of her tunic an inch and looked at it. "I can get over the fashion, it's the mannerisms I have a hard time with. Why can't this ship make any other clothing styles?" She scoffed and dropped the fabric back down onto her lap.

I laughed out loud. "Themia moves slow. If you want new styles, you have to tell the computer. It's not much different from inserting a picture. We could get someone to work on it." I leaned forward in earnest.

She smiled a tired smile, "That would be nice." She rubbed her hand down the side of her face and closed her eyes for a moment before they snapped open to stare me down.

"You know, it doesn't always have to be a fight. Emmaline is right. You don't have to order everyone around." I murmured low enough so just Sydney and I could hear.

She sat back and heaved a sigh. "It doesn't. Emmaline gets my back up with her drawl and she knows it. She's nothing like Grace. I miss Grace. Maybe, I wish she was more like Grace. I don't blame her for being here when her sister isn't. It's just…" she sighed again.

"You should tell her about her sister. She would want to know. You can't think it was easy for her to live on Alethea for 40 years while everyone she loved slowly died." I said.

Pointing out the obvious sometimes brought it to the forefront.

"I know it wasn't. I can't think about Earth or everyone we left there. If I do, I may never be able to do anything else. Zack, Maria, Nonna, Trish…"

She turned away from me. Her forehead pulled down creating wrinkles all over her face. For a moment, I saw Sydney from the inside out. She was scared, but her wall quickly went back up and she pushed to her feet.

She had called me ruthless. I was willing to be ruthless but she was so much more than that. Sydney would fight to the end of the Universe for a cause and we had become her cause.

She stared out the domed ceiling at the star cluster in the distance with her arms crossed. These stars were old friends of mine. I had stared at them for most of my childhood. They called them the Fates. They were three bright white stars of equal size, clustered in an obtuse shape.

"When you stare at the vacuum of space, what do you see?" She asked resting her head on the back rim of the chair.

"I see what can be," I replied letting the hope of life with my children fill me.

"I see what can be and isn't," she stated then turned back to me.

"Together we can make it what it should be," I offered with a weak smile.

"Do you think that looking for the original Homeworld is the right choice? We could just pick a planet and settle down." She was looking for something from me, but I wasn't sure I could give it to her.

"My gut, the one I've always been told not to listen to, tells me it is right. We can always leave the lion's share of our people on a world and continue the search." I moved to stand next to her, letting the chair sink back down into the floor.

"No, that isn't the right choice either. We have to stick together. We can't leave anyone behind." She smiled and took to her feet then turned to leave the shifting room and I watch her glide out into the ship.

Ixis stood as a guardian on watch by the center podium. His long black braid hung down his back in stark contrast with the white fabric of his tunic. I glanced around the room for Emmaline, but, of course, she wasn't there.

"How does it feel to be the only Themians on board?" His voice cut the air surprising me.

"I hadn't thought about it like that. But it is strange. Humanity and hybrids are so different. And you, did you think you would stand here, mated to a non-Themian?"

He turned slightly and glanced over his shoulder. "I never thought about it. Emmaline awakened and my Universe changed." His simple answer awakened that place in my heart that was alone.

"You could have taken her at anytime and kept her with you. The High Council would have been none the wiser," I ventured.

He barked out a laugh, a sound I had never heard from him. Ixis was always quiet and soft spoken. "It never crossed my mind to do otherwise. That was my plan from the first. I would complete my assignments and go to my mate. I didn't understand how fragile humanity was until she almost died. But even that wasn't enough to wake me from my Themian stupor. Athena threatened to cleans them all, to kill my Emmaline..." The words came out even and calm, but the expression of emotion behind them was a shock to me.

Themian stupor. As if their very thoughts were nothing more than a drug to be awakened from. They do live in a world lacking change or empathy in any form.

I shook my head. "Is finding Homeworld 1 the right choice?" I asked.

"It is our best choice. Themia will not start a war but one will come. Humanity will expand into the Universe as will the Hybrids and it will be as if the Titans have returned. The cosmos is vast but conflict always finds you eventually. I watched the second human World War through Emmaline's eyes." He pivoted on one foot, and our eyes met. "They butchered each other over an idea. Can you imagine what they will do over a star system?"

My mouth dried. It was never part of the plan to stop human progress.

The hybrids can and will change. I can lend a hand in that. But humanity, in space, wreaking havoc...

I trembled at the thought.

Ixis' voice was low as if to keep our conversation private, even though Emmaline could hear it all. "The last time I saw a carnage of that kind was on Tartarus and the Great Division. I had hoped to never see it again." He never wavered in his countenance while his dark blue eyes bored into me.

The only things I knew of the Great Division came from my education and the bits and pieces in Poseidon's mind. He had gripped those memories tightly, giving out only flashes of a face— but nothing more.

"While you are in the library, I want you to look something up for me," he said in the same even tone of voice.

"I would be happy to help you in any way I can," my reply came automatically, but I realized that I truly was happy to help him and a small smile touched my lips.

"Find out everything you can about a man named Anu." He stared me down for another moment and a shiver of fear reached me. Then he turned back to the podium and his watchful stance.

Who is Anu? And why does Ixis fear him?

CHAPTER 22

HERA

The dreamwalk coalesced around me and the great columns of my one-time home took shape. I was standing outside one of the main colonnades in Zadria, the central city. The stark white buildings glared back at me against the green grass. It cut a beautiful contrast and I sighed. My home was unchanged in every way. Themia never changes. They thrive on the sameness of everything.

I have lived with constant change for so long, I realized that I didn't know any other way to be. Even Alethea changed. The coral grew, the ocean waves moved atolls, trees grew and died. The spaceship became a part of the planet, to the point where you couldn't see where Earth ended and Alethea began.

But not here. Zadria is the same. Even the air tastes the same.

The dark-haired, Vika, stood across from me and next to a man in a half tunic. His golden curls where closely cropped on his head. But the set of his shoulders and the tilt of his head, I knew him. Even from behind, I couldn't forget Hyperion.

My breath caught in my throat. I wanted to call to him and see the light in his eyes, but I stepped back into the shadows of the columns.

Hyperion is not why I am here.

The desire to be with my twin would always be there and no amount of space or time could take it away. He turned his head to scan the area and I broke the dreamwalk.

*****

My bed was covered in sweat, as tears streamed down my face. My chest heaved with pain, the pressure inside threatening to tear me in two. Hyperion sensed me. I locked my mind down to keep him out, because the feeling of him prodding at the edges was like ice cutting you in the bitter cold. I curled on to my side and heaved with my pain.

If only life had gone so easy for me, as for him.

I wasn't jealous, only regretful. I don't know how long I laid there, but when I got up and bothered to look in a mirror, my face was swollen from the tears.

You knew this was a possibility.

I had hoped I could be in and out quickly, but fate never works that way. At least it never worked that way for me. I always had to face everything head-on without any chances to hide.

I washed my face and straighten my clothes, but my dress was a wrinkled mess, so I hosted it over my head and threw it in the recycler. I called for a new one and waited for the computer to supply it. The compartment dinged and I slid the door to the side and found my fresh tunic.

I quickly donned my clothes and laid back down on the bed, then gave myself the injection. I wouldn't be able to wake myself this time. I would be forced to stay in the dreamwalk no matter what.

I am not a coward. I have a job to do.

Vika had moved on from the open air of the colonnade into a room filled with data chips and just as in the vision Ixis had sent me, she was crouched over a display screen reading. I coughed so I wouldn't startle her and she lifted her head to stare at me.

"I locked the door. Did you override it? I *have* left the building today," she remarked, then turned back to her screen.

"I didn't break in. Ixis sent me," I responded then placed one hand over the other and waited.

"Did he? I wonder when was that. Half an orbit ago?" She asked and leaned on one elbow squishing her face into her hand.

"No, five turns ago," I replied.

Her eyes grew to the size of a dinner plate and her mouth formed an O. She sputtered for a moment. "Um, he did? Why?"

I approached her work table. "May I?" I asked and pointed at the second chair. "We are looking for Homeworld 1," I stated.

She leaned back with both hands touching each other and her lips. "You came for Elysium?" It came out as a whisper and awe.

"Yes, that is exactly what I came for. Can you help us?" I asked laying my arms on the table.

"What do you need?" She smiled and glanced around.

I cocked an eyebrow at her. It was not a Themian facial expression but one I'd come to use anyway. "Full access to the library for as many people as I can dreamwalk."

She pushed her chair back, grabbed my hand and lead me from the room into the outer one. This room was covered from floor to ceiling with nothing but data chips that sparkled in the Alexandrian light.

The high windows arched up into so many floors above I couldn't count. But I didn't need to. I already knew how tall this building was - 72 floors reaching into the sky. In front of me was a stone railing and I gazed down into the abyss of the structure.

We must be 20 floors off the ground.

The ground floor was a checkerboard of black and white crystalline stone with the electronics shot through. The gold-colored Orichalcum threaded its way around the room, blocking out any hum from an errant mind. Humans called that pattern a 'Greek key', but it was the pattern to control our abilities, keeping us from invading each other's minds, or so the High Council thought.

I wonder what they would think if they found out it no longer works on me?

Vika lead me back into her workroom and closed the door, pressing a pattern on her bracelet, locking it.

"What is your name?" She laid her back against the door with both hands behind her.

I'm sure she is touching her bracelet.

"Hera," I simply replied.

I didn't feel the need to use my old name — I am no longer that woman. Vika moved away from the door and went back to her table. She piled the data chips off to one side and patted the tablespace in front of the chair I had vacated only moments before.

"Should I tell you that I spoke to your twin earlier?" She asked retaking her seat.

I shook my head and swallowed back the small lump threatening to form there.

She believes I want to see him. I can't! Hyperion works for the High Council and I would compromise him.

"I am not here to see Hyperion." I respond in an even voice.

She didn't say anything else regarding the subject. She just gave me a strange look and then changed the subject.

"I have been searching for Elysium for as long as I've been alive. I have a long list of data chips I haven't read and maps I haven't checked, but to tell you the truth I don't believe what you seek is here." She states.

I opened my mouth to speak but found I had little to reply. I closed my lips and ran my tongue over them and tried again.

"I have a group of people willing to read for you or with you. We can cover more ground in ten days then you could in twenty years. The hybrids are quick-minded and inventive." I quickly replied.

She shook her head in a manner that didn't transpose as a decline but as an issue of my wish.

"I've had to change my search from Elysium to Pythia. She, I believe is the key." Vika responded in a conspiratorial tone.

"Sydney will want to meet you. May I bring her into the dreamwalk?" I asked.

She agreed and I closed my eyes and listened.

CHAPTER 23

SYDNEY

< I need you, properly dressed, in a dreamwalk. > Hera's voice echoed in my mind.

Before I could reply I was standing in my own room next to my bed. Adrian was lying sprawled on top of the sheets wearing nothing more than a smile.

I cocked an eyebrow and hitch my mouth to one side. "I like the view but I don't like being moved without notice," I remarked.

"Hera needs you. I was helping," he said and patted the space he'd made on the bed next to him.

I let my eyes check him from his hair roots to his toes. "I have work to do, so no hanky-panky while I'm gone," I said.

He faked a shocked look and did the 'who me?' move.

I changed into a long tunic dress and wrapped the traditional ribbons around my waist. I laid down next to Adrian and he kissed my lips. A second later, a gun-like device appeared in his hand. I remembered that Hera had the same one. I looked at it and the blue liquid from inside sloshed from one side to the other.

"Does this hurt?" I asked and bit my lip.

"I've never forced a dreamwalk, though I have been forced…"

I playfully smacked him and he laughed.

"I never forced you," I huffed.

He smiled and kissed my lips. The moment the injector snapped my skin, I lost consciousness.

*****

It was foggy. I didn't remember that dreamwalks I had with Adrian beginning like this. I groped in the white mist looking for another sound or person. I was about to scream when Hera appeared.

"This is the in-between, a construct. I create it to bring everyone into the dreamwalk. It is like a vestibule. It also keeps you from arriving naked. Yes, that can happen," she said.

"Oh, cool," I said, aware that I was blushing because I arrived naked in Adrian's dreamwalk several times.

I found a new respect for Hera and her abilities, "How did you learn to do this?"

"There is no way to teach dreamwalk. I had my brother to experiment on. We taught each other. I can explain that better later, Vika waits on the other side."

She closed her eyes and the fog dispersed and the white crystalline walls of Themian technology formed around me. The woman seated across the room took to her feet and approached me with her hand out.

"So, you are the famous Sydney, the mated hybrid. Do you know how truly rare you are? They speak of you on all the Homeworlds. If it's possible, I want to join you. I know you're looking for the original world. I don't know if Ixis told you, but I'm a historian." Her lips faded into a thin smile as she searched my face and then she continued. "For thousands of years, I've studied the books and texts. I can stay here as long as you wish. However, I can tell you that I don't think that the answers you seek are here."

"Why not? Where do you think they are?" I asked.

I knew that I should have also said something nice, a greeting, or a thank you, but her matter of fact statement had knocked the wind out of my sails. The only thing that would have hit me harder was throwing an anchor over the side.

"I think we need to go Homeworld 2," she supplied and tilted her head back to look up at me because she was a little shorter than I am. "I have already begun making arrangements for transportation. There is something they are hiding on Delphi. It's supposed to come from Homeworld 1 and should be our most ancient painting or artwork." With that, Vika walked over to her table and picked up a tablet with writing across the screen.

"There are no pictures and its extremely difficult to receive permission to view it. I have petitioned to have access at it for many years and been denied."

"It's a painting? If you are the most foremost historian on Homeworld 1, how come they wouldn't let you see it?" I asked confused.

"It isn't just a painting. Actually, I don't know exactly what it is because there are no known pictures. It is just referred to as the 'original artwork'. The word itself does not necessarily refer to a painting. It could be a sculpture, a building, anything, but it's something from or about Homeworld 1, Elysium. It is prized and kept under lock and key. It is a shame the ancient one Poseidon has been expelled. He would know where it is." She sighed.

I shot Hera a sharp glance and she nodded her head perceptibly. I didn't interrupt Vika. I was sure that she liked the sound of her own voice. Melinda had the same problem.

Spending too much time alone makes you talk to yourself.

"Poseidon would remember the time before the Great Division. He has probably seen the ancient writings that go with it. I'm told that there is a prophecy too. I don't know what any of them say but it refers to a woman or a woman child, or a young woman perhaps. It is an obscure reference. It's an ancient word they use for a female that is not fully grown or had children or something like that." Her forehead wrinkled and she began to pace the room.

I smiled to myself.

What would Melinda do if she found out there was a Themian version of herself?

"So, you believe that our trip here will be a waste of time and we should simply wait till you reach Homeworld 2 to dream walk you?" I asked, then I ran her words back around in my mind.

"Did you say Delphi and Elysium?" I quickly asked.

With my question, Vika stopped pacing. "Yes, Delphi is Homeworld 2 and Elysium is Homeworld 1."

I suddenly felt the blood running out of my head. Hera took over and led me to a vacant chair. She then changed her focus from me to Vika.

"That will not do. I will search the library for as long as you're here on Homeworld 10. When you leave, then, we will worry about the artwork, but until then, we're going to search every night and take every chance we can for as long as we can," Hera's reply was firm and decisive.

I gulped air into my body hoping to regain my perspective.

Why did it all have to have this surreal feel to it?

"You're welcome to use me as a conduit as you need. However, my arrangements are not for 3 months. Search the library and after that, I'll be in transit. Once I arrive on Homeworld 2, you will be able to dreamwalk me there." Vika replied.

"Every person you dreamwalk weakens you and it will become more like walking through water," Hera warned.

I found my voice and replied, "Vika, we appreciate everything you're willing to do for us and if you really do wish to come with us, we will pick you up on Homeworld 2, but unless we find something tangible, you may be more valuable to us amongst the Themians," I offered my hand as a thanks.

"I'm undeterred. I know we will find our answers. We simply have to find the object, whatever it is that they're hiding from the rest of us." Her firm assurance was an interesting comfort.

I just was not sure that taking her without permission was wise or that cherry-picking Themian citizens wouldn't start an intergalactic war. That sounded crazy even thinking it.

They won't go to war over eight hybrids and one historian. At least, I don't think they will.

Hera pulled Issy into the dreamwalk and her high sweet voice put me at ease and on edge all at the same time.

"Don't worry, mom. It is not that big of a deal. All we're going to do is looking over a bunch of manuscripts, scrolls, books, computer entries and hopefully we will find something. I'll be back before you know it," Issy giggled.

"Issy, Hera intends to keep you here for at least 16 hours. I wish you luck and please don't do anything stupid," I cautioned.

Hera picked up a rectangle chip from the table and held it out to Issy.

"This is a data chip. There are no scrolls or books here. These are the books."

Vika pulled out two more tablets and inserted a chip into the side of one of the screens. "This is a book on the teachings of Pythia."

CHAPTER 24

ISOLDE

The pressure in the back of my mind had been building, along with the whispering and the murmur. We have been on Odyssey for months but it was never like this. There were waves of emotion, panic, relief, anger, and frustration. I was a yo-yo to the onslaught.

"What is going on? I constantly feel like I'm being bombarded and just want to get them all to shut up. Just when I get one shut out, a new one comes to take its place." I'm wining, its my default setting when I'm in pain. I want to stop, but self-control takes practice and right now I spend all my time pushing out the emotions of others. I barely have time to think.

Rubbing my temples was an act of futility. It didn't take the pain away, but I rubbed them anyway. I wanted to sit down, but this was the first day in five that I hadn't been in a dreamwalk and I needed the exercise.

"I'm getting the same thing, Issy," mom snapped. She didn't bother rubbing her head, instead, mom paced like an animal.

Hera and I dreamwalked for five days then took two off, but she never stopped working. Like my mother, she kept moving forward, toward an unknown goal.

I stretched my arms and legs in my sweatpants, thankful that I was not wearing a tunic or a toga. Themian fashion was nothing more than a sheet thrown over a shoulder. After all the tank tops and swimsuits on the boat I wasn't used to all that fabric encasing me and tripping me.

My mother had still not mastered the art of blocking, and the bleed-over from her sends to Adrian sometimes made me want to retch. She loved him, and a part of me was happy for her because I had always sensed the sadness that clung to her. However, the other part of me hated Adrian.

He was not my father, only Tristan's. When you perceive life one way and then are forced to see it the way it really is, it can kick you in the ass. I had always seen Tristan as my other half, the completion of me. We were two sides of the same coin, but now I knew that was not true. Tristan and I, we were not the same. We are more like a coin made from two different metals, each side with its own metallic mix. Mine from mom and dad, his from mom and Adrian.

< Adrian, are you hearing everything I'm hearing?> My mother's broadcast overpowered the background murmur.

< Yes, there's a new voice being added every couple minutes. I think you need to check with Hera. > His response was at a lower level, but still came in over the din in the background.

I didn't bother to wait for my mother's call. My feet moved toward the C ring and the labs.

< Hera, where are you? > My mother called, blasting it into everyone's head.

< Down in the labs. > Hera called back in a conversational tone.

< Issy, can you meet me in the labs…Please! > The tone came through loud, but she didn't mean it as an order.

Thank God, for that!

She usually barked at me for what she wanted, but in the last few weeks, she had changed. I think 'they' had sex.

Yuck!

Mom would never let on.

My path left the pyramid and I entered the main connection hall, leading from the center of Odyssey to the outer rings. From that point, it was just a matter of reaching the ring you wanted. The rings were rotating around a circular base in the center while the pyramids sat on either side of the base, creating the effect of a rhombus. It wasn't a rhombus, they only looked that way. There were two separate pyramids.

The actual science that went with Odyssey and the logic of the design were all lost on me. Tristan had tried to explain to me how the ring movements were creating gravity and the crystalline building materials were re-enforcing that, but it all became gobbly goop once it hit my ears.

The only part of the ship I didn't like was moving from the connecting hallway to the C ring. It wasn't just that the ring turned. You could watch the ring sliding through the end of the shaft, with access halls appearing every so often. What I didn't like was the way everything was turned on its side, perpendicular to the rest of the ship. Every time I stepped over the threshold and found fresh footing in the ring, a wave of nausea swept over me.

I stood just outside C ring waiting for it to turn to the closest location for Hera.

"Good! You're here and you beat me." Mom gave me a sideways hug and kissed my temple.

"I was already on my way here when you called," I smirked and glanced over at her before turning back to the moving ring. Numbers flashed by with each passageway and I mindlessly counted in my head how many we had to go.

"Was I broadcasting again?" She asked, as her ears turned red.

Ugh, I didn't want to know what was the reason she was so embarrassed.

"Yes. Maybe you should have Ixis or Emmaline tweak your bracelet to help you out?" I replied, hoping she would save us all from her mental bleed.

Our turn came and I stepped from one form of gravity to the other. My feet were pushed sideways. My mind said down was one thing, but Odyssey said it was something else.

The floor became a wall and a wall became a floor. My belly fluttered with unease.

For a moment, I stood in the long corridor between the labs and criminals to get my bearings. Mom, on the other hand, didn't lose a step. She trapezed off down the hall toward Hera's lab and Melinda's domain.

I moved to follow her, trying to avoid the faces that were peering through the glass. All the rooms were heavily shielded, they couldn't send or receive anything. That didn't cut down all the chatter.

One man stood with his hands pressed on the glass, mouthing words. I stopped to look at him and manage to understand '*I want to see her. You can keep me from her. We're not any different than you and your mate.*' There were tears in his eyes. For a second, I was touched, but then his hands slammed against the glass.

I must've stepped back. Even without sound, it frightened me. He slid down the glass wall, begging, with clasped hands. I reached out the pressed the intercom button.

"What did you say?" I asked.

He repeated his raw plea through a voice box, then I pushed the button closing his cries off from the hallway.

"Did you hear what he said?" I asked mom.

"He's one of the mentals. You have no idea what he's talking about," she replied then waved her bracelet in front of Hera's door. The low sucking sound filled the space between us as the door slid open.

"Yeah, but how would he know that you are mated to anyone? And we can't keep him from whom?" I inquired then pushed the intercom again.

"Who are you looking for?" I demanded.

"Her. Can't you hear her? I can! She's out there somewhere. She's scared. I need to protect her," he retorted then slumped to the floor.

"What is your name?" Mom asked. Her curiosity was getting the better of her.

"Scott, my name is Scott." He was on his feet again staring at us through the glass as if it wasn't there.

"Why are you in here?" Her brow pulled down creating wrinkles on her face.

"I see things sometimes. They say they're not there, but I know it's true. I hear voices too. Little quieter up here than out there. Now, I just mostly hear her. I'm not crazy. I know the voices I heard they were from other people. I know that, but I can't convince anybody," he moaned.

"I believe you," mom and I chimed together then smiled at one another.

His eyes lit up and he pressed his hands to the glass.

"Oh, Capitan, my Capitan! You're Sydney! Everyone heard you. You made the announcement telling us who and what we were. That was the happiest moment of my life. That was when I realized that wasn't crazy. Can you please let me out of here? I've been locked up for a long time and I'd really like to go now." His eyes were clear and he sounded sober.

If I didn't know better, I might have believed him. But the clinically insane are often clear-minded and sober.

"Okay, Scott. We have a process to go through. Tell your mate to come down here, so we can see the validity of your claim." Mom weighed her words carefully.

"Her name is Sylvia," he supplied with a smile, rubbing his hands together.

"I'll come and check on you later. Okay?" She asked.

"Yes, thank you! Now, if I could just get a bigger meal...I'm really hungry," he said.

We both burst out laughing. "I'll have my brother send you something!" Mom responded.

He beamed back at us. We both waved and headed down the hallway. Other people came to stand by the glass. Some were pounding, others were yelling. I wanted to stop and check each one, but at that rate, we would never make it to Hera.

Hera's lab was next door to Melinda's. Melinda was in her labs, doing whatever Melinda does with her face glued to the microscope.

The hiss of the door opening and the pressure change was all it took for me to be blasted with every bit of noise coming from the space Hera occupied. The untrained minds filled the space and I looked at Hera which I believe had her mental shielding on high.

"Oh, Sydney! Good. You're here, I'm so glad. This woman, here, claims there is a man named Scott who's talking to her," Hera indicated the girl across the room sitting in one of the chairs.

The girl was fidgeting and every few minutes her eyes were darting around the room, searching for something. When she didn't find it she bit her lip and fidgeted some more.

I burst out laughing, "Is your name Sylvia?"

"Yes! He said he was just talking to you. Where is he? I mean, I just started hearing him. Why am I hearing him?" She asked, then began her nervous cycle again.

Mom approached her and intervened, "Did Hera give you a drink of water?"

Sylvia nodded her head, "Yes she did. She also gave me some vitamins." Her hands fidgeted with the edge of her shirt.

I glanced over at Hera and she smiled raising her shoulders in a shrug.

"You started hearing Scott after you drank the water and took the vitamins?" I asked.

"Yeah! I suddenly feel like I'm whole. We are meant to be, you know? Those stories that talk about love at first sight and finding your soulmate, I always thought they were crap, but then, I heard his voice and everything changed."

I'd seen the look before. It was the one my mother had when she was talking about Adrian.

"Step out the door, turn right, keep going down the hallway and you'll see him on the left-hand side," I said and turned back to Hera. "How many of those have happened?"

"Last I checked...412," she replied. Her smile was full but didn't reach her eyes.

"After you give them the water, do you hear every single one of them?" Mom demanded and paced to the window and back.

"Yes! It is like a light just turned on and the sun shone in the realignment of their genetic structure. It's amazing! Everything happens almost instantaneous. It is like taking all that was never right and suddenly turning it on. Every single one of them lights up. She's the third one mated today," Hera finished, then turned back to the hybrid in front of her and handed him a glass of Primordium.

His mind lite up right in front of me. I could almost see the physiological changes that rolled over him, then he yawned.

My fingers rubbed the bridge of my nose. A headache was rising.

"412. How many do we have left?" I asked.

Hera spoke to the man and sent him on his way, then pulled us into a side room. The din in the background stopped, giving me the relief, I couldn't find anywhere else.

"Thousands!" Hera responded enthusiastically and glanced back at the long line of hybrids down the hall.

"Every time one of them lights, I get another headache. I understand what we are doing. We already discussed it and agreed on it, but how much longer can it take?" Mom heaved a sigh of relief herself.

Hera touched her personal bracelet and pulled up a schedule, but I couldn't make out the holographic image from where I was standing. Placing her finger gently on the holo display, she looked up at the ceiling, then her blue eyes locked back on mom's.

"One week and two days. That is if I don't dreamwalk Issy to the library."

"Holy shit, mom! I don't know if I can do this for another week or so," I squawked without thinking.

Mom turned to squint at me. "Really, Isolde, did you have to curse? I know I curse a lot but that doesn't mean you have to do it too." She sighed, then rubbed her forehead. She paced to the other side of the room and looked out the window into the black void of space. Other than the three stars clustered together, there was nothing else to see.

"Sorry, but I'm not sure I can handle another week, Hera," she murmured mostly to herself, then turned back to us. "Okay, change of plans! You will not be turning people on in the laboratory anymore. Every person needs to be turned on in a separate shielded room. When they turn on you will be the only one who hears them. From there, I want them to go into another shielded room and be met by someone who will start training them to block."

Hera began tapping the holo display from her bracelet. The people that were in the hall, shuffled over to the door of a new room after touching their own bracelets.

"Also, get someone to take the mated to another space and have a long talk about matings. Did I miss anything?" Mom asked and placed her hands on her hips.

"Not everyone can join their mates," Hera remarked then leaned back on the glass of the window while the light from the stars rimmed her silhouette.

"What are you saying? That some of them mated humans or someone else?" I gasped and the shock of it rolled over me.

"One person mated a Themian." Hera's lips spread into a tight smile while she crossed and uncrossed her arms.

I'd seen Emmaline do that enough times, so I guess she'd picked it up.

"Homeworld 2. Her mate is on Homeworld 2. Her new mate told her that he was on Homeworld 2 and he also asked if we're coming to get him." Hera continued.

The light behind Hera blinded me just enough I couldn't make out her face, but her body spoke of sadness. I cast a glance at mom and both her hands were on her temples, rubbing them vigorously.

< *Adrian, did you hear what Hera just said?* > My mother boomed.

I shot her a dirty look just before I heard him as well.

< Yes, beautiful girl. We're not the only mated couple on the ship, beside Ixis and Emmaline. It's good. The more mating's between us and Themia, the safer we'll be. They won't attack if they think we hold the key to their future. > Adrian's reply calmed my mother.

I almost thought that she let me hear him just so I would like him more.

"Where is this chick?" Mom asked and plucked at her tunic.

"She went up to the observation deck. She said she wanted to look at the stars and be alone with her mate," Hera supplied.

My mother paced the room for a few minutes, then turned to me. "Issy, you can't stop our research. Hera, you can't be in two places at once. The Primordium business will have to continue as before. So, bright an early tomorrow, both of you will have to keep reading. But Hera, get Caroline and her family to help with the Primordium. Also, it would be nice if your kids would do something." Mom hates lay abouts and Hera's kids hadn't left their rooms since they arrived.

She didn't say it to be mean, but my mom wasn't always the most diplomatic.

"It is true. All of this could be handled by one of my children. I have left them to their own devices long enough." With that, Hera turned and left the room without another word.

I walked the ship aimlessly for another hour. Tristan was sleeping and I was alone with my thoughts. I stared out one of the glassed windows longing for the days on the boat. I never thought for one moment I would miss them. The ocean of black didn't soothe me the way water did. Though I didn't have quite the call my mother did, I still missed the cool breeze and a brisk swim.

It was getting late and I needed real sleep before my next dreamwalk, so I headed back to my rooms. I knew that I should mingle with other people, but I couldn't keep the mental barge at bay long enough.

I built up my mental walls and wove my way passed the cafeteria and the various rooms that had been turned into a small village-like area. The glass walls revealed an area that looked like a bar and another one where people were playing games. There was a room filled with children and equipment to amuse them.

I'm an outsider. I don't want to be one but I am. Even here, with all the other hybrids, I'm different. I can't touch them, or I'll know too much, feel too much, see too much.

I stopped and gazed at the simple life of the children. I looked at their laughing faces and smiles.

They will never feel what I feel. They will grow up in a world where it is okay to be a hybrid, with people teaching them how to live and how to be safe.

I was jealous and surprisingly happy because I would help build that world. They wouldn't know the fear I'd lived with. My chest swelled with a feeling I'd never had before and I realized it was pride. I was proud that I would be a part of this new civilization.

The door to my quarters slid open and rather than the dread of sleep and another dreamwalk I was light and happy to face my dreams in whatever form they took.

CHAPTER 25

HERA

They stood around the common space between the rooms in pairs, as always. Perseus gazed out a window, while Eris was across from him. Part of the time she looked out the window, the other part she stared at Perseus, taunting him.

Ares paced the surroundings like a caged animal, unwilling to leave the room and desperate to do so at the same time.

Eros and Hebe sat quietly on a double recliner reading from their bracelets. The human past fascinated both of them. They combed the archives for stories about all of us. I found the myths to be just stories, but Hebe was like a child, giggling at the inaccuracies and huffing at the truth.

Hercules was the only one who didn't resist my prodding.

"You cannot just stay in your quarters. You must get out. Everyone here is one of your children, grandchildren, and great-grandchildren. They don't know you and they don't expect anything from you. Most of them have no idea who you even are and might not even care. Maybe they'll just meet you on your terms on an even playing field. This won't be like your experience on Earth and Themia."

I looked at Hephaestus. He would never join the hybrid race without his siblings. I needed a leader, so I turned to Ares. His blues eyes carried not only fear but also anger. It was senseless, but it was there nonetheless.

My words fell on the ears of the newly freed and unsure.

"They are not going to treat you like Gods." I said doing my best to hold back the irritation blooming in my chest.

I glanced from one child's face to the other. They did not seem the least impressed with my words. Eris even gazed away. Perseus was the only one to step forward.

"Mother, we've all sacrificed to get here. We all agreed to father children, none of which I personally, ever saw. So, even though it's been thousands of years, we followed the plan. We were loyal and dedicated to its success. Now, we should be resting on our laurels. So, I am not hiding from our civilization as a few others here might be. However, I do question what is happening on this ship." He turned away from me back to the window and three stars of Fate, only to continue. "I hear the awakening of minds even as we speak. You're giving Primordium to all of them. You are changing them," he said and turned back to me crossing his arms.

When I didn't answer, Perseus started talking again. "I can't say I disagree, but I'm not sure I agree either. One thing I do know. I hear their minds and they are awakening to each other, and many have become mated, yet we all stand here and not one of us mated," he replied.

There it was. He was jealous. I didn't blame him. I too was alone and have been since Zeus left me on the side of Olympus. I could still hear his mocking laughter ringing around the village.

Perhaps by loving Zeus I will never be mated? I thought but didn't reply to my son's statement.

"I have never loved, not truly, not a deep abiding love." He continued, "Part of my heart has always been out of reach. I cared for the women I made children with, but I did not love any of them. I could not. It would have torn me up inside every time I had to leave," Perseus finished and stared me down with his harsh blue eyes.

My ready answer flowed from my lips fast and easy. "I do not wish to spend the rest of my days alone–"

Perseus cut me off. "However, if even one of us could find a mate, my faith in life would be renewed, but for now, our hard-fought freedom is like ashes in my mouth. I can see and hear our, my offspring, finding that very happiness I have sought for myself for thousands of years." He shook his head and then left the room.

Heads nodded around me. They had too much of their humanity in them and they clung to it as a small child does to a toy. It comforts them. I understood what they were saying. They were jealous. I was not jealous. I could not say why, but I was not jealous. It was simply not an emotion I felt. Perhaps it was because I have faith or my Themian side.

"I have faith and you all have the green-eyed monster upon you. I see it in you, these children of your children, they haven't been alive as long as you have. They haven't fought as hard as you did. They didn't lose as much as you have. They do know what it is like to have their entire way of life taken from them. Everything they thought they knew, has been proven a lie." I stood over my children dominating them in a way I never had before. They needed it.

Ares stopped pacing and took me in. My words brought them all to a standstill.

"They were told 'you don't belong here' and it is something I'm sure they felt their entire lives. They all felt that they didn't belong, that something was not quite right," I continued.

Hebe reached out and gripped Hercules hand with tear filled eyes and trembling lips. Her child like emotions unable to take in the truth of my words without crying.

"I never hid from any of you who and what you were. You knew, but they did not. You grew up with the thought that one day a perfect mate would come along. They would be born and their mind would meet with yours, then you would spend all of eternity together. What a beautiful picture! I could not have made it more beautiful, even if I had sculpted it with my own hands for several thousand years. And now, you grow jealous because you see your children receiving the fruits of your labor. Listen to me carefully!" I glared at each of them. "To be jealous of your children is evil. If you really want to hear my opinion, well I predict every one of you will mate." I took in their grave faces with my pronouncement.

I touched Eileithyia's hair and ran my hand down her cheek to wipe the tears away. I wanted to hit them, to wake them up. Themia had them all locked in its dreamworld, but that would not work. They must choose to rejoin society.

"Perhaps, there is more to do before your matings happen. The one thing I do know is that you can't stop trying, or stop looking. If you do, you will stop growing, and it will never happen. Humans have a saying, Sydney has actually said it to me several times already. They say 'if it's got to be, it's got to be me.' It means that whatever has to be, you must make it happen. You must get up and fight for it, no one else will fight for you, not like you will fight for yourself." I took a breath and gauge the room.

They were really listening now. "If you must have a love for your happiness or war or companionship in order to feel as if your life has meaning, then you have to create it.

Whatever 'it' is, 'if it's got to be, it's got to be me'. You cannot wait for someone else to magically appear. If you are waiting for magic, you will wait for all eternity. Magic is not real. That is simply an old story that humans tell to explain the unexplainable." I huffed.

Perseus opened the door to one of the bedrooms and leaned on the jam with one leg crossed over the other. Eris crossed and uncrossed her arms, her lips pursed and pouted, then rolled her eyes. Eros' mouth was open and her eyes were wide.

"I guess we have fostered the magic idea," Eris ventured with a small smile.

I laughed under my breath and they joined me.

"It was magic. That's how Hera did it," Hebe giggled and covered her mouth with her hands.

"I told numerous humans over thousands of years that it was magic. That everything I did was magic because I could not explain to them in terms they could understand that it was simply evolution and my mind. Something I was born with." I shrugged, "But I am telling you the truth. If you want something to happen, it will not magically happen. You must go out and seek it for yourself. Sitting in this room doing nothing, staring at each other for thousands of years, you have already done that."

Love. That's what Sydney said. She specifically stated that sometimes children do need love and all eight of mine certainly needed it.

Hercules stood up and paced the room several times clenching and unclenching his fists.

"I will leave the room, mother. I cannot stay here another moment. Is there a life chamber on board?" He demanded his nostrils puffing air over the stubble on his upper lip.

He opened a storage door and pulled out his leather battle skirt and belted it over his short tunic. My heart smiled at him. His favorite clothes were still his battle gear. Yet, he had not been in a true battle in thousands of years.

"Yes, there are several. Go look for one. I will tell you where it is or you can find it for yourself." I turned back to the rest of my brood, "I can't give you all your answers. I can only point you in the right direction," I said and patted Hercules' back.

"Do any of you wish to come with me?" He arched an eyebrow looking toward his brothers.

Ares crossed his arms and shook his head, while Perseus stood his ground clenching his jaws, also shaking his head.

Hephaestus was the only one to actually speak. "I have no need to explore. I simply wish for a forge and metal to work, because I feel I must bludgeon something. So, rather than finding a person I preferred my metal. Give me my hammer and I will take out my frustration where it will be most useful," he supplied.

I nodded to him. If we didn't have a forge, I had the feeling that a 3D printer would have to build it.

The girls stared at us. None of them were going to move from their places.

"You are all behaving like cowards and I didn't raise cowards. Are you telling me that Hercules is the only one willing to leave this chamber to face the world again? He is the only one that wishes to have felicity with strangers and adventures of his own?" I demanded.

Eros raised her hand. "I am jealous. What I feel is the same as Hercules. I should scream if I stay here, but I am also trapped by my own fear. Let me prepare myself and I swear that within the next three days, I will leave this chamber and I will go and commiserate with the other hybrids. Perhaps I will discover something I have lost, like the art of conversation with people I'm not related to," she said and then smiled.

I laughed dryly. "Oh, my silly girl, you are related to every single one here. Other than the Themians and the few humans, you're related to 99% of the population on the ship so I suggest you open a discourse, and do it soon."

She nodded her head in acquiescence. I was tired of it, so I turned and stormed out of the room. The door slid open and closed with a sucking sound and I realized that was exactly how I felt. They were in there, just sucking the air. Wasting away all those years pining for their freedom had become a habit.

Now they have it and don't do anything with it.

To say I was disappointed was probably the least of my feelings. The door opened and closed again quickly.

"I am sorry, mother! We all feel this way but I believe you are right and I will go find a life chamber and see if I can renew my vigor in it." The hulking figure of Hercules lumbered down the corridor while the slapping of a scabbard against leather followed him.

He wandered off in the wrong direction. I wanted to call out and inform him that he was heading the wrong way, but he was a grown man and had been for a long time.

He must find his own way.

They only needed a mother to tell them when they were making mistakes these days. They didn't need a mother to hold their hand, regardless of how much I would have liked that.

I turned and headed back towards the shifting room and my lonely quarters. Somewhere, there had to be a mate for me. I did not feel the melancholy they do. I was not hankering for the other person to love.

The last human I loved is dead and he was a monster. I would rather wait and be alone than give myself to such a beast again.

CHAPTER 26

ISOLDE

I read Pythia until my eyes bled and then I read some more. Being stuck in that room was like Chinese water torture. I wanted to see the rest of the library. I was not like my mother. I didn't love books just because they were books. I loved the knowledge. I knew it was silly but it was my thing.

I finally set the tablet down and stared at Hera until she glanced up at me.

"Do I need a special bracelet to enter the library system?" I demanded with my foot tapping on the floor. It had been six weeks of dreamwalking to this room and I wanted out.

Hera laid her tablet down on the table and placed both hands on either side of it. "No, the library is open to everyone who wishes to study. Nothing is restricted," she said while cocking her eyebrow.

I wanted to smile at her. It was uncharacteristic of her to copy such human mannerisms, but I didn't. "Yes, but you haven't been there in tens of thousands of years. Things could have changed."

She added a smile to the cocked eyebrow. "Your statement shows your ignorance, Isolde. Things do not change in the Themian world. They remain the same. That is one of the problems my people have. They do not grow. They are like bumps on a log, as you Americans like to say. They pride themselves on the changes brought to the Universe but Themia does not change. If there is a restricted section it has been here all along and I have never seen or heard of it."

Now, that was an answer I could wrap my head around.

"Vika, you've been here for thousands of years. Is there a restricted section?" I asked.

Vika roused herself from the deep thought she had been locked in at the sound of her name. "Yes, I have been here hundreds of thousands of years, but I've never even heard a whisper of such a thing. Science cannot achieve under the cloak of secrecy."

Hera's sardonic smile grew a half-inch, "I think you might add this to your knowledge. Vika is not an ancient, but she is very old, so if she says she's never found such a thing here, she is not lying."

"Are you sure?" I asked.

I knew that I was being rude, but for scientists, they really were thick.

"Themians, generally, as a rule, do not lie, Isolde, and I would be very, very careful about throwing such statements around. To call someone a liar is more insulting than you can possibly imagine. Honor and truthfulness are held in extremely high regard according to Themian society. To say those things is like striking at the heart of every Themian. You are attacking who and what they were raised to be. Science is the pursuit of alethea or truth. To accuse someone of lying, not only are you saying that they are not a scientist, but you're also questioning their honor because only the dishonorable would lie," Hera stated and I realized that she truly believed that drivel.

'Only the dishonorable would lie'. What a load of crap!

"Hera, I understand what you're saying, but I'm human and humans lie. We're naturally suspicious of everyone. It's part of how we've survived. You lived long enough and being suspicious is what kept you alive. After all, haven't you Themians betrayed each other a bunch of times?" I retorted.

My muscles bounced in readiness, a readiness I didn't understand.

"Yes, many times and yes I have been betrayed by Themian. All of them were infected with emotions, human emotions and the onslaught, I think, was more than their psyche could bare. In the case of Poseidon, I think he was just too old."

"As I said, people lie. I don't care what race you're from, what planet or the environment you're raised in, eventually everyone lies a little bit of a big whopper."

"Even your mother and your brother?" Hera inquired.

"Especially my mother! My mother is a talented liar. She lies by omission and by action. Tristan, on the other hand, is not a liar unless you count that he simply fails to mention the important parts. But truthfully, Tristan has a very hard time hiding anything from me," I smirked.

"Do you think your brother would lie to you to save your life?" Vika asked.

I looked at her and she was taking notes as if I was a new project she was studying.

"Yes, yes, I do. I think he would tell every lie there ever was to save my life or my mother's. I think you would lie to any one of us if it meant saving our lives."

I didn't realize I stood up, but I was standing and leaning over the table. Adrenaline jetted through my veins and made my heart pound.

Why am I so uptight about this? It's not like I didn't ask myself these very same questions and came to the same conclusions.

This wasn't new, but my feelings were. It was almost as if they weren't my own. I gulped back my retort, turning it into a calm reply. I push the strange reactions down in an effort to control them.

"I too would tell all the lies in the Universe to save everyone I love," I whispered.

"No matter the cost," Vika said then made another note on her tablet.

"I don't know," I replied as I was pacing. The other hybrids looked up from where they were working. I only gave them a glance before continuing, "I don't know, but Tristan is noble and complex and extremely logical. When I hear his thoughts, I understand but... I think that is a situational question 'would he save us even if it cost him his life?' the answer is a definite yes if the persons needing saving is either me or my mother. Regarding any other person, I don't know."

How did we get from a secret room in the library to lying to save the world?

Hera pushed her chair back and moved to my side. "These are all deep questions with no immediate answers. Most may never be answered. But as for the question of a secret room, that we can look for today."

I wanted to interlock my arm into Hera's as if we were sisters even though she was the great matriarch, but I pulled my hand back. I didn't want to live her life in a flash. I wanted to become stronger.

Maybe she can teach me to control my abilities, so instead of this lonely isolated life, I could really live.

The grand library looked like the Parthenon, only on a scale that most humans couldn't even begin to imagine. There were massive Doric style Greek columns everywhere. All of Themia was pristine, with clean lines and no writing on the buildings. The statues and carvings were all in alignment like a colonnade and it looked nothing like Ancient Greece.

I wandered the lower floors and trailed through the surrounding plazas. All of Themia was white with their idea of perfection and balance. Once I got over the awe of it, the mundane boredom of it grated on me. The aesthetic of perfection created a sameness.

Other than the statues, it is all the same, but every style and blended into one another.

In the center of the Library, on the ground floor, there were statues of three women. They were standing in a circle with their arms raised and their hands almost touching. Their faces were covered in heavy veils and their faces were turned aside from one another. Each one had sagging shoulders as if they carried a heavy burden.

I stared at them for as long as it was acceptable, then hurried back to Vika's room.

"The statues on the ground floor, what are they? Somehow it looks familiar," I asked breathless for no reason.

"Those are the fates. You've probably seen them before because Greece has them everywhere. I talked about them often when I lived there. They are part of our history. The three fates talk about three women who control the fate of our people, all of our people, I guess," Hera shrugged as if none of that mattered.

I went back to my reading, searching for any hint of where the lost world could be and how to get there, but at the end of my shift, we were no closer to finding Elysium. I racked my brain to make the information coalesce into something I could use, a direction to go, but no matter what I read, it slipped like sand through an hourglass.

We took a three-day rest. I searched the database on Odyssey for anything the library didn't have, but my queries turned up nothing.

The moment Vika boards the ship to Delphi our chance would be gone.

I fingered the side-seam of my dress and muttered, "The wealth of knowledge here is unbelievable, but there doesn't seem to be a great deal about Elysium itself. From what I've read, it sounds as though Elysium is not much different than modern-day Earth."

I threw it out there for Vika, Hera, or my mother to pick up and all of them lowered their tablets.

"You mean… squabbling countries with politicians, all angling for the most power and the most riches?" Mother asked.

My mother was probably the most jaded person I have ever met. She despised most people. She was very wealthy on Earth, but I don't think that she saw herself that way. She always donated a great deal to charity, mostly women's shelters and places for abused or homeless women and children. She also donated to legal funds to help defend them. However, her comment didn't faze me.

"So, there were multiple nations or how was Elysium run?" I asked.

"From what I can see, they were all united under one banner of governance. When the first powerful shifter arose, he petitioned the government for something. The leaders rejected his request so he took his followers and left," Vika replied, but it was not quite the answer I was hoping for.

I glanced around the room at the other readers, all of them engrossed in their assigned data chips.

"Do you think that he had abilities similar to ours?" I didn't whisper, but I didn't want to say it too loud.

"Yes, I do. I think he had a great deal of them. He took the best and brightest and put them on a ship. He convinced them all to join him and leave the planet and I don't think he had any intention of returning." She leaned in as if this was a story she'd told before.

"I do know that one of the reasons why Themians never returned to Elysium was because he never recovered from the first shift," Hera added.

"You mean he stayed in a hospital?" I asked while the fluttering in my belly grew.

This, this is the right path. I can taste it.

"No, they refer to him as the statue," Vika whispered like it was a ghost story one that children tell each other, but this didn't strike me as a 'Bloody Mary' urban legend.

Hera continued, "He became a statue, stationary and never moved again!"

I shivered, anyway. I hated that ghost stuff.

"Yes, they say his skin became stone and he stared off into the distance unseeing and never spoke another word," Vika added as if she couldn't let it go.

"Is he still alive today?" My mother asked, smacking her lips together dryly. Her distain for ghost stories bled through in her every move.

"Perhaps," Hera answered, "but he would've died of hunger and thirst if nobody kept him alive." She shrugged and turned back to her tablet.

"What if this guy, who is the first intergalactic shifter, what if he wasn't strong enough?" I asked and looked around only to continue. "And what if he worked so hard to shift the giant spaceship, that he actually short-circuited? He then turned into a statuesque vegetable, not dead, but not really alive." I bit my lip and then forced myself to stop. My mother was the lip biter, and I didn't need her habits.

Hera sat back in her chair and crossed her arms while Vika stared off into the distance, with her fingers tapping a rhythm on the table.

I didn't want to lose them. All the information that rolled around in my head suddenly locked into place.

We had been looking at this all wrong.

I leaned in, "The Oracle, she becomes this really great and powerful seer, right?" I looked from my mother to Hera then Vika and they bobbed their heads in unison.

I whispered my idea to them. It was my cracked form of logic, but mom smirked.

"This would be the first time I followed you on a wild goose chase to go find something that may or may not exist. Last time I was right, so do we want to do it again or not?" She smiled at Hera who nodded her head vigorously.

"Yes, mom, but I think the last time you were just trying to find your boyfriend," I snickered.

She blushed and ran her hand down one cheek, "This time we're looking for a whole planet. Go big or go home, baby!" Mom winked at me and chuckled.

Mom grabbed my hand at the same time as Hera's and I touched Hera's hand in return.

My body flexed into the rigidity of steel.

*****

Three women stand before me. The light reflects off the razor-sharp edge of an ancient form of shears one of the women holds. The woman next to her hums to herself weaving on a giant loom. The rhythmic sound of a shuttle sliding from one side of the frame to the other.

On the other side, stands a woman measuring a piece of fabric from a bolt. She holds a stick up to it, then she marks the spot on a chart. I cannot see her face because her hair hangs in the way. It has a beautiful honey-gold color.

The woman weaving on the loom is turned away from me. Her hair has the reddish gold of a strawberry blonde and the waves hang down past her waist. The sound of her shuttle slides through like the lulling of the sea. I watch every piece of thread that is woven into the fabric and as the fabric slowly rolls off the loom, the next woman reaches down and adjusts it so it's laid properly. I cannot see their faces, but the ring of metal rubbing against metal forces me back to the shears. The blonde hair woman hides her face, but with every strip of fabric that she cuts, a drop of blood drips to the ground. Under her feet is a pool of red.

My heart pounds in my chest.

*****

"Isolde, why are you staring off into space?" Mom asked.

I jerked back into my own reality. I shook my head to clean the macabre scene from my mind.

"I haven't slept much in the last few days. I should go rest. I'm tired of dreaming on my feet," I muttered.

"Are you sure you're okay, Isolde? You disappeared," Hera said.

I pulled my hands away from the two of them. I had expected to see Hera's life flash before me, but what came instead was just as frightening.

"I'm okay here I...I just—I think I should get to my quarters and sleep for real," I replied with a tight smile.

The dreamwalk dissolved around me, and I stared up at the ceiling of my room.

*****

"Sis, you look pretty tired," Tristan called from the open door.

I sat up and met his searching eyes. It bothered me because it seemed almost as if he knew something I didn't.

"You know I've been thinking, Issy, maybe I should go down to Delphi with you. There will be no need for you to dreamwalk. You would just visit, like a normal person." He strolled over and sat on my bed.

"Right now, I can't think about it. Can we talk about this later maybe?" I asked.

He nodded his head and then he reached up with his left hand and twirled his hair almost as if he expected it to be longer.

I did a double-take to make sure I actually saw him do it, but when I tried to probe his mind, every door slammed in my face.

"Tristan, why are you shutting me out?" I demanded, then got up off the bed with all thought of sleep gone.

"Oh, am I? I'm sorry. I'm just used to keeping everybody else on the spaceship out. You're tired. You don't need all the stress of everything I've had to put up within the last few days. Just go to bed."

My door slid open and Tristan gave me a weird pat on the shoulder and walked away. Actually, it was not a walk. His stance was wider and it was more of a swagger. Tristan had never swaggered. He always had a very firm and determined way of walking, like a man with a purpose, not a showoff. I hadn't been around for the last couple of weeks and I had no idea what he'd been up to.

Maybe he met someone, but Tristan didn't look like a lovesick fool.

I took a shower and put myself to bed for real, deciding I would work that out later.

CHAPTER 27

HERCULES

I wandered the corridors aimlessly. The last ship I'd been on was Alethea but that was thousands of years ago and I was a prisoner there with no chance to explore. I bit back the memory of Athena's betrayal. My distaste for Themian technology had only grown from there. I could request my location, and allow the computer to do its job, but my mother was right, I needed to find my way in the world again and using to a computer as a crutch was not my idea of self-reliance.

I did not need a walking stick to find my way. I was not blind, but the very nature of technology blinds you. I couldn't see the trail or smell the change in the air. Having the foliage of an earth chamber surrounding me as I sensed the soil and heard the sound of animals was the only time I truly felt at peace. It was the only time I was ever reminded of Earth and my childhood on the side of the mountain. My shoulders relaxed at my mental visions of Hebe and Eileithyia chasing goats and birds, fishing with nets and spears in the cool mountain creeks and rivers. Carrying Jorhan down to the river to bathe...

I push the memory away. I couldn't think of Jorhan or his fate.

The curved corridor finally led me to the opening of a large chamber filled with many tables and chairs but also with people that were talking and laughing. I immediately spied several that I was sure were from my line. It was almost like the calling of blood to blood. I did not need to search to find my children because they were easy to spot. I watched them sitting, laughing and joking and I realized that my mother was right.

We must get out.

The desire to speak with some of them pulled at me, but I held back. I couldn't say why, but I didn't want to break the spell.

"So, which one are you?" A jovial voice inquired.

I had not heard the man approach and was taken aback by the direct forwardness of his tone.

"I do not know what you are referring to," I replied never taking my eyes from the scene before me that reminded me of our village. If not for the windows to the cosmos I could have believed I was there.

"I'm sure you know what I'm talking about. You're one of Hera's kids. Don't worry, I won't tell anybody. It is obvious, a big brawny guy standing in the doorway as if he owns it while wearing a leather battle skirt—kilt. My sister said that you would be here or that Hera's children would be here, somewhere. I didn't think it would be hard to spot you and it looks like I was right."

The man carried the blue eyes of Themia and hair as black as Ares. But something about him told me that he was not from his line. He was of a height that I could meet his eyes without looking down. I'd always been larger than humans, and it was a relief to have someone of my own size, other than my brothers. His youthful laugh reminded me of Hebe and I found myself smiling at him.

"And who may I ask are you?" I inquired.

He stood too close so I playfully shouldered him. The man chuckled and regained his footing.

"I'm Tobias. You can call me 'T', everybody does. I'm Sydney's brother." He thrust his hand out to for a greeting.

No one had offered a hand to me in such a fashion since Earth. He didn't appear to be carrying a weapon, but I grasped his forearm to assure him I was unarmed anyway.

He laughed at me and in a rather awkward fashion, he returned the shake then pulled his hand back so his palm was holding mine.

"No one shakes hands like that anymore. I'm not carrying a knife. It's a greeting, a way to say 'hi', or 'hello'," he informed me.

I returned the gesture in kind. "Why aren't you carrying a knife? Isn't humanity a bloodthirsty lot? That is what all of Themia say," I return laughing without releasing his hand, but squeezing it a little tighter.

He hitched a half-smile and returned the pressure. His grip was strong, and our fingers began to turn red with the pressure. I repositioned my feet for better leverage, never taking my eyes from the young man's face.

His smile grew, as he too took a better stance. Then he locked his elbow and pushed using his whole arm forward.

I, in turn, added force to oppose him. "You have played in the games!" I stated and a thrill ran down my spine because I've wanted a good fight for years.

"Wrestling, yes. I wrestled. But, I don't think the cafeteria is the best place to hold a match." His nostrils flared as he pulled in more air.

The noise from the room behind us ceased and metal scraped against the floor as chairs changed position in the room.

I released his hand. "Perhaps you are right, but I would like a match."

He slapped me on my shoulder, like a longtime friend. "Absolutely, but not today."

T's easy-going manners were a relief from the constant pacing of Ares and the silence of Hephaestus. You can only fight your brothers so many times before it becomes a repetitive dance move and counter moves. Pursues, was the most challenging. My heartbeat rose at the idea of sparring with someone new.

"Well, Tobias, would you take me to the nearest life chamber and tell me how life on the ship is," I asked.

"Sure, I'd be happy to take you, as soon as you tell me what a life chamber is. I'll take you right to it," he chuckled under his breath and stepped back into the corridor where I followed him.

"A giant cavern filled with plants and animals similar to a planet but inside the ship," I replied.

"You mean the bio-domes? I'll take you to one, only we can't go in bio-dome 3," he informed me then moved in the opposite direction I had come from and I moved to keep pace with him.

"Why can't we go there?" I asked keeping instep with him and trying not to glance through the glass into every room we passed.

I slowed at the sight of children. There was an entire room filled with them, more than I'd ever seen in my life. They ran and played, jumping and giggling.

"Oh, Tristan said there's a whole group of very dangerous animals called Nemean Lyons," T said.

I snapped back to the conversation and Tobias.

"If we go in there, well…apparently, they're partial to Themian blood and of course, you know we're all hybrids. So, we taste good… if we go in there," he added and ran his thumb across the hollow at the base of his neck.

I smiled. It was good to know that somethings had not changed and the slicing of a throat was one of them.

"I'll take you to bio-dome 1 or 2 or maybe 6. I hear that one's really nice," T said and picked up the pace.

My forehead pulled down narrowing my eyesight.

Nemean Lyons.

"No! Take me to three!" I ordered.

Adrenaline flooded my veins. He glanced over at me and the smile drained away from his face.

"Are you sure?" Tobias asked.

"Yes!" I returned with a determination I've not felt in eons.

CHAPTER 28

SYDNEY

Elysium is supposed to be the golden field where heroes lived on. That was the human version, anyway.

Issy left the dreamwalk and I left not long after her. But Issy's idea wouldn't go away. I found myself unable to sleep and Adrian was grumbling next to me as I tossed and turned.

Adrian husky voice whispered in my ear. "I could put you to sleep if you let me." He ran his hand down my body messaging and squeezing as he went.

My breath caught in my throat and for a moment I was going to let him, but sex wouldn't find us a home or allies, so

I just rolled over and kissed him. He pulled me to him for more, but I wiggled away.

"Always running away, beautiful girl." He yawned, stretching one arm over his head.

"I'm not running away from you. I can't sleep. I need to do something, to think or just to walk. I don't know." I scoffed at my inability to shut my brain down.

He waved me off in the dark and I got dressed and left. The halls on the ship were never really empty or quiet. People still milled about, the cafeteria had food and there were always people there eating. I wandered in and grabbed a coffee.

I sat at one of the tables and watched. It was what I was always doing and for the most part, I was left alone.

"Can't sleep?" *T* asked, then took the set next to me.

"Yeah! Where's the girls?" I glanced at him.

"Asleep, with their cousins," he replied and took a sip of his own coffee.

I cocked an eyebrow at him. "Do we have cousins on this tub?" I smirked.

"They all are really. You know Emmaline's brother, Dewy? His grandkids...we've been claimed."

We both laughed. The idea that anyone would claim our dysfunctional family was funny.

"Anyway, they babysit and the girls have sleepovers. I get free time, so I mostly stay here. You have no idea how many interesting people I've met," he said and gave me a secretive smile only to continue his thoughts. "Dewy's a good guy like that. You would like him." *T* leaned over and whispered, "He's more like Grace."

My throat tightened. I threw a tight smile over my shoulder at him, then changed the subject.

"Issy has this crazy idea, and I've said I'll follow her down that road. However, doing it, will take all of us there, so I don't know if I should," I said then took a gulp the hot acidic taste of coffee mixed with sugar and cream and I immediately felt its energizing effect.

"Didn't you say that 'dream map' was crazy? She went with you, nevertheless." He shoved me a bit with his shoulder.

"Yeah and we were chased by God knows who. Not even Hera knows who they were or why they were after us. Not that it matters now," I mumbled.

"It's a leap of faith, Syd. You can't second guess everything. Sometimes you have to close your eyes and jump. I miss my wife, but I came anyway. I've made friends, the kind I never had on Earth. I can move stuff with the wind. It's pretty cool. And most importantly, I got my sister back," he said and smiled.

"I'm your cousin," I stated and his fist hit my shoulder like a hammer.

"Ouch! What the fuck was that for?" I asked then rubbed the red spot. He hadn't done that since we were kids.

"You will always be my sister," he replied, then pulled me in and kissed my forehead and stared into my eyes. "Do you trust your daughter?" he asked.

I bobbed my head without actually saying anything.

"Then listen to her. We..." he moved his hand around in a circle to indicate the room, "All of us will be fine. There is a whole lot of whoop-ass walkin' around these halls. Trust us! We trusted you." He took a long gulp of his drink, which I don't think was coffee. But at this time of night it shouldn't be.

I smiled and once I finished the last of my coffee, I headed to Hera's rooms. The door slid open to reveal a rumpled Hera. I smiled and asked her if she could dreamwalk me. She looked left and right before answering.

"Yes, but I thought we were doing that in a few hours."

I didn't answer immediately so she shook her head and pulled me in. Only after we entered the dreamwalk in the library did I start speaking.

"Isn't Elysium supposed to be like heaven and those who lived a good and honorable life are allowed to go there? Or if they died for a glorious cause they can go there to live in all eternity?" I asked and rubbed my tired eyes.

"Yes, that is how it's described. I know that the Greeks had their own ideas. I told many stories of Elysium. Humanity has such wild imaginings, so they may have changed many of the details," Hera responded but never looked up from the tablet she'd claimed as her own.

I should have slept more. I had only been at this for a few days, but I am already over it.

"Don't you have to go to the river Styx or something like that?" I pressed.

"We don't know where the river Styx is. You don't have to go to the underworld to reach Elysium. Elysium is a planet. We just don't know where it is." Hera rubbed her forehead and stretched her arms.

I looked at Hera. She was tired and was the worst version of herself I had ever seen. Ever since Issy came up with her crazy idea, neither of us had slept.

"Let's say that we do find Elysium. Should we expect to find a paradise, a Homeworld where we can live out our days in internal peace?" I kept at it.

"I feel it's important like I was meant to do it," Issy piped in.

I glanced at Hera. She didn't warn me about adding Issy, but Hera shrugged and went back to her tablet.

Vika's eyes opened wide like saucers and her mouth became an O.

"There's something you should know about the search for Elysium. I told you there was a prophecy connected to the landing on Homeworld 2, the story of the Fates," she said and glanced around.

"I know about the three Fates. There are three ladies. One weaves, one measures and then one cuts, right?" Issy asked.

I always thought it was the cycle of life story.

"That's the gist of it, yes, even though I think your human version is a little off," Vika stated and the dark circles under her eyes told me we were all running on borrowed time.

Issy's arms crossed over her chest while she stood there staring, She didn't like being wrong. I hitched my lips to the side and glanced down at the chair next to me. Issy plopped down and huffed.

"You're getting some human version of the three Fates," Hera remarked without looking up. "The story I told many thousands of years ago has changed many times, but the role of each Fate never changes." She lowered her tablet with a look of a school teacher on her face.

"That's just it, Hera, it is not just a story. It's a prophecy about three women," Vika stepped in and her eyes darted around the room again. Though I can't think why, we hybrids were the only ones here.

"One weaves, the other measures and the third changes the fate of people. That is why I made my preparations to leave. As I already told you, some of the books describe a painting or an artwork. I've read it is many things, a statue of three women even. Apparently, the Oracle - Pythia, she was considered a great artist with a fabulous talent that was able to render such lifelike statues that even the owners had a hard time defining between their mirror image and the actual statue. Many times, the Oracle was questioned about her prophecy and her vision was always the same. They never changed, but they only describe what the Fates do, and never describe the actual prophecy." When she finished, Vika was trembling.

Prophecy-smophecy. I don't believe in fate or prophecy.

"If everyone is looking for Elysium and there's some prophecy connected to it, why can't anyone see it?" I asked.

"I think that if we're going to find the prophecy, we may have to do some very clandestine things," Vika whispered furtively.

I noticed that she couldn't stop glancing around. It didn't scare her that there were six hybrids sifting through the library records, but a prophecy did.

"Thoth wrote the original histories of the Themian people. He made an obscure reference to the art being the prophecy, that in a way they are the same. He said *'you cannot have prophecy without art'* or sculpture. The references are very obscure. The Themian language has changed. His writings are two million years old and he disappeared along with his brother before the Great Division."

Vika handed me a chip then pressed her lips closed. She returned to reading her tablet.

I glanced down at my own and the words that splashed across the screen told a story of three men on Elysium. I was not interested in, so I yanked the data chip out of the machine and slid the new one in.

The three fates.

The first of the three is Clotho, the spinner. She weaves the threads of the universe into a piece of fabric.

The second Fate is Lachesis, the allotter. She measures and analyzes it, determining its value and worth, the length and breadth, all its achievements and the time allotted to each mind.

The third is Atropos, the inflexible. She cuts the cloth or destroys it. She appears as a crone and she chooses the manner of each person's death, deciding when their time is up. She is also characterized the most terrible in various accounts. She is the judge of all Fate, the bringer of death, and the changer of the universe.

The three goddesses are crowned as a symbol of dominion.

As I was reading, I wanted to giggle at the absurdity of it. The idea that three chicks would control the 'fate' of the Universe was silly. They were knitting old ladies, sitting in a circle chatting to each other, yet Vika quaked at the thought of them while Hera too appeared unsettled.

People always say that you cannot avoid fate, you cannot change it, it is inevitable, it is and will always be predetermined. Many believed this, but I didn't. I rejected the concept that everything was predetermined, that I couldn't make a change. The very idea that my entire life was predestined and I had no control over my choices, that all my moves had already been made for me, I would never believe that. Not ever.

I kept on reading and discovered that Pythia was the first to arrive on Delphi and she claimed it as her own. She was inspired to create art for her people. Pythia was called the Oracle and was asked to lead the people. She declined, instead she turned that honor over to Themia.

Themia, in turn, created laws and brought order. One could only lead for one hundred years then must step down for all time and never lead again. Themia said that rule by council was better than a tyrant. Eleven were chosen from among the Elysian to join Themia and they sat in council. Themia set the example, and all followed it, until the Great Division - those who followed the teachings of Themia were on one side and those who followed Anu on the other.

I skipped through the Great Division. It was over and everyone died, leaving only the Themians. I didn't want to waste time with that.

However, the Oracle was brutally murdered and it was a bloody public mess. She left in her wake a testament foretelling her death.

Why did she go if she knew that was the day she would die? People are dumb!

Many claimed it must be the work of the Fates for knowing her skein had been measured with all her sorrow and joy. It was time for Atropos to cut the skein of her life.

Rumors were spread about how she'd been visited by the Fates and how she knew that her death was inescapable and so she surrendered to it with her arms outstretched and ready for the embrace.

Ridiculous!

'*Death is not the ending*' she claimed. I smiled to myself when I read that.

It wouldn't stop me, that's for sure.

She referred to the Fates many times. Reading her testament was like reading a sad story about a beautiful death. No new Oracles have stepped forward since the Great Division. Her testament said there would not be another. She said '*there would be no new Oracles until the Fates arrive.*'

Fate intervening in people's lives, scares small children, making them behave or comforts old people at the end allowing them to believe it's okay to let go.

The idea that your life is already predestined and you have lived it because of already written fate can be freeing, but as I read the testament, I started to believe that she was referring to something else. I scooted my chair closer to Vika and whispered, "In her testament, Pythia said until 'the Fates arrive'. She didn't say until 'Fate arrives'."

Vika leaned over and said shaking her head, "The Fates, the three women. Language is everything and she had a great grasp of the language."

I realized that Vika didn't get what I was implying and that Pythia said exactly what she intended to say *'no new Oracle until the Fates arrive'.*

I continued reading, but most of it meant nothing. There were stories of the building of the first city on Delphi, Abydos, and the rise of abilities and schools to control the forces.

Since Pythia's death, there were many who claimed to be an Oracle, but all were found to be false. In over 1 million years, the great prophecies made by the Oracle at Delphi have stood the test of time. The first of her prophecies was the Great Division. She told only a few about the rift and it happened thousands of years later.

Thoth detailed her visions. She claimed that there would be great loss on a level such as none had ever known and that the battlefield would be filled with the bodies of millions of Themians and Anunnaki alike.

Many years later, her second prophecy was the discovery of a world filled with life and that this new world would bring disease. However, this disease would free Themians, causing them to do harm to themselves and others. Only she described the disease as '*dis-ease*'.

Her third prophecy was of her own death which she wrote down and kept secret and was only delivered to the High Council after her murder.

Her fourth and final prophecy was not written at all but created.

"How old was the Oracle when she died?" I asked.

"Is age really an issue? After all, we are Themians and Themians live forever," Vika said the words as if reading them from a school lesson.

It reminded me of the moment when I'd asked what year Columbus sailed the ocean blue—1492.

"Yes, but it sounds like her life was extremely tragic. Until she went to Delphi she was a normal person," I remarked, more to myself than to them.

Issy wasn't paying attention. She was hunched over her tablet, her eyes darting left and right rapidly. She devoured the data chip and reached for another. It appeared that Isolde had zero interest in my line of questions. I already knew what she was after, regardless of how crazy I thought it was.

"When she left Elysium, she was but a girl old enough to receive her bracelet. Or at least that is what they say. Something about the shift changed everyone. Specifically, the moment when they arrived in the new galaxy and couldn't return to Elysium," Hera remarked.

This all sounded great, but it was more like a Themian school lesson. I couldn't shake the feeling that something wasn't quite right.

The truth is always somewhat different from the history books. Only survivors write history.

"The Oracle stepped forward in the aftermath and guided them to Delphi. She never left Delphi. They built an entire city to her. She was their savior and she was held up as a hero," Vika added with a smile on her face.

Actually, both women seemed happy to recite the history lesson they'd been taught.

She never left Delphi, she was their savior, their hero and someone murdered her. What would they do to a trouble maker like me?

CHAPTER 29

ISOLDE

After spending months inside a library and years on a boat, now I'm stuck on a giant spaceship. Every day was laid out before me with more work. I felt less like an 18-year-old and more like a 50-year-old lady. Everyone I've ever known was gone.

The people on the ship seemed to actually have a fine time, but every time I turned around, I had more work to do, more data chips to read, more ridiculous clothes to wear and another long nap to take for a dreamwalk.

The longer I laid in bed dreamwalking my life away, the itchier I became when I finally woke up. I needed to do something, to go somewhere, to talk to people my own age. I needed to have fun.

My mother was hyper-focused on saving us, and she would never back down. She would never stop, even if that meant killing herself. She would do anything to keep Tristan and me safe.

She can't save me from myself.

Before I knew where I was, I'd wandered into the shifting room looking for Tristan.

"Aunt Emmaline, have you seen Tristan?" I asked.

He wasn't there. My eyes told me that, but I had to ask. Maybe he stepped out for a moment. Tristan didn't walk much anymore, he simply shifted from one spot to another. Also, ever since Adrian showed up and announced his paternity, Tristan had been avoiding me. I missed my brother and our friendship.

"Ya, honey, he went to bed, I think. He finished his shift in the shifting room — wow that sounds dumb — anyway he said he was tired." She tilted her head to the side and looked at me funny. Her toga drifted around her like a fluffy white cloud of cloth.

"Honey, you okay? You look like your fixin' to pitch a fit." She stated the obvious and I hesitated for just a moment. I could talk to her.

She ran her hand from my shoulder to my hand, lacing hers fingers into mine. I stamped my foot. All I wanted to do was to hang out… with someone.

"Aunt Emmaline, if you wanted to go and have some fun on this rickety old boat what would you do?" I asked.

She raised an eyebrow, hitching up one side of her mouth in a half-smile. "Oh, first of all, this ain't no rickety old boat," she replied. "I know you want to have fun and being stuck on a spaceship or rickety old boat, as you say, or in a library, all the time doesn't sound like a whole hell of a lot of fun." Her lips smiled but her eye pitied me.

I don't want that.

She narrowed her eyes and glanced around the room and continued. "Your brother scoped out a bunch of bio-domes or ecosystems or whatever he's calling them," she whispered.

"So, he went to these Garden of Eden places looking around, so what?" I already knew that.

"Said they're filled with some pretty wild plants and animals and stuff. And a boat, that you know pretty well. Why don't you get out of town?" She raised her eyebrows. We went from standing in the shifting room to the cafeteria.

Then she tilted her head at a couple of young men. "You can always find some good-looking young stud to protect your virtue or your person from all those mean wild animals." She snickered for just a second then continued to stare at the guys.

I have to confess, there were quite a few of them. For eye candy, the ship wasn't hurting and there were guys of all shapes and sizes and colors. Every single one of them smart. I liked smart guys, like my dad. That sounded like a lot of fun, but ever since the whole Jacques incident I was just not interested in boys or men.

"Emmaline, I like half of your idea. The getting out of town i.e. going to bio-dome, but as for taking someone to protect my virtue, no thanks! I think I can do that all on my own. Anyway, the first guy that starts annoying me, I think I might scare the shit out of him," I snickered.

Emmaline laughed out loud. "I do believe, my dear, that any man who decides to hitch his wagon to you ott' to be scared. After all, you are the daughter of the great and powerful Sydney and the first hybrid shifter Adrian," she said.

The smile on my face bled away.

"Adrian's not my dad. My dad is Gabriel. Adrian's just Tristan's father. I know it's an easy mistake to make, it's okay." I replied in a low voice doing my best to keep an even tone.

I liked Emmaline and I didn't want to push her away. I was aware that everyone thought that Adrian was my father. My mother didn't do explaining to others well.

"Pardon me! I was mistaken and you're right, Adrian's not your dad. But you called me 'Aunt Emmaline', which means you have to accept both of us into your family. Can't have one without the other," she finished, then pinched my arm.

"Ouch," I said and rubbed the spot.

I liked Emmaline. She was feisty and tough. I was sure that she'd never take anybody prisoner that she could take down and kill. Hell, I was pretty sure that if you handed Emmaline a bowie knife she'd gut you and stripped the hide right off your backside.

"I guess actions do speak louder than words. Still gets me pissed that mom was doodling him while still with dad," I mumbled.

"You can't blame people for things they did in their dreams. I'm sure you've done something in your dreams you don't want anybody to know about," she replied and elbowed me.

"Yeah, I have done things that I don't want anybody to know about. I also don't have any physical proof walking around that I was diddling someone else while married," I retorted, smoothing my dress in false modesty.

"Do you really think your mom would have done that if she had known?" Emmaline growled out.

"No, I know she wouldn't." I glanced down and away, "She would've been faithful to my dad, no matter how much it cost her. I don't blame my mom for what she did to Adrian or with Adrian. It gave me my brother and I love Tristan. Life would be boring without Tristan. It just weirds me out," I remarked squinting at her.

She smiled her self-satisfied smile before speaking. "Well, Issy, are you going to one of those bio-domes? I highly suggest you tell somebody and you make sure you wear your bracelet. If you have a problem, you want us to be able to get you out of there. There are wild animals in some of them," she finished her sentence with a wink.

I nodded my head. She was right. Tristan said there was a lot of dangerous stuff in there, but the truth was, he also said there was a massive Ocean sized lake and I knew Calypso was on it. I just wanted to sit on my boat for five minutes and feel normal. To pretend that the horizon I saw in the distance isn't the edge of a spaceship or some kind of technologically engineered room, but instead the curvature of Earth. The pressure in my chest lifted as the memory of that big blue ocean washed over me. That was what I really wanted. I just wanted to pretend everything was normal again. To feel the swell of the waves and see a dolphin jumping in the water.

I gave her a fake smile and left the cafeteria. I followed the curve of the corridor watching for the main hallway back to the pyramid. When it arrived, I jumped from the B ring into the connecting hall.

"Odyssey, show me the way to a bio-dome!" I ordered without slowing my pace.

"There are six bio-domes. Which one do you want?" The voice inquired, without the inflection of a question.

"The one with the catamaran sitting on a lake."

The ship didn't respond to me, but my bracelet lit up and I began following it playing the hot/cold game. In some ways it was fun, but when you're doing it all the time it gets rather stupid.

Twenty minutes later, I made it to the entrance, but the doors were sealing closed as I approached, so I picked up my pace.

"Hey, hold the door!" I shouted.

Whoever had gone inside, clearly either didn't hear me or didn't want to. Raising my bracelet, I waived it over the touchpad, but nothing happened and I was surprised that it didn't immediately open.

"Odyssey, why is this door not opening for me?" I demanded and stamped my foot.

"Security lock has been instituted. No one is permitted to enter this bio-dome," the ship replied.

"What level of security does this person have that they can override me?" I demanded again while irritation flooded my system.

"The person carries a higher security clearance than you," the computer replied.

I scoffed.

That can't be.

The only people with higher security clearance than me were Hera, my mother, Ixis, Emmaline, and probably my stepdad, Adrian.

Screw that! I don't think anyone of them is in there. Someone must have hacked into the system.

< Mom, can you please do a security override on bio-dome 3? I just want to go see the boat. I think somebody hacked the system and locked everybody else out. > I said.

< *Don't worry about it, Issy! I'll have the door open in a minute.* > My mother replied.

< Thanks! >

I leaned against the door to catch my breath. Between the long walk and the dreamwalking, I was out of shape.

Having your mom in charge of your entire population does have its good points. However, the fact that I hadn't seen her much on board this ship was ridiculous.

Just then, the doors slid open and I was immediately blasted with moisture. It carried the scent of decaying plants that wafted out the door, surrounding me. I closed my eyes and drank in the scent from the lush jungle before stepping over the threshold. The freshly chopped ends of vines and branches that clearly had been impeding the access to the hatch, had been hacked away. Some of the plants still dripped their liquid blood. Whoever it was probably came through in the last 15 minutes.

Determined to figure out who hacked the system and locked everybody out, I headed inside.

It was beautiful, like being back in Panama or with mom on one of the Caribbean islands with all the lush foliage, heliconia looking plants growing everywhere spiky and vibrant.

I smelled something that was suspiciously close to jasmine, but it was daytime in the bio-dome, so night-blooming jasmine wouldn't be flowering.

There were vines everywhere. Birds chirped in the trees and sang on the wing. Something moved in the overhead canopy, but I didn't care.

I missed the tropics. I hadn't realized how much. Life on the boat was so long ago.

How long had this entire bio-dome existed?

The ship had never been used before, but the growth in there could've been growing for 20 years or more easily, without any sentient intervention. It had been long overgrown with the amount of neglect I was looking at. It was a fresh jungle waiting to be explored.

Emmaline's words rang in the back of my mind. '*Make sure you tell someone where you're going.*'

I asked mom to open the door, so obviously, they should know where I am.

That was about as close as I was going to get to telling anybody where I was. It was like asking permission.

I'm 18, an adult. I can do whatever I want, within reason.

I looked down at my clothes. The short toga they called a chiton I was wearing wasn't really jungle gear, neither were my sandals, but I didn't care and trudged into the leafy madness.

After standing and drinking in the sunshine for several minutes, I could clearly see the path that had been cut through the jungle by my 'hacker'. It led off to the right.

One path is as good as another.

I shrugged. I had no idea which direction the lake was and without a map, I decided to follow the hacker.

Trudging through all of the underbrush in the heat hadn't crossed my mind as being a possible problem. Giant leaves slapped me in the face, while furry plants tickled my calves, freaking me out. I pushed my hair out of my face and the sweat on my forehead with it. I tore a strip from my dress and wrapped it around my head to keep my hair in place.

I finally shucked off my Greek revival clothing and stood there, dripping with sweat in a bra and camisole and boy short panties. I shrugged wrapped the fabric of my dress around my waist to protect my lady parts and kept going.

My feet squished into the mud and it oozed up over the sides of my sandals and in between my toes. I pulled my leg up and my foot came free with a sucking sound.

I was beginning to think this wasn't a great idea. I didn't have any water and I was dying of thirst.

I stopped and took in the landscape, but there was no lake in sight and I didn't see anything like a water source. I smacked my lips together and moved my tongue around to wet my whistle until I spotted some large elephant-shaped leaves.

The upswept heart shape was perfect for catching water. One of them was drooping in a funny fashion. I picked my way off the path and pulled the leaf down, cupping the sides. The center of it was filled with water and I tilted it toward my face. The warm water poured onto my face and down my throat. It was enough to push the thirst back.

For now, at least.

The deeper I went into the bio-dome, the louder the sounds of the creatures grew. I listened and realized that in the background there was a heavy humming. Snake-like beasts hung from the trees. Several birds perched on branches not far from me. They watched my movements, tilting their heads from one side to the other, letting their single eye take me in.

One of the birds, black with a vicious curve on a bright orange beak, seemed to be following me. Its claws were pointed as if they were the tip of a knife. It hopped from one branch to another, keeping within fifteen feet of me. Soon, it was joined by a few friends and I found I had company. One of them swept down like it was going to divebomb me and instead landed on a bush behind me and started pecking at a fruit.

I laughed, to keep me from screaming. My heart was beating hard through my chest. The bird scared the shit out of me and this was the most fun I'd had in months.

'*Always get the lay of the land before you find yourself dead in the water*'. Mom's words echoed in my mind. Even when I was having fun, she was there. Dad called it a conscience, but I ignored the little voice. I was having fun and didn't want my imaginary mommy butting in.

My belly grumbled and I looked around for anything edible. I spotted a giant tree off to the right, that looked suspiciously like papaya but with a trunk like a coconut tree. However, the fruits definitely looked like papaya. I'd learned to climb a coconut tree years ago, so I picked my way over the ground cover to the base of my coco-papaya.

A six-legged monkey-looking creature grabbed one of the fruits and swung away. That sealed it for me. If the monkey-looking thing could eat that, I could too. I pushed at the base, shaking it, but the tree only swayed like it was made from rubber. I called the forces of wind and added that to my efforts, but the tree held firm.

I took my dress off and wrapped it around the trunk and used it to lever myself up as I climbed. The closer I got to the fruit, the more I realized there was no way to get it down. Not without smashing it on the ground. When I reached the top and the cluster of fruit, I put it in my camisole and began to shimmy back down the trunk.

I was three-quarters of the way down and about 10 feet up when the entire jungle went quiet. It was like everyone went to sleep. I realized— it's always bad when you don't hear the jungle—I gulped. It could only mean that there was something bad nearby.

Fuck, Fuck, Fuck!

I whipped my head left and right, looking for something, anything out of place, but it was all a wall of varying greens. My arms began to shake. I had to make a choice - either get down and run or climb and see how long I could hold on.

I bit my lip, as adrenaline jetted into my system causing my heart to hammer through my chest. I couldn't see behind me. I only had 280° view. Whatever was going on, it had to be going on behind me, because I could not see one Goddamn thing that was out of order in front of me.

My legs were shaking too and sweat was dripping from my temples running down between my breasts. At some point in time, I wasn't going to be able to hold on any longer, so I didn't want to waste my strength. I sucked my tummy in and changed my leg position, then wiggled. The fruit slipped between my thighs landing on the ground with a splat.

I took a deep breath, closed my eyes for just a moment and listened to the silence of the jungle. I released one side of my dress and jumped, falling the last 10 feet.

I called the forces of wind to ease my landing, but one foot ended up on a branch. My mud-coated sandal slipped off and I lost my balance and landed on my butt.

A growling rumble vibrated the air around me like something out of a night club mixed with a bit of National Geographic, and a cat, a really, really big cat. I slowly slid my back up the trunk of the tree. The bark clung to my camisole and scraped my slick flesh.

Crap, I should have climbed the fucking tree!

I gazed out into the foliage. My eyes were darting this way and that.

What fucking color is this damn thing? How do you spot a creature, if you don't know what it looks like?

"Odyssey, is there a creature in the bio-dome with me?" I asked in a calm voice.

"Yes, there are many. Please specify," the answer came.

I gritted my teeth, "Are there any predators in here?" I squeaked.

"Yes, the Nemean Lyon," the ship replied, in the same tone as if it was a bunny hopping around looking for a carrot.

"Are they dangerous?" I asked and bit my lip.

Oh please, don't let them be dangerous!

"Nemean Lyons are extremely dangerous. They have been known to eat Themians as their preferred meat. They are also known for their extremely soft fur and their willingness to defend their territory. Nemean Lyons are endangered." Odyssey provided the preprogramed school lesson in death by kitty-cat.

Great, that's just great! Extremely dangerous, but soft and cuddly. Why the fuck are we carrying around a dangerous Themian eating Lyons?

"And why exactly did the High Counsel think it was a good idea to put one on the spaceship?" I asked as my knees knocked together with fear.

"A Nemean Lyon Pride was added to the bio-dome in an effort for transplantation on new worlds. The High Council was hoping to repopulate them on another planet if it was possible."

I gulped back the bile creeping up my throat.

If there's a whole pride of that, it means there's more than one. They're all hunting me. and have been for the last hour or more.

< Tristan! > I called in my sing-song voice, the one I liked to use to get my way.

< I'm a little busy right now, sis. Can I talk to you later? > He replied.

< No, Tristan! I really need to talk right now. > I shouted.

< I really can't talk to you right now, sis. Let me get back to you in about five or ten minutes. > He said.

< I need my brother for real, okay? The one time, no, this is the second time I really need my brother for real. > But the connection slammed closed.

Fuck! He pushed me out.

< Mom! > I called, as panic climbed up my insides.

< *Isolde, we're all in a meeting. You have to wait.* > She barked.

< I'm being stalked. > I whispered.

< *There are no creepy people here. All the mentally ill were checked, so stopping being overdramatic. I will get back to you in 20 or 30 minutes.* >

The firmness of her mental voice said she was done talking.

< I don't think I'm being stalked by a human. > I retorted, but she didn't reply.

I swallowed back my cry and hot tears rolled down my face. I'd been sweating for hours, so I was sure I stank. There was no way I could hide my scent.

The lump in my throat felt more like a bowling ball than a lump.

How many cats are in a pride? Five or six? God, why didn't I pay more attention to biology or zoology?

I bit my lip and felt the coppery taste of blood on the tip of my tongue.

The nature shows are always so boring and the likelihood of running into a lion in the middle of the ocean was zero. It hadn't been important at that time.

But now, I'm in the middle of the spatial void and the likelihood of running into a pride of Alien Lyons is apparently very high. How the hell did this happen?

I glanced around for the out of place. Neon green orbs beamed at me from behind giant leaves then blinked. The green eyes looked like they were split in the middle by a knife creating an X, making up its pupils. It was creepy!

I darted my eyes around and found four sets of green X's staring at me. My mouth went dry.

Who does all the hunting in a pride?

I scratched the side of my leg and removed a small insect that had climbed on my thigh. I couldn't recall what I'd read or heard. It never seemed important enough. There were at least four Lyons out there, hunting me.

I could turn around and run away, but the moment I move, they might attack. They wanted to wait until I was in a position where I literally had nowhere to go then pounce on me.

Glancing around, I realized climbing a tree was a waste of time.

They're cats, they climb too. I closed my eyes and took a deep breath to study my nerves.

Deep in the background, low on the auditory range, a rumbling vibrated in the base of my spine and climbed its way into my chest. I trembled as the sound grew louder.

I remembered watching a movie about a true story once. It was about Earth lions that were maneaters in Africa. Apparently, the guys who hunted down those lions, took a long time until they finally found their den. The two males had developed a taste for human blood and killed thousands. Their den was filled with skeletons.

How long have these guys been without some good Themian meat?

I was too far from the entrance to make it back alive. I furtively surveyed the foliage for anything. I finally spotted a dark impression that resembled the entrance to a cave. None of the landscape was natural, so the Themians must have put it there for a reason.

Maybe it masks an exit?

I slowly inched my way in that direction. The deep rumbling in the background turned into a loud voracious roar and it rebounded off of every surface.

"Odyssey, is there an exit near me?" I whispered, keeping still.

"Yes, 12 meters to your left," the matter of fact machine replied.

12 meters. I can make 12 meters alive, maybe, hopefully. Okay, so what's 12 meters again? Approximately 3.3 feet, 3x12 is 36 feet. I can make 36 feet. That's not even the length of the boat.

I moved in a slow but determined fashion, foot over foot. I made it look like I was foraging. It seemed like a good way to get there, or so I thought.

I can do it!

I didn't turn around because if I turned around, I probably would have started running. My heart was beating out of my chest and my breath came in gulps. The pounding of my blood roared as loud as the creatures in my ears.

The insatiable deep rumbling coming from the male and deep purring from the females in anticipation, harmonized into this rhythmic music of cat. It was almost hypnotic. I could feel myself wanting to turn around and look at them, to stand still for them, so they could eat me.

It was insane. They were trying to hypnotize me with their sound or maybe I was just imagining it. I couldn't be sure of anything.

Slowly, easing my way through the foliage, I finally reached the entrance to the cave. My bracelet glowed bright, emitting a soft ding.

I entered the cave, letting the cool darkness descend over me. A deep sigh of relief flooded my veins.

Just then, two hands wrapped around me. One was on my waist and the other over my mouth, dragging me back into the dark gloom.

CHAPTER 30

HERCULES

The foliage at this door was overgrown and thick. I drew my sword and began chopping away, but before the door closed behind me, I thought I heard a woman's voice calling out to me. I smiled to myself.

I'm not desperate for a woman, not enough to be hearing things.

After a month of study, today was the day. T said I was 'cray, cray'. I was still not sure how that translated to insane, but it didn't sound like a bad thing.

The sound of the insects buzzed in the background while my bird friends worked as an alarm, letting me know where my prey was and also the danger level. Sweat poured down my chest and temples, running into my ears and tickling the back of my neck. However, swinging a sword for real work and not just practice felt right. All those wasted years on Homeworld 14 slipped away.

I lost myself in the physical work of hacking a new path to the cave. As long as I kept moving I could be there in an hour.

Off, in the distance, the sucking sound of a door opening and closing made its way through the jungle. My blood turned to ice.

I'd told T not to follow me here.

He agreed that I could capture the beasts on my own. Without stopping my movements, I ran through the events of my morning.

Does anyone know I am coming here today?

I didn't think so, well at least no one other than Ixis and T. There was no need to check in with anyone else. The lockout was for everyone but Ixis, Sydney and my mother. They understood the danger, well my mother and Ixis did. I wasn't sure about Sydney.

However, I knew that Tristan put the first lockout on so it wouldn't be him behind me. The jungle still sounded safe. Maybe the Lyons were on the far side of the dome…

I will clear my path unless something changes.

I couldn't change my plans at that point. I chopped the plants back and turned to survey the area behind me, hoping to catch a glimpse of the suicidal fool.

My birds had quit keeping track of me and the flock was hovering over an area just out of my view. I caught flashes of white amongst the green and a bit of blond, but that was it. The halfwit was bumbling through the jungle. The white fabric flashed through the foliage again, almost as if they were waving a flag.

I stopped cutting the vines and took a deep breath. I was almost at the cave. The rocky outcropping loomed up ahead. I pulled the water jug from my back and took a long draw, letting my muscles rest for a moment. The electric zing from labor and straining muscles felt good, better than a mock fight or the use of a weight machine as T called it.

If the village fool is still wandering around safe after I reach the cave, I will come back.

The leather greaves on my legs itched from the heat and sweat, as did my breastplate and spalders. I rolled both shoulders and began swinging again. The sooner I cleared this path, the sooner I could have Ixis pull this imbecile out of harm's way.

The plant life thinned the closer to the cave I got. The dim light of the cave and the cool air was an illusion, but I greeted the respite from the hot sun-like light. I double-checked the door on the far end and its lockout held. The space was undisturbed, so I paced the area one more time to assure myself of the spacing.

The vibrating began in the distance and I dashed to the edge of the cave. There, not 40 meters away, was a girl, wearing almost no clothes, she was climbing a tree with a piece of white fabric. I froze at the sight of her.

If I move to save her, I put myself in the line of the hunt. If I do nothing, she will die.

I rubbed my temples and tapped my bracelet. Ixis wouldn't be ready for another thirty minutes. I closed my eyes.

< Hebe, I have a problem. > I called.

< You are free. What could possibly be wrong? > She giggled.

My sister would never see the serious side of life.

< I'm trapping Nemeans and a hybrid has wandered in. > I replied.

< Oh my, Herc! I'm sending the others. > She whispered and for once she sounded sober with the gravity of it.

< They will not make it. > I remarked.

The hypnotic rumbling rose and the jungle fell into silence. My breath caught in my throat as I watched the girl stop climbing down the tree and glance around. The Lyons were well hidden and even I couldn't pick them out.

She let the fruit slid between her legs, then jumped to the ground and fell on her ass. I repositioned the sword in my hand.

A buzzing began in the back of my head. I shook to throw off the fuzz it created and concentrated on clearing my eyes. Bending my knees into a crouched position, ready to leap, I could cover half the space between us.

The girl's eyes were the size of dinner plates, but then she narrowed them and slowly moved in my direction. I thrust my dagger back into its sheath, freeing my left hand. I inched closer to the edge of the cave, keeping just inside the safety of the shadows.

Her bracelet lit up and grew brighter as she moved closer to me and the safety she thought she'd find in the cave.

The Lyons hunting calls grew in intensity and with their sound, the hair on my arms reached for what it thought was the sky.

The girl moved slow and steady, with no sudden movements. Perhaps she wasn't as foolish as I first thought. Her skin was covered in sweat and grime, but she never wavered.

I sheathed my sword and pressed my back against the cold rock as she entered the cave. Then, I grabbed her.

CHAPTER 31

ISOLDE

I struggled against the strong arms wrapped around me. The hot breath of whoever was holding me, burnt my ear. The light from the entrance of the cave slowly disappeared as we backed away from the opening. I stopped moving as the X shaped irises came into focus and double blinked two sets of eyelids.

I sucked in air through the hand that was covering my mouth. I couldn't tell whether they were looking from left to right or stared straight ahead. It was almost as if it could see three-dimensionally. I still couldn't make out the shape of the creature. All I could see was the strange eyes, as my captor and I melted into the darkness.

The breathing in my ear slowed, as did the rise and fall of the chest I was pressed against. The heartbeat from whoever was holding me captive was slow and steady, not petrified, not like me. My feet dangled above the ground and yet the man only held me by my waist with a hand cupped over my mouth.

He was large and strong. His hair hung down, over my shoulder, laying on top of mine as the scent of leather and soil came with him.

I couldn't defend myself, not against him. If I use my ability to send out fear… it could enrage those creatures or they could be completely immune which would irritate them further.

A sharp intake of breath and then words came out of his mouth.

"I don't know who you are," the voice growled, "or how you overrode the security lockout on this bio-dome, but you have got to be the stupidest son of a bitch I ever heard of."

With that, his arms tightened around me and he loosened his hand over my mouth.

He called me stupid.

I wiggled in an attempt to get free and my heart jumped to my throat.

"Stop!" He ordered. "They have a three-dimensional night vision. They can see what we're doing in the cave. They're like a Tyrannosaurus Rex. They can't see you if you don't move." He stopped only for a second before he continued. "Now, I'm going to let go of you and take my hand away from your mouth. And you're not going to get us killed. Speak quietly!"

He released me and the human wall that was behind me slid to the right. I wanted to turn around and yell at him, but the X-shaped eyes were fixated on me.

He took my hand in his. It felt like being a child and holding your father's hand. It was so large. I stepped back into the wall and he began speaking again.

"Who are you and how did you come by the ability to unlock that door? I locked everyone out of this bio-dome," he whispered through his teeth.

I wiggled my hand free of his, "I should ask you the same question," I retorted in a low voice.

He looked at me, "There are only three people who can override the command I put on that door," and with the last word he reached for my hand.

I balled it into a fist and he just closed his meaty paw over the top.

"Well, then you should know who I am," I spat.

"No, I know all three of those people and you are not one of them," he replied squeezing my fist in his own.

It brought tears to my eyes and I sniffed.

"Obviously, one of those three opened the door for me," I retorted.

It doesn't take a lot of brainpower to figure that out.

"None of them would break the seal," he stated and I whirled around to look at him.

The Lyon cried and a loud rumble of a roar followed. In the deep gloom, I could make out the shape of a giant man with long honey gold hair and crystal-clear blue eyes with the dark ring. I could make out enough of his facial features to see he was terrified of what I just did. Just then he pulled me into his embrace.

"Let go of me!" I shrieked.

"You really are a moron. I told you to hold still. They've seen you. Now, they know you're in the cave. And they'll camp out hoping you'll come out. Or they will come in and get you. You just destroyed all my plans," he growled, holding me tight against him.

"What plans? This doesn't look like a plan, hacker," I barked.

He shushed me right in the face.

"I'm not a hacker! This bio-dome has been closed off to everyone on the ship for over a month. There was an announcement. Where were you when that happened?" He demanded with a little shake.

"Doing my job. Why are you acting this way and who are you?" I seethed.

"I'm Hercules. Sydney sent me here to either kill or capture the Nemean Lyons. My plan which you have fouled up was to capture the entire pride in this cave. But now, since you're in here, I can't trap them, so you just ruined a month's planning."

"Oh, sorry!" I whispered as the reality of my fuckup slammed down on me.

I am a moron.

Mom didn't say anything. She opened the door, she didn't even think about it.

"Sorry, I was doing my job with Hera. I've hardly been awake in the last month," I moaned and I felt my face heating with shame.

"You've been dreamwalking for the last month with Hera?" He whispered.

"Yes, I couldn't possibly have heard an announcement of any kind. Sorry, I wouldn't have asked my mother to open the door, if I had known," I mumbled staring at the cave entrance, hoping the X shaped irises would suddenly disappear so I could go hide in shame.

"Sydney's daughter, Isolde?" He asked.

"Yes, I thought everyone on board knew who I was. What kind of a name is Hercules? What you think you are some kind of Demigod?" I snapped to cover my guilt.

"I am the son of Hera and Zeus, I am a Demigod," he retorted with pride.

I swallowed back the giggle that inched its way up my throat. But the sound didn't go down and escaped anyway.

Ha, I'm being saved by Hercules who's hunting a lion.

I wanted to belt out a laugh because everything was so corny. This guy had to be lying.

"We can continue to discuss who fouled up who's plan and die, or you can shut up and do everything I tell you and maybe live. Pick your poison." He shook me a bit to pull me out of my mirth.

"Life of course," I responded swallowing back the hysteria that sat at the back of my throat.

In the deep gloom, a smile spread across his face and I really looked into his eyes. Suddenly there was a clamor in the back of my mind and everything around me turned blue, like the blue glow carried by all Themian technology.

But this time, it wasn't just a blue glow, it was lightning followed by thunder, and an electrical charge, that radiated out from us. I looked back into the sunlight reflection in his eyes. His pupils were dilated and his smile changed. I squirmed. I wanted to pull away from him because something in his smile bothered me.

"Don't fight it, Isolde," he whispered in a deep voice.

"Let go of me! Let go of me now!" I demanded in a low voice.

At any moment I was going to live his entire life because our skin was touching. I squeezed my eyes closed and a cry replaced the giggle I had a moment before. I tensed for the onslaught of his life vision, but it never came.

Slowly his hands dropped down to his side and we were just a hair's breadth apart. We were still, but not touching. The blue lightning, the electricity disappeared and the world snapped back into place. The buzzing in the back of my mind remained, but it was all a low-grade hum.

My mouth was dry.

What the fuck just happened?

"You need to get behind me and stay behind me. Press yourself against the cave wall and don't move." He ordered in a deep husky voice.

The anger and frustration that had laced our conversation before, was replaced by a fierce tenderness. I didn't argue but slowly worked my way around his hulking form. He angled his shoulder to protect me and guided me with his left hand. Every time he touched me, it was just enough for the blue electricity to flash again. I yanked my body back suddenly.

"Don't make any sudden moves. You hear the sound they're making?" he asked.

"Yes, the low-grade rumble," I responded as the cold of the faux stone dug into my back.

Actually, the sound made my head want to turn inside out. I didn't know what was worse, the blue lightning or the hypnotic rumble.

"It's a form of echo-location. They use it in the same way the Earth's bats do. The noise guides them, revealing a three-dimensional image. As soon as you move, they have a perfect image. Then they'll attack. Right now, the sound is low, meaning they're still trying to position us. The less we move, the less they see." His hand moved to my hip. "Sudden movements, give them instant sharpness. So, don't yank away again or they will kill both of us."

He turned his head slightly and I could just make out the light reflecting from one eye.

"There in one pride of Nemean Lyons out there and I can probably kill one third but I can't take them all. You may have just signed both our death warrants," he said while his hand caressed my hip.

I wanted to pull away, but until that moment I didn't understand what we were facing.

One entire pride of Lyons! He can kill a third?

I couldn't even hope to kill one.

We slowly wormed our way back against the wall of the cave. For every step back I took, he took one also. We were never further than a hand span apart.

His clothes were leather, in a style I'd only seen in movies, such as the 'Odyssey' *harhar*.

"Why did you come to this cave?" He asked.

"I thought it was an exit from the bio-dome. I knew I was being stocked by those catlike creatures, so I wanted to get the hell out of here," I whispered.

"Now, you will be lucky to get out with your life. You shouldn't have breached the seal." He chided.

He was right, I should have asked more questions instead of just insisting on my own way.

My back met the cold rock of the wall and I pressed myself deep into a little alcove. Hercules, did not stop stepping back. As a matter of fact, he was now at the point where he was pressing into me.

"Is there a reason why you feel the need to squish me?" I asked.

"There won't be enough room in the cave for Ixis to transport in the cages," he supplied.

"Cages?" I squeaked.

The edge of the rocks were digging into my exposed flesh.

"I intend to catch the creatures, assuming they don't attack before I have time to get them."

The more flesh that came into contact with him, the more blue electricity it provoked. The humming in the background never went away. One of his hands was up, facing out and lightly glanced off of the edge as his wrist while turning slightly. It was a sword.

He is going to defend us against Lyons with a fracking sword!

"Why don't you have a gun?" I demanded as the tooled leather of his backplate firmly pressed against the side of my face.

"What is wrong with a broadsword? And what is a gun?"

I had to rack my brain to describe a gun. "It shoots projectiles."

"You mean like a bow and arrow?" He asked.

"No! Yes! No!"

His huffed but was intrigued by my stupid response, so I had to give a proper description.

"A bow and arrow would be a very primitive version of a gun. It's more like a stone that's thrown at a high-speed."

"And you kill animals with this? Sounds like a sling and a sling doesn't kill large animals," he scoffed.

"We're defending ourselves, from their attack. The stone goes so fast, it penetrates the hide and kills the animal, so not a sling. Humans use them to hunt."

I was already sorry, I said anything.

"It's a good thing we're not humans. However, the last time I was on Earth was more than 10,000 years ago. All we had were swords and daggers. Men would carry around swords and shields. I've never killed without seeing the whites of a mans or beasts' eyes. What you described sounds soulless," he scoffed and his fingers gripping the handle of his sword, repositioning again.

"Many people think killing animals is soulless, but if we had a gun you could shoot every single one of those Lyons and be free," I finished.

The vibrating of the creatures rebounded around the cave at strange angles pummeling my brain. I had to open my mouth to breath from nausea that welled up.

"Just one problem, Isolde. I'm not trying to kill them. I am trying to save them from being killed," he said and his shouldered tensed.

"Why? Because they're endangered and from another world?" I demanded.

"No, because killing them would just be senseless and they wouldn't need to die if you hadn't come in," he responded.

I shook my head and the sharp increase of rumbling in the background told me they knew exactly where we were.

"They're going to attack any moment now. Whatever you do, do not move out of this alcove. Do not track my moves. As a matter of fact, you would be better off if you close your eyes and just stand there like a statue. If you can do that, you might survive," he took a deep breath.

Why didn't I ask my mother why it was locked? Fuck, fuck, fuck! Mr. Perfect trying to be an ecologist and save them all and he thinks I'm a soulless killer.

Maybe he was right, maybe shooting these creatures with a gun was soulless. It was certainly not very sportsmanlike. When you can kill a defenseless creature from hundreds of yards away, and there's nothing they can do about it except runaway and it is kind of soulless, and cruel.

If I hadn't come in here, these creatures would not need to die. He found a way to trap them, so they wouldn't hurt anybody on the ship.

Fuck, fuck, fuckity, fuck!

I hated when people were right.

I looked at Hercules. Other than the rise and fall of his chest, he stood there like a statue waiting. The deafening roaring in the background that came from the Lyons reached a point where I wanted to cover my ears. It felt as if my ear drums would burst.

Other than the X'd green eyes, I still hadn't seen one of the beasts, but I realized that one inched its way to us. Two sets of X'd eyes moved in with a third stationery.

The closer they came to the entrance of the cave, the deeper the vibration in my chest grew. Even the ground all around us shivered. It was like the bass in a nightclub. It permeated every part of my body and it was all I could do not to move, flinch, or cringe away.

They talk about being frozen in fear, but that was not what I felt. Fight or flight. I wanted to flee. The sound pulled at me, making me want to jump up and run away, to feel the hypnotic motion of it pouring over me and filling me with the desire to run.

"Do you feel the power of their hypnotism?" Hercules asked.

"Yes."

"You want to run—don't. Fight it!"

He pulled his hand back and the spot turned cold.

"They have the ability to make you not only feel like you want to run but fill you with enough terror to run in circles. It makes you easier to catch. The moment you give over and start running, they will kill you," he said then slowly pulled a dagger.

In my mind, his voice rang loud and clear.

< Ixis, move the cage. Now! >

The two Lyons leaped and a cage appeared in front of them. Their bodies filled the enclosure and slammed into the side closest to us. They screamed in anger and swiped at each other.

It was a cage unlike one I'd ever seen before. I had no idea what kind of metal was made out of or if it was even made out of metal, but it glinted with the crystalline technology typical of Themia. The entire structure was permeated with the color red and woven into a mesh tight enough to keep a claw in.

The third Lyon pounced at the same time but its trajectory was different and the giant cat was able to realign and leap out of the way. I watched in horror as the cloaked creature landed and entered the cave.

< Ixis, now! > Hercules voice called out in my mind.

The cage disappeared leaving us alone with one very large Lyon.

"Isolde, if you want to live don't even breathe," Hercules said through his teeth.

I was terrified. I couldn't tear my eyes away from the X shaped irises. The rumbling sound was deafening as it rebounded off every square inch of the cave. I was desperate to push the man in front of me out of the way and run. My brain was consumed by that one thought.

Hercules stepped away from me and for a moment I thought I might dart out of the cave, but I clenched my teeth and pulled a shallow breath in through my nose. Hercules moved between the creature and me.

"Well, aren't you a pretty girl? Why don't you come and see what I brought you?"

Suddenly it wasn't just the eyes. An entire body displayed itself. It was striped with black, gold, green, red, a large rainbow-colored cat. Everything on it was in a deep jeweled tone and it shimmered as the creature moved. Its fur was increasing its cloaking ability. The only way to track it was its eyes. The hypnotic rumbling lessened and she crouched up on all four paws raised her tail. She opened her mouth wide and she let out an ear-piercing scream.

"That's right, pretty girl." His tone of voice caressed the feline.

Her fur rippled over muscles. She leaped into the air, jumping up and over Hercules. He was quick and he knew what she was up to, so he whipped around while thrusting up. Almost like a ballet dancer, he splashed with his dagger at her face. As she landed, her green blood oozed and she screamed. She extended her paw towards Hercules and I cringed back, but quick as lightning, she raked every one of her five claws and dug them into my chest, ripping down my torso and then my thigh, while the other slashed my face.

The scent of copper and burning pain filled my senses and my throat grew raw with my screams.

< Holy crap, Isolde, where the hell are you?> Tristan screamed in my mind.

I answered with shrieks of agony. Through pained eyes, I watched Hercules. He roared and drove his sword into the beast, then hacked at the creature cutting off both of its blood-soaked paws. Only then, he went to the beast's throat, slicing it with his dagger causing green blood to spray everywhere.

I could hear myself screaming but I couldn't stop.

< Ixis, get her out of here! > His terrified mind shouted.

With a quick movement, he was at my side, staring at me, into me, while his hand gently touched my face as his words filled my mind.

< Don't worry, Calla! I won't let you die. >

And with that darkness descended.

CHAPTER 32

HERCULES

I should've asked Ixis to get her out sooner but I was afraid. My greatest fear was that one of the cats would pounce before I had a chance to get either of us out of here.

I slid along the wall to the exterior of the cave. The rumbling of their hypnotic roars still filled the jungle although they weren't as close as I thought they would be.

Maybe she had only been tracked by three of them.

As soon as I thought of that, I knew that was wrong because they never travel in numbers lower than five and that there's always three sets in the pride. One lyon for every set of four lyonesses. Three lyonesses were gone or dead, but where was the other female and the male? I slid my way along the wall back towards the opening hoping to spot the X-shaped pupils.

I scanned the variegated greens in the jungle, it got me thinking.

Maybe today is just a loss and maybe I won't get one set of the pride. I came here to capture at least a third of the pride today, but it all gone to shit. All...except Isolde.

Why hadn't I asked Ixis to take her out sooner? After she touched me, I couldn't make him take her. If I die, she would too. My eyes were darting around, taking in the area, but not paying attention.

Death comes to the distracted, Hercules.

Isolde screamed in the back of my mind and I squeezed my eyes closed to push out her agony, then reluctantly closed my mind to the woman I'd just met.

I opened my eyes to survey the area again. This time I really was searching. Just then, the tip of a tail flicked.

Why do cats always do that? It is a dead giveaway.

Nemeans could only cloak colored fur. The tip of their tails are white like the cottontail of a rabbit. My eyes picked out the fluffy white from all the green. And then I saw its friends, especially one that had the tip larger than the others.

That must be the male.

I pulled the muscles in my face back into a grin.

The female moved around and I followed her movements with her tail and the X's of her eyes. She was prowling and pacing. They both knew where I was. They were on guard because they'd seen what happened to the other three. I was sure they could smell the blood of both Isolde and their packmate. The male moved off to the right, while the female broke left.

I guess they planned to squeeze me in a pincer move. Hoping, I'd exit the cave for safety. Little did they know that this was where I'd already decided to make my last stand - capture all or die.

Only when I made that choice, I didn't have anything to live for. Now I do.

The male opened and closed his double lids and the rumble notched up a few decibels. I listened for the female and if my ears weren't tricking me, she was doubling around and up over the top of the entrance. She was going to jump down as I walked out.

First, they were assuming their hypnotism worked on me and I would run out of the cave.

Maybe I should step out and dart back.

It would spring their trap and force them to chase me. That sounded like a plan, but I would have to move quickly.

I was strong. The stories about me said I was stronger than 10 men and that part was true. I was also pretty smart, smarter than the average human. However, the one thing I had learned among Themians, was that I wasn't as clever as I thought. They were much cleverer.

But when it came to hunting, I've been told I could rival even Athena and Artemis themselves, that were famous for their hunts and warlike tactics. Not that Ares would ever agree. He would deny it emphatically. He was still drunk on the idea that everyone considered him to be the God of War.

Raw rage blossomed in my chest with every step that I took to the edge of the cave opening.

< Ixis, be ready! > I called.

I took a deep breath and tensed my muscles. I was sure the cats did the same.

One small step out and a turn, and dash.

I thought it through and visualized it several times.

I took the step and a roar greeted me as the sound instantly intensified from the male. The air changed as the female leaped down toward me, so I turned and bolted into the cave.

< Ixis, now! >

An empty cage appeared behind me and the female leapt into it while chasing after me. The male followed her but he refused to enter the cage, darting around to the other side instead.

< Ixis, get it out of here. >

I could kill this male, but there were two others. I had captured three females and I could come back later for the rest of the pride.

The cage and its occupant vanished and the male reared back. He took a tentative step to the right. His X shaped pupils examining every avenue of attack. His deep hypnotic rumbling continued at a constant level. He wasn't raising or lowering it, he was just testing. It didn't matter what level he used, it would never work on me. I was completely immune to all of it. That was part of being human, sometimes the best part.

His tail twitched as he paced and I timed myself to it. With every shift of his head, I was mirroring his every move, until finally, I saw his game. He was pacing to build up momentum. He wanted to use that built-up momentum to pounce. He was hoping I would go right when he went right, giving him an extra-long jump before he landed on top of me.

He slowly rippled his camouflage away and it was like watching water fading from a rock as he revealed his vivid colors.

He reared his head back and released a piercing roar. He moved right and then left. He retraced to the right and with a double leap he was heading toward me but I dove left and he missed. I managed to slash him with my sword arm, cutting deeply into his shoulder. He screamed in pain and in his anger he leaped straight at me without even pretending he was trying to do anything other than use brute force.

He raised the hypnotic decibels a hundredfold. My eardrum burst and hot blood ran out of my ear and down my neck. I crossed both my sword and dagger as he leaped and use them like scissors to hack his head off mid-leap. The weight from his body hurled into me and we both fell.

My hands were trapped under the weight of the dead cat and my back slammed into the ground with a sickening thud. Stars danced before my eyes and blackness pulled at the edges. The adrenaline from the battle bled away, only to be replaced by pain.

The head of the cat fell into my face, still attached by its thick fur at the scruff of his neck. I was trapped beneath the lion carcasses. Before it died, the beast had buried both front claws into my shoulders.

< Ixis, now! > I moaned in pain.

< I cannot move you with his body on top of you. You must remove him. His cloaking ability makes it impossible for me to help you. > The old shifter replied.

I pushed with all my might, but I could not dislodge him. With my sword hand, I levered and push to one side. He rolled off and his claws pulled free of my shoulders ripping and tearing flesh and muscle as they went. His green blood covered my face and hands filling my wounds, burning me. The pressure changed around me and I was inside one of the laboratories.

"Well then, you've gotten yourself into a fine pickle, haven't you? Don't worry Mr. Hercules, I will get you patched up," a red-headed vixen said.

Her hand held a thin vial that squirted liquid from the tip.

"Isolde? Is she alive?" I moaned.

"Go to sleep, big boy. We'll take care of all those issues later."

She patted me and the last thing I remember was a stabbing pain in my thigh.

The end

Killing Gods II

FATES

https://amzn.to/2T739QQ

If you've enjoyed what you've read here please give it a little

love and leave a review or feel free to follow me on Amazon

Or send me an email slmason1889@gmail.com or follow me

on Instagram @s.l.mason_author

For the most up to date information on the Killing Gods

Universe or These Hallowed Hills visit:

Quickquillpublishing.com